Dreaming of Italy

T.A. Williams lives in Devon with his Italian wife. He was born in England of a Scottish mother and Welsh father. After a degree in modern languages at Nottingham University, he lived and worked in Switzerland, France and Italy, before returning to run one of the best-known language schools in the UK. He's taught Arab princes, Brazilian beauty queens and Italian billionaires. He speaks a number of languages and has travelled extensively. He has eaten snake, still-alive fish, and alligator. A Spanish dog, a Russian bug and a Korean parasite have done their best to eat him in return. His hobby is long-distance cycling, but his passion is writing.

Also by T.A. Williams

Chasing Shadows
Dreaming of Venice
Dreaming of Florence
Dreaming of St-Tropez
Dreaming of Christmas
Dreaming of Tuscany
Dreaming of Rome
Dreaming of Verona
Dreaming of Italy

Escape to Tuscany
Under a Siena Sun
Second Chances in Chianti

T.A. WILLIAMS
Dreaming
of
Italy

CANELO

First published in the United Kingdom in 2020 by Canelo

This edition published in the United Kingdom in 2021 by

Canelo Digital Publishing Limited
31 Helen Road
Oxford OX2 0DF
United Kingdom

A CIP catalogue record for this book is available from the British Library.

Print ISBN 978 1 78863 941 5
Ebook ISBN 978 1 78863 932 3

Look for more great books at www.canelo.co

Printed and bound in Great Britain by Clays Ltd, Elcograf S.p.A.

EXT. VENICE WATERFRONT – DAY

EMILY and ROBERT standing face to face on the quay. Tears running down EMILY'S face. A launch is waiting in the water alongside them.

EMILY
Is it really time for you to go?

ROBERT
(struggling with his emotions)
I wish we didn't have to part like this.

EMILY
So do I, but it's out of our hands. (sobs) You have to go one way. I have to go another.

ROBERT
(stretches out his hand and lays it against her cheek)
If only things could be different. If only we could stay together.

EMILY
I wish that were true... These past days have been so wonderful. I can't believe it has to end. I'll never stop dreaming of Italy and of you.

ROBERT
Meeting you is the very best thing that's ever happened to me.
(reaches out and embraces her)
I love you, Emily, from the bottom of my heart.

EMILY

And I love you too. So very, very much. Goodbye,
Robert… my love.

ROBERT steps down into the launch.

ROBERT

Goodbye, my darling. I'll always love you.

Launch starts to pull away. Cut to close-up of **EMILY'S** face as she stands on the quay.

Camera follows launch until it disappears. Final close-up of **EMILY**, distraught.

Dissolve to credits.

THE END

Chapter 1

'So, what did you think of *Dreaming of Italy*?'

He dropped the final pages back onto the well-thumbed pile of A4 sheets lying on the polished surface of his glass and steel desk and looked up at her. Through the window behind him Emma could clearly see the Hollywood sign on the hill in the distance, but her full attention today was focused on her boss. His fingers drummed on the screenplay as he asked her the all-important question.

She answered immediately and without hesitation. 'I liked it, JM. I liked it a lot.'

She gave him an enthusiastic smile, still trying to come to terms with the fact that here she was sitting opposite the big boss himself. Although she had been rising pretty quickly through the ranks during her twelve years with the company and had met him on a number of occasions, this was the very first time she had been summoned to the top-floor inner sanctum of the man universally acknowledged to be the twenty-first century's answer to Sam Goldwyn or Louis B. Mayer as the current uncrowned king of Hollywood.

Of course, she reflected, JM did have his ever-present right-hand man, conveniently named Dexter, perched on a stool at his side to fill him in if her name should escape him. With his minute stature alongside his six-foot-six employer, Dexter had always reminded Emma of one of those little fish who swim around sharks, even venturing into their mouths to remove parasites and keep the predator healthy. His encyclopaedic knowledge of the company, its many productions and its staff from stars to sound engineers, from costume designers to camera operators, was unsurpassed, and she knew that her name was only one of hundreds upon hundreds stored inside his computer-like brain.

As for the screenplay, she knew she would probably have felt obliged to tell JM she liked it anyway, seeing as it had to a great extent been the brainchild of the big man himself, but in this instance, there was no need to dissimulate. She actually had been very impressed with what she had read the previous day. She smiled again and added a bit more.

'It's the best screenplay I've read for a long, long time.'

In return, her boss's mouth curled into what was the closest he ever got to a smile. The first time she had witnessed this phenomenon, she hadn't been able to tell whether he was genuinely pleased or just preparing to bare his fangs and sink them into her throat. Fortunately, it had been the former. Jan Miros, the legendary founder, president and major shareholder of JM Global Productions (JMGP) had a reputation for being a tough guy. The movie business was a dog-eat-dog affair and she knew full well that this particular dog wasn't afraid to use his teeth if it came to it. But today he appeared friendly, even though he was quick to challenge her.

'You're not just saying that because I came up with the idea, are you?' She started to shake her head but he hadn't finished. 'Cut the bull. Give it to me straight. Is this the Big One? God knows we need one.'

He wasn't wrong. Over the past few years, the fortunes of JMGP had taken a turn for the worse, mainly after an ill-advised foray into the world of zombies and vampires just as that genre had started to decline in popularity. Only this winter's romcom, *Love Me Only*, with which Emma herself had been heavily involved, had kept the money rolling in and the shareholders reasonably happy. She took a deep breath and told him the truth.

'It's good, JM, really good, and I mean that. Whether it becomes the Big One will depend on who we can get to star in it. We're going to need the biggest names we can get hold of… you can get hold of.' She caught his eye and cast him an enquiring look. 'Anybody in the pipeline?'

'How about Laney Travers and Ethan Dukes? How does that grab you?' His lips did that curling thing again and she dropped her eyes, assuming it indicated he was pleased, but surreptitiously brushing her fingers across her jugular just to check it was still intact.

'You mean both together?'

He nodded and Emma was genuinely stunned. Laney and Ethan were currently the two hottest properties in the movie business, but they had never appeared together in the same film. Yet.

Media speculation had been growing for well over a year now as the anticipation increased. Emma had never met the fantastically beautiful Laney, but Ethan was on contract here at JMGP and she had got to know him well. If JM had managed to get the two of them together, then *Dreaming of Italy* really did stand a chance. Emma felt a sudden shot of excitement run through her.

'In that case, I reckon it could well become the Big One. In fact, the ending reminded me a bit of *Casablanca*.'

'Contracts were signed yesterday. It's gonna happen, Emma. If it could become our *Casablanca* I'd be well pleased, I can tell you. In fact, I'd be over the moon.'

He nodded a few times to himself and then Emma saw Dexter lean towards him and whisper in his ear. JM nodded more decisively and looked up.

'Listen, Emma, I want you to do something for me. I know what you did for *Love Me Only*. Some of those locations you found on the wild coast of Ireland were breathtaking. You have a great eye. That's why I want you to go to Italy.'

'Go to Italy?'

She did her best to hide her surprise that he was aware that the choice of locations for *Love Me Only* had to a large extent been down to her, rather than her then direct superior; who had spent most of his time while in Ireland inside a bottle of Old Bushmills. A few weeks later he had appeared at the weekly admin meeting in a Roman gladiator's costume and spilt a full bottle of Johnnie Walker into his superior's lap. As a result he was no longer with the company and rumour had it that he was now working for a small-scale porn production studio in the Hollywood Hills.

As for taking a trip to Italy, Emma was currently deeply involved with *Sweet Memories*, another romantic comedy that was about to go into production in the next few weeks, and she had expected to find herself very busy as this took shape. She started to protest, but JM was in full swing.

4

'That's right, Emma. Italy. The film roams all over Italy as our two main characters follow each other around. I need you to find me the best, the most scenic, and the most atmospheric locations. I don't just want the old favourites like the Sistine Chapel or the Ponte Vecchio. I want places that people don't already know. I want the visuals to be so stunning, the audiences will fall in love with the scenery every bit as much as they fall in love with the story.' JM's piercing blue eyes met and held hers. 'Can you do that, Emma? Can you?'

'I'll do my best.' Feeling that more was needed, she added a bit of emphasis. 'I'll do my very best.'

'Do you know Italy?'

Emma could hardly believe her ears. Dexter, the pilot fish, had spoken out loud. Even JM cast him an uncertain glance as if to be sure he had heard right. To be on the safe side, Emma addressed her reply to both of them.

'I don't know Italy terribly well, but I've been there. When I was doing my degree back in England, I spent a summer doing a course at Cinecittà in Rome. I took a few trips to places around there and travelled down to Naples and the Amalfi Coast for a few days when the course finished.'

JM looked at her approvingly. 'And do you speak the language?'

'Enough to get by and to tell men to stop bothering me, but certainly not well enough to wheedle my way onto private property or to deal with all the red tape over there.' She shook her head ruefully. 'And one thing I did learn is that Italy has one hell of a lot of bureaucracy.'

JM waved dismissively in the general direction of his lieutenant. 'Dexter, get Emma somebody to act as guide and interpreter.' His expression hardened. 'And make sure it's someone really, really good. There's too much riding on this.'

Emma decided she had better make it clear she couldn't just up sticks and drop everything.

'But, JM, I'm right in the middle of finalising everything for *Sweet Memories*. Shooting starts any day now and I need to be here for that. I've got sets being built as we speak.'

'*Sweet Memories* isn't gonna be the Big One, Emma. We both know that.' The big man shook his head sorrowfully. 'More's the pity. I'm hoping it'll be good, but it's not gonna be box-office gold. *Dreaming of Italy* has to be our number one priority. Don't worry, we'll get somebody to take over from you with "*Memories*".'

Emma didn't like the sound of this one bit. What if this 'somebody' ruined all her carefully prepared plans? Her increasingly important role in the company was as a fixer, ensuring that everything from lighting engineers and wardrobe staff to location shooting permits and road closure orders were in place and ready for the director to step in seamlessly as the cameras began to roll. She knew only too well that every lost day on a shoot would cost the company thousands upon thousands. She made another attempt to tell him how much work she had on her desk at the moment, but JM had already turned to his right-hand man. 'Dexter, make it happen.'

Dexter nodded and tapped something onto his phone. Emma gave a surreptitious sigh. *Sweet Memories* might not be the Big One, but she had been working flat out to ensure it was going to go as smoothly as possible. Now, if problems cropped up and she wasn't there to fix them, it would be her fault, seeing she had done so much of the logistical groundwork. At the same time if everything went well, she knew the praise would be heaped upon her replacement. For her, it was a lose-lose situation.

However, she didn't have a chance to object again as JM had moved on.

'And we're going to need a history guy. How's that coming along, Dexter?'

The movie was set in the early years of the twentieth century, and she knew how important it was to ensure that the film was historically accurate and for everything to be as authentic as possible. Nothing would be more potentially embarrassing than the occasional glimpses of watches on the wrists of Apaches to be found in old movies or vapour trails in the sky above Napoleon's retreating army, the characters shouldn't suddenly find themselves in a building that hadn't existed back then or taking a ferry built in the nineteen fifties. Reluctantly accepting that she and *Dreaming of Italy* were now irrevocably linked, she nodded her agreement and added a plea.

'And if you can find somebody who speaks good Italian as well as English, Dexter, that would be great. Like I said, I can order a pizza and a glass of wine, but I wouldn't have a clue when faced with a deep historical treatise.' Another thought occurred to her and she turned towards JM. 'Are you going to be happy with stills or do you want video? If so, you'd better send a cameraman.'

JM shook his head. 'Stills are good. I prefer stills. Just make sure you take lots of them. Now, let's get this straight. This movie is the studio's number one priority for now, and I mean number one.' He slapped the desk with a massive palm to emphasise his words. 'How soon can you get onto it?'

Anticipating the question, Emma had already started thinking about this. 'Well, if you can find somebody to take over from what I'm on now, I'll need a few days – say a week – to talk them through everything so, in principle, I could be ready to go a week after you find my temporary replacement.'

She made sure she added a little extra emphasis to the penultimate word. After her years in the company, she had too much experience of what could happen when people took over other people's jobs. She knew full well there were any number of hopefuls a rung or two below her on the ladder who would be only too happy to get their hooks into her job – and hang on tight.

JM wasn't the boss of a billion-dollar company for nothing. It was immediately obvious he could tell what was going through her mind. What he said next had her rocking back in her seat.

'Listen, Emma, in this company, we reward talent. That's what got me where I am today. Get this right and you won't be going back to your old job.' He caught her eye and nodded again. 'That's what I said. Find me the very best locations for this movie and there's a corner office with a vice president's nameplate on the door for you. That's how important this movie is for me, for you and for the whole company. Get it right and the sky's the limit for you.'

And if I screw up... Emma had no doubts about what the alternative scenario would be. She gulped, savouring the tantalising prospect of such a massive upward step, but only too aware what the penalty for failure could be. Even worse, she could be on the wrong end of two failures, if her replacement on *Sweet Memories* also screwed things up. However, JM didn't give her time to dwell upon what lay before her.

'So you could be ready to go this month?' As Emma nodded cautiously, he shot a glance across at his PA. 'Dexter, find us a replacement for Emma as soon as possible so she can get them bedded in. Okay? As for you, Emma, no husband or boyfriend who's gonna miss you?'

Emma answered resolutely. 'No, sir, nobody. I'm good to go.'

For a second she read that same expression that often crossed people's faces when they registered that she was in her mid-thirties, reasonably bright and good-looking, and yet unattached. Yes, there had been a few men over the years, but none that had provided any more than temporary entertainment. She was increasingly approached these days by random men – and a surprising number of women – but she knew only too well that as her status in the company rose, so her appeal in their eyes was almost certainly not just for herself, but for what she could do for their careers. As a result, she had become ever more wary, especially in an environment like Hollywood where little was ever what it appeared to be. Besides, there was no doubt in her mind that her career was far more important than any random man.

'Great. Well, thanks, Emma. I know you'll do a great job.' Just in case she hadn't realised the gravity of the situation, he reminded her once again. 'Make this our *Casablanca* and we'll all be winners. Got that, Emma?'

'Yes, sir. Got it.' He was dead right. There was a great deal riding on this – for the company but even more for her.

However, just as she was about to get up, assuming the meeting was over, JM said something that raised the stakes a thousandfold.

'And I'm gonna send my son to Italy along with you.'

'Your son?'

Like most of the staff of JMGP, Emma had heard of the existence of JM's son, but had never met him. Such was the secrecy surrounding him, some had even started to doubt whether he actually existed or whether he was yet another Hollywood myth. She sat up and listened with rapt attention, her mind churning over the implications of this bombshell.

'He's fresh out of college and I want him to learn all there is to know about the company.' He caught Emma's eye again. There was definitely something almost hypnotic about his gaze. 'And I want him to learn from the best. Yes, I mean you, Emma. I want you to teach him all you know.'

'Erm, right, yes sir, of course...'

He must have heard her hesitation. 'But there's something you need to know right from the start. I don't want you treating him with kid gloves just because he's the boss's son, right? He's a foot soldier and you're his commanding officer. I've told him that and he knows it. Get him to make your coffee, carry your bags, go out and fetch the pizzas. I don't care. Just make sure he learns. That's what he's there for. Got that? No special favours.'

Emma swallowed hard. 'Right, sir, no special favours.'

Who was she kidding? Suddenly the idea of a tour of Italy – which had been developing considerable appeal – was looking far less attractive. It now appeared clear that she was going to find herself saddled with what was in all probability going to turn out to be a spoilt brat who would be reporting back every mistake she made to his all-powerful father. Still, she knew she had no choice in the matter, so she swallowed her reservations and accepted with as much grace as she could muster.

'I look forward to meeting him.'

Dexter was once again talking sotto voce in his boss's ear. Nodding in approval, the big man looked back across the desk at Emma. 'And you can meet him tonight. My wife and I are throwing a party at our place this evening and we'd like you to come.'

In spite of her reservations about JM's son and this whole project, Emma was genuinely overwhelmed to find herself invited to the legendary Villa Milagro, built for silent movie star Harold Lloyd, briefly occupied by Greta Garbo, and now home to one of the richest men in Hollywood. She knew that very, very few of her colleagues at JMGP had ever been inside the place and that this was an honour bestowed upon only a very select few.

And now this number was going to include Emma Taylor from a tiny little village in Norfolk, daughter of Sid and Martha Taylor who ran the local post office and shop. Twelve years earlier, her mum had been very doubtful about the wisdom of Emma's decision to head halfway across the globe to work on another continent, but there could be no doubt now that the decision had been the right one. What, she wondered, would they think when she told them their only child was going to be mixing in such rarefied circles? That would come later. For now, she didn't hesitate.

'That's very kind, sir. I'd be delighted.'

'Great. Eight o'clock. We'll send a car. Dexter has your address.'

For the second time that morning, the pilot fish spoke out loud. They were only two words, but they struck fear into Emma's heart.

'Black tie.'

Chapter 2

Emma wasn't the sort to panic, but she was as close to freaking out that afternoon as she had ever been as she raced home from work to get ready for her boss's party. She had been to a number of formal events since coming to Hollywood to work, but never anything at this level. For the men this just meant buying or renting a tux, but for women it was more complicated, much more complicated. She knew she was going to find herself in the midst of untold wealth, unimaginable beauty (often the handiwork of the most expensive cosmetic surgeons on the planet), and extravagant designer clothes and jewellery.

She still had all her own skin, no surgical enhancement, no valuable jewellery and a seriously limited stock of 'smart' frocks. Her job had always been more important to her than her social life and she didn't really enjoy all the palaver involved with dressing up and, as she had always told herself, she saw no reason why she should dress up to attract a man when that was the last thing on her mind.

However, as she fought her way through the rush hour traffic in her Mini, she found herself toying with the idea of breaking all her resolutions and dashing into one of the big-name boutiques to pay a small fortune for a dress she would probably only wear a handful of times in her life. Of course, dressing up tonight was a work imperative. Her boss would expect her to make an effort, and turning up in jeans and a T-shirt would no doubt impact very poorly on her career. No, there was no question about it. She was going to have to slap on the war paint and suit up. The question was what to wear and her apprehension grew once more. Fortunately, as she spotted a police car in her rear-view mirror and lifted her foot off the gas, she came to her senses.

There was no way she could, or should, try to compete with the rich and the famous. For a moment she reflected that she and Dexter, the pilot fish, probably had more in common than she had hitherto realised. He would only be there because he worked for JM and she was only going to be there so that she could meet JM's son, whatever his name was. Nevertheless, she had to look smart – that much was clear – but that was that. As she carried on driving at a more sedate pace across town, in her head she ran through the contents of her wardrobe, such as it was, and decided to go for one of the only two long gowns she owned. Fortunately, she was tall and this meant she would be able to wear comfortable shoes and not find herself having to totter about on the sort of high heels some of the other ladies would be wearing.

By the time the doorbell rang, a few moments before eight, she was as ready as she could be. She was scrubbed and polished and she had even managed to put her hair up for once, although she had cricked her neck trying to check the result with the hand mirror. She was no longer close to panic, but there was a cold empty feeling of nervousness gnawing at her gut. Even after more than ten years here in Hollywood, she knew she was going to be far outside her comfort zone tonight. Her apprehension grew as she came downstairs and stepped out onto the sidewalk in her scruffy, but wonderfully comfortable, sandals. The 'car' JM had promised was almost as long as the whole block. A uniformed driver gave her a smart salute and opened the rear door.

'Miss Taylor? Good evening, ma'am. My name's Luis. I'll be your chauffeur tonight.'

She climbed gingerly into the massive limousine, doing her best not to crush her gown – or display her 'sensible' shoes as she did so. As she sat down, so the glass partition in front of her hummed smoothly down and Luis's smiling face appeared.

'Can I get you anything, ma'am? A glass of champagne, maybe?'

Emma shook her head. One thing was for sure, she was going to need to keep a clear head tonight. Getting hammered was not an option – however tempting it might be. 'Thank you, Luis, but I'm fine. How long's it going to take us to get to Mr Miros's house?'

'Traffic's not too bad tonight, ma'am. Half an hour, tops.'

He was dead right. It took exactly twenty-six minutes for them to get to the neo-classical gatehouse of JM's palatial home. Here they were met by a bulky security guard with a pistol in a holster at his side. More frightening than the pistol, however, was the sudden explosion of flashes as photographers materialised around the car, some even pressing their lenses right up against the double-glazed window beside her. Clearly, JM's not so little bash was going to be plastered all over *The Hollywood Reporter* and the internet by morning. Emma sat back and surreptitiously wiped the sweat off her palms against the leather upholstery beneath her.

After checking her name on the list, the guard waved them through and the limo glided smoothly up the winding drive to the house. This ran between meticulously trimmed box hedges, behind which there was a subtropical extravaganza of exotic plants and trees. She wouldn't have been surprised to see monkeys swinging through the branches, maybe even followed by Tarzan himself. This was quite some place.

The front of the villa was bathed in floodlight and she did her best to keep her shoes out of sight as she stepped from the car and murmured a quiet 'thank you' to Luis. To her surprise, he gave her a big smile and allowed himself a personal comment.

'You look great, ma'am, if you don't mind me saying. Just great.'

She smiled back at him, genuinely grateful for the morale boost.

'Thank you, Luis. I needed that.'

As she started to make her way up the broad stone stairway to the front door, an immaculate servant appeared, dressed in a smart grey waistcoat and freshly-ironed white shirt. He gave her a little bow.

'Welcome, Miss Taylor. If you'd like to come with me, I'll take you to Mr and Mrs Miros.'

Vaguely wondering how he had recognised her, Emma thanked him and followed as he led her into the marble-clad lobby and onwards into an enormous lounge. In spite of its size, the room was crowded, and within just the first few seconds she recognised no fewer than half a dozen A-list celebrities. The waiter led her to the centre of the room where she immediately saw JM's head looming above the others around him. Alongside him, barely reaching his chest, was his wife. Unsurprisingly, stationed at his other side was none other than Dexter, the pilot fish. As Emma approached, the little man leant forward and drew JM's attention to her arrival. Excusing himself from none other than the Governor of California, the great man held out a welcoming hand towards her.

'Emma, good evening. Thanks for coming.'

His lips even curled into a pretty good approximation of a smile and she wondered if the glass of champagne in his hand had maybe helped to relax his face muscles.

'Thank you so much for inviting me to your gorgeous home, sir.' For a moment, she came close to curtseying, but managed to control the impulse.

'Let me introduce you to my wife, Rachel. Rach, honey, this is Emma, She's the young lady who's gonna be accompanying Richard to Italy. She's one of the brightest talents in the company.'

The elegant blonde lady produced a smile of her own and extended her hand, politely ignoring Emma's blushes at her boss's compliments. As they shook hands, she glanced back at him.

'Jan, you didn't tell me how pretty she is.' Even through her embarrassment, Emma registered the first time she had ever heard her boss addressed by anything other than his initials. 'It's good to meet you, Emma.'

'Thank you so much, Mrs Miros. You have a wonderful home.'

Mrs Miros directed another reproving look at her husband. 'And you also didn't tell me she's English. I do so love an English accent.'

As she spoke, Emma studied her surreptitiously. She knew for a fact that she was nudging sixty, but there wasn't a line on her face. If her hair was dyed, it had been done amazingly well. She was wearing a simply stunning light grey silk dress and she looked little older than Emma herself, who only the previous month had reached the ripe old age of thirty-five.

'Rach, have you seen Richard?' JM's eyes were scouring the room from his high vantage point, but without success. 'I want him to meet Emma.'

For a second the smile on Mrs Miros's face slipped a notch, but just for a second. 'I haven't, Jan, I'm afraid. I suppose he must be outside in the garden.' She glanced across at Emma. 'He's not a great one for crowds. I expect he's gone into hiding.'

That sounded strange and unexpected and was followed by a momentary silence. Emma decided to help out. 'I'm sure you have lots to do welcoming all your guests.' She followed the direction of Mrs Miros's eyes and spotted open French windows at the end of the room. 'Why don't I go and look for him? I can introduce myself.' A thought occurred to her. 'You'll just have to tell me what he looks like.'

To her surprise, it was Dexter who responded. 'Don't worry, I'll come with you.' He shot a quick glance at JM, presumably to seek his permission, and then came over to Emma and pointed towards the French windows. 'The garden's this way.'

'See you later, Emma.' JM gave her a little wave. 'And, Dexter, get the girl a drink. She looks like she could use one.'

As they walked away through the crowd, Dexter added under his breath. 'I think we could both do with one.' Although she knew he was originally from England, just like her, his accent now was completely neutral, which perfectly suited somebody whose job it was to melt chameleon-like into the landscape. In fact, she had no idea even of his age. He could have been forty or he could have been sixty and she vaguely wondered if he somehow magically morphed into whatever role he happened to be playing at the time. This was Hollywood, after all.

A passing waiter supplied two glasses of freshly poured ice-cold champagne and Emma took one willingly, pausing to clink it against Dexter's before taking a sip. She didn't know a lot about wine but she had no doubt this would be real French champagne, and the expensive stuff as well. She gave Dexter a smile.

'Thanks a lot, Dexter.'

'You're welcome, Emma. Listen, there's something you need to know about Richard.'

Emma was immediately intrigued, mainly by his some-what hesitant tone, and the fact that his voice had dropped to almost a whisper. He led her across to the far corner of the room where they were able to take up station behind the massive white grand piano, out of earshot of everybody. After a surreptitious look around, he launched into his exposé.

'Richard's been in a spot of trouble. The thing is, the reason he's only now graduated from college is that he disappeared off the grid for a few years in his early twenties and since then he's been in rehab, on and off, for quite some time, trying to break a serious drug habit.'

Wow, Emma thought to herself. 'And how old is he now?'

'He's twenty-seven. He'll be twenty-eight any day now.'

'And his drug problems, are they all behind him now?'

Dexter shrugged. 'We can only hope. The fact that he's managed to get himself together enough to finish his studies is a positive sign, but it's still early days.'

As she listened, Emma was turning over in her head the ramifications of this disclosure. So she was going to be expected to act as nursemaid to a recovering drug addict. What was he going to be like and, more to the point, what would his father's reaction be if Richard were to fall back into the habit while on Emma's watch? Suddenly her forthcoming tour of Italy was looking less and less inviting. She toyed – only for a moment – with the idea of telling her boss she didn't feel like taking the job after all, but she had no doubt what the result of that act of rebellion would be. Like it or not, she was going to be stuck with Richard or she would torpedo her whole career. She took a deep calming breath and followed it up with a very welcome mouthful of champagne. Beside her, she saw Dexter reach into his top pocket and pull out a card.

'Listen, Emma, here's what we're going to do. This is my personal cell number. You can get me on that any time of the day or night.' He caught her eye. 'But I'd be grateful if you kept that number confidential just between the two of us. Okay?'

'Okay, it's a promise. Now, just so we're clear, what you're saying is that you want me to notify you, rather than JM, if anything happens in Italy involving his son, is that right?'

'Exactly. You tell me and then I'll break it to JM in the best possible way.' He produced a little smile. 'You should be pleased. I'm volunteering to be the messenger. I get shot instead of you if it all goes belly up.'

'And you think it will?'

Again he shrugged. 'Who knows? Richard's not a bad boy. I've worked for his father for twenty years now and I've watched Richard grow up. He was a pretty naughty kid, but it was only when he went off to college that it all fell apart for him. I think his problem was that he came from a family background where everything was done for him, where he could have whatever he asked for, but ultimately, it was always his father who called the shots. Don't get me wrong, there's no doubt both his parents thought and still think the world of him but, whatever the reason, he went AWOL. On the face of it, he had everything, but in the end he just rebelled and the results were ugly. He disappeared so effectively that everybody thought he was dead at one point.'

'Where did he go?'

'Europe, apparently, and some very unsavoury parts of it from what I hear. Ironically, the very fact of having so much money made it all too easy for him to afford the drugs that have had such a devastating effect on him. In the end it was by following the money stream that his parents finally managed to locate him again. He was found in some squalid slum in the suburbs of Berlin, I believe.'

'Wow, what a mess!' Emma nodded in sympathy. The poor little rich boy syndrome was all too common in this glitzy world of excessive wealth. 'And what about after-effects? Has he done himself any permanent harm?'

'I don't think so. I hope not. I haven't spoken to him much since he came back home a few weeks ago. He seems pretty much his old self again now, but just a whole lot less bubbly, more introspective – quieter. You heard what his mother said. He hates crowds and finds even the most superficial conversations challenging. He used to be the absolute opposite – always going to parties, having parties, and wanting to be the life and soul of them. But not any more.' He swilled the last of his champagne around in his glass before swallowing it. 'You needed to know that before you met him.'

'Thanks, Dexter. I owe you. Tell me, does his father know you're telling me this?'

Dexter nodded. 'He's the one who asked me to tell you. To be honest, I would have said something to you anyway, but he took me to one side this evening and made me promise to tell you the whole story.'

Jan Miros went up in Emma's esteem. 'If I don't get a chance to talk to JM alone, please will you thank him? You're right. It's much better for Richard, and for me, that I know.' She finished her drink and set the glass down alongside his on top of the piano, hoping they wouldn't mark the pristine surface. She slipped the card with his phone number into her purse and gave him a big smile. 'Thanks, Dexter.'

'You're welcome. Now, if you're ready, let's go and find Richard.'

Mrs Miros was right. Richard had indeed chosen to hide. As they walked down to the enormous pool, hidden from the view of the other guests by a high hedge and a bank of sweet-scented lavender, Dexter caught her by the arm and pointed. 'That's him there. Want me to introduce you?'

At the far end of the pool, sitting on a springboard at the water's edge, was a figure dressed in a dark tuxedo. Emma made a quick decision.

'No, that's fine, Dexter. Thanks a lot. I'll take it from here.'

He nodded and turned on his heels, while Emma set off down the side of the pool to the far end. As she reached the springboard, the figure stirred and looked up. Emma took a good look at him as she approached. He was a good-looking man with thick, dark hair like his father's, but he had inherited his mother's fine facial features. Yes, he was handsome all right, and with his wealth she had no doubt he could have had the pick of any available girl in Hollywood – and there was no shortage of them. His face was only marred by dark rings below his eyes. As he saw her, an expression of recognition crossed his face.

'You must be Emma.'

She nodded and smiled. 'Dead right. What gave me away?'

He managed a half-smile in return, not dissimilar to the attempts his father also made in that department. 'Dexter told me you were tall, blonde and drop-dead gorgeous.' Then he let his eyes fall once more to the water below.

She did her best to control her blushes, still amazed at being described in such glowing terms by the pilot fish. She had never really thought of Dexter as possessing any kind of aesthetic sense. In fairness, she hadn't really thought of him up to now as anything more than an appendage forever linked to the big boss. Her opinion of him rose as a result.

'Well, you can see he was exaggerating, but surely that description could apply to any number of the women here tonight?'

He looked up again and she noticed for the first time that he had the same piercing blue eyes as his father. The difference was that his were much bleaker, prematurely aged. 'Maybe it's because you look different from the others.'

'Is that a polite way of saying I look a mess?' She was determined to keep it light.

He shook his head. 'Not at all. You just look a bit more serious than the average Hollywood blonde.' He gave that same dismissive gesture of the hand as his father did. 'Anyway, my father said you were coming tonight and you're about the first person to speak to me so it wasn't that hard to join the dots.'

'Mind if I sit down?'

He shifted across the warm wood of the diving board to make room and she sat down beside him. As she did so, her 'sensible' shoes suddenly hove into view.

'Cool shoes. Is this the new fashion?'

She wasn't sure if he was serious or if he was poking fun at her; she could feel herself blushing again. She thought about trying to hide the shoes, but the cat was out of the bag now so she did her best to bluff it out. 'Maybe I'm setting the trend. Anyway, Richard, I thought I'd come and talk to you about Italy.'

He nodded but made no reply. His eyes had dropped once more, maybe to the water or maybe to her sandals. She did her best to dismiss thoughts of her *bloody* shoes and concentrate on work.

'Have you read *Dreaming of Italy*?'

He shook his head.

'Then I think that's the first thing you should do. Will you do that for me? I'll ask Dexter to get you a copy of the screenplay.'

'My father already gave me a copy, but I just haven't got round to reading it.' He glanced up. 'But I will.' His eyes made contact with hers once again. 'Is it good?'

'I'll leave that for you to judge. For my money, I think it's very good. Certainly your father's hoping it'll turn into a blockbuster.'

'What's it about?'

'It's a love story set immediately before the First World War, around the same period as *A Room with a View.* Seen that?'

'No, but I've heard the name. That was set in Florence, wasn't it?'

'That's right. Well, this is sort of similar but it strays all over Italy, or rather northern Italy, from the Alps to Tuscany and back up to Venice. It's the story of a young Englishwoman who's been packed off on a tour of Italy by her father, accompanied by her governess who's a bit of an old battleaxe. The girl had got herself involved with the suffragette movement back in the UK and he didn't approve.'

'Didn't one of them run out in front of a race horse and get killed?'

'That's right.' Emma was impressed. Clearly he had paid attention in his history classes. 'Anyway, in the course of the tour, she meets and falls in love with a young British army officer who's on leave over there in Italy. What we've got to do is to find the most beautiful, emotive, atmospheric locations possible. Your father told me he wants people to fall in love with the scenery as much as with the characters.' She paused. 'Have you been to Italy?'

He nodded. 'Yes, but the places I went to were anything but beautiful.' He raised his head again. 'It was a bad time for me. Did they tell you about my problems?'

Emma took a deep breath. 'They told me you'd been in rehab, but that you're clear now. Is that right?'

'That's what they tell me.'

'You're not convinced?'

He shrugged. 'I'm taking it one day at a time.'

Emma decided to steer away from this topic but not before she had given him some encouragement. 'Well, you're looking good from where I'm sitting.'

He didn't acknowledge the remark so she stood up, smoothing down her dress and checking that her sandals were once more hidden from view.

'Feel like coming in with me for a drink?'

He shook his head. 'I'm staying off the booze, thanks. To be honest, I'm not that fond of crowds these days. Besides, nobody'll talk to me. Nobody knows who I am.'

Emma couldn't let that one go.

'What do you mean, nobody knows you? This is your house. You're the son of the host and hostess.'

He gave her a wry smile. 'I've pretty much been painted out of the picture over these past few years. They did it to protect me, but it also eliminated a source of embarrassment for them.' He hesitated for a few seconds. 'I don't blame them, I really don't. I've been an embarrassment to myself.' He sounded genuine and Emma's heart went out to him.

'So you're telling me most of the guests here tonight have no idea who you are?' He nodded. 'Well, that makes two of us. I'm almost completely unknown amongst all these big names as well. I've got an idea, let's pretend you're my little brother from England. Can you do an English accent? Come on, let's go and have some fun.'

He looked up again and this time she felt she could discern a spark in those lifeless eyes. 'Did you say *little* brother?' As he spoke, he stood up and Emma couldn't miss the fact that he had definitely inherited the height gene from his father. She wasn't small, but he towered over her.

'I stand corrected. You can be my *younger, but taller* brother.' As she took a better look at him, she reflected that if she were ten years younger, she could quite easily have been attracted to this handsome, troubled boy. No sooner had the thought occurred than she dismissed it, just as she dismissed the thought of any man. She determined to concentrate on thinking of him as her little brother, six foot six or not. 'Come on, let's see if we can both find something non-alcoholic to drink. Don't forget, I'm in my boss's house. The last thing I need is to get plastered.'

This brought a real smile to his face and it took years off him. 'Well, if you insist, my dear, I totally agree. Do let us go and have fun.' He sounded like Lord Whatshisname out of *Downton Abbey*. She was impressed.

'Wow, you do a good English accent.'

'I had an English girlfriend for a while.'

There was a strange note in his voice and she should have picked up on it. Instead, she chose to keep the conversation going and immediately regretted it.

'And what happened to her? Why did you split up?'

His answer suddenly changed the whole mood of the conversation.

'She left me because I couldn't quit the drugs.' His voice was studiously level. 'It was the right thing for her to do. I was a waste of space.'

'Oh, Richard, I'm so sorry.'

'Call me Rich. My friends call me Rich.'

Taking this as a positive sign, she caught hold of his forearm and set off towards the house.

'All right, Rich, come and help your sister find a glass of water.'

A few minutes later, as they mingled with the crowd back in JM's huge lounge, she felt a tap on her bare shoulder. She looked round to see none other than Ethan Dukes, one of the most recognisable faces – and bodies – on the planet. She had known him ever since he was a young actor just after getting his first big break and they had become good friends. As he was under contract to JMGP, they often met and they got on very well together. Unlike a lot of superstars, he had remained pretty grounded – insofar as you can be grounded when you do most of your travelling by private jet or helicopter.

They often spoke on set, or over a coffee, and she felt she knew him as well as anybody in the business. She got the impression that he enjoyed talking to her and, in fact, she sometimes felt more like an agony aunt, or a big sister, to him as he often came to her with his problems. In fact, she knew him so well by now that she genuinely managed to forget he was a global megastar when they met up and he probably appreciated being treated as a normal human being.

'Hi, English. How you doin'?' Ethan knew her name, but had always called her that, and when he greeted her he always imitated Joey from *Friends*.

She gave him a big smile and a kiss on the cheek. 'Hi, Ethan, I'm fine. How's life in your stratosphere?' She pointed to Rich beside her. 'Do you know Richard?'

Ethan nodded and shook Rich warmly by the hand. 'Hi, Richie, I haven't seen you since you were a spotty teenager. All good with you?'

Emma was pleased to see Rich respond with a real genuine smile. 'I'm good, thanks, Ethan... now.'

Emma caught a glimpse of comprehension in Ethan's eyes. She knew that very little escaped him here on his home turf and he had probably been one of the very few to know of Rich's struggle with drugs. He clapped Rich on the shoulder and gave him an encouraging wink. 'That's great, Richie. Keep it up.' He turned back to Emma and she felt his eyes on her, checking her out. 'You're looking gorgeous tonight, English, you know that?'

Emma had enough experience of Hollywood hype by now to be able to sidestep the compliment almost without blushing. Almost. Whether she thought of him as sort of her little brother or not, this was, after all, the man *Cosmo* readers had voted the sexiest man on the planet.

'Why, thank you, Ethan, you say the nicest things. And you aren't looking too shabby yourself.'

He grinned. They both knew that was the understatement of the night. 'Hey, they tell me you're on your way to Italy to scout out some romantic places for me. Is that really true, English?'

'That's right. Have you read the script of *Dreaming of Italy*?' She lowered her voice as this was still a closely-guarded secret.

She saw him hesitate for a moment and it didn't surprise her. He had probably received a one paragraph summary of the plot from JM or his agent and he wouldn't start in on the whole thing until just a matter of weeks or even days before shooting began. Even so, she knew from past experience that he would be word perfect when he came on set.

'Not quite all, but it sounds great.'

'It *will* be great with you playing the lead.' She smiled to herself. She was getting quite good at this Hollywood hype herself. 'And I imagine you've heard who your co-star's going to be?'

A look of apprehension crossed his face. 'I know. Laney Travers. That's amazing… I think.' He dropped his voice. 'I just hope she isn't going to act me out of the movie.'

Emma slipped seamlessly into her agony aunt persona. 'Don't do yourself down, Ethan. You'll knock 'em dead.'

'Here's hoping. Anyway listen, while you're in Italy, I need you to find me somewhere sexy in the moonlight. I love those scenes.' He grinned for a moment. 'That way, nobody sees the wrinkles in the half-light.' His eyes flicked over her shoulder and back again. 'Sorry, sweetie, but that's my agent over there beckoning. Looks like I need to press the flesh. No rest for the wicked…' He waved at Rich, blew her a kiss, and carried on making a tour of the room. Needless to say, there wasn't even a hint of a wrinkle on his face.

Chapter 3

Their flight landed at Turin airport in the early afternoon and Emma was glad to get out into the fresh air. They had flown from LA to Munich earlier in the day and had had to wait there for a couple of hours before getting their connecting flight. Although the transatlantic part of the journey had been in business class with a lie-flat bed, Emma hadn't been able to sleep much and was looking forward to an early night.

First things first, however, she pulled out her phone and called Elliot. He was the executive Dexter had found to take over her work at JMGP and she had spent twelve hours a day with him every day over the past week, doing her best to ensure he was going to be able to take her place – as much for her sake as for his. It wasn't that she didn't trust him to do a good job, but it would be her reputation on the line if things went pear-shaped, and after the years of toil, sacrifice and burnt midnight oil it had taken for her to claw her way up to her current position in the company, she wasn't going to see that thrown away by somebody else. Still, grudgingly, she had started to come round to thinking that he might be all right, but she was determined to keep a close eye on him, even from six thousand miles away.

'Emma, hi. You've arrived?'

'Hi, Elliot, what's new?'

He reeled off the latest developments and she felt reasonably reassured. For now, at least, things appeared to be running smoothly but with shooting starting on Monday, she knew the real acid test still awaited. She threw him a few queries about thoughts that had occurred to her in the plane and his answers were what she wanted to hear. As she wished him luck and ended the call, her fingers were firmly crossed.

The hazy June sunshine was not dissimilar to Los Angeles and she was looking forward to the warmth after the air-conditioned interior of the aircraft. Unlike LAX, passport control here in Turin took barely a few minutes and they were soon reunited with their bags. Richard piled them onto a trolley and they made their way out into the terminal building where they found their guide waiting for them. To Emma's surprise, this turned out to be a woman, and a fairly young one at that, certainly a few years younger than her. Emma hoped Dexter had got it right. They needed somebody really good.

No sooner had the thought crossed her mind than she gave herself a mental telling-off. Just because this woman was younger than she was didn't make her any less likely to be good at her job than if she had been middle-aged.

As she saw them, the young woman waved the sign marked JMGP and hurried towards them.

'Good afternoon and welcome to Italy. I'm Marina and I'm going to be your guide. Can I give you a hand with your luggage?' She had a noticeable Italian accent, but her English was very fluent and Emma gave a surreptitious sigh of relief.

Seeing as Marina barely came up to Emma's shoulder it was debatable how much help she would be able to provide when dealing with the two hefty suitcases, but it was nice of her to ask. Emma shook her head and went over to her while Richard pushed the trolley along behind her.

'Hello, Marina, it's good to meet you. I'm Emma and this is Richard.'

They all shook hands and Emma was quick to find out what Marina had in store for them. The reply sounded reassuringly organised.

'I was told you're on the lookout for beautiful, romantic places that are a bit out of the ordinary and you want to start in the Alps somewhere. That's right, isn't it?' Emma nodded. 'Well, tonight we're booked into a comfortable hotel right in the centre of Turin and there's nothing planned. I'm assuming you'd both like a rest after your flight. But tomorrow we start work if that suits you.'

Emma nodded again. 'I'd certainly like an early night. What about you, Rich? A quiet night in or are you thinking of hitting the bright lights of the city?'

'Something to eat and then I think I'll head for my room.' He gave her a little smile. 'I've been reading the screenplay on the plane and I really want to finish it.'

Emma was glad to see him smile and glad he was reading it, but slightly disappointed that it had taken him over two weeks to do so. After all, this was her job on the line here, not to mention the bottom line of his father's company's balance sheet. She was more than ready to show Rich the ropes as his father had instructed, but she had hoped he would show a bit more enthusiasm. Still, she told herself, they were both jet-lagged and, the main thing was that he was reading it.

'Are you enjoying it?'

'Yes, I am, more than I thought I would. I haven't really been in a romantic mood for a good long while, but I've really got into the story now and I want to find out how it ends.' He glanced across at Marina. 'Have you read it?'

As she shook her head, Emma explained. 'It's for our eyes only for now. Sorry, Marina, but the precise details are very hush hush.'

'That's all right. My boss already explained that to me. I know it's set just over a hundred years ago, but that's about all. You just tell me what you feel I need to know. Now, if you'd like to follow me, I've got the car outside.'

The car park was only a short distance from the terminal and the late afternoon air temperature was high, but not unpleasant. The sky was cloudless and they could clearly see the semicircle of the Alps curling away to the horizon on both sides of them. Although it was June, the tops of the mountains were still covered in snow that sparkled in the sunlight. She took a deep breath and felt a burst of excitement flood through her. Here she was, back in Italy after so many years and the memories came flooding back. The last time she had been over here, she had been right at the start of her career, filled with hopes for the future, but even she couldn't have imagined back then that she would find herself here; now in charge of a team scouting for locations that could make or break a multi-million dollar project. There was a lot riding on this, but it gave her a terrific feeling of responsibility and she felt a shiver of pride. All those long hours at work after everybody else had gone home, all those missed parties, refused invitations and cancelled dates were paying off. Her eyes flicked up to the snowy peaks. Yes, the sky was the limit.

The car turned out to be a very new-looking, large people carrier with three rows of seats which easily accommodated the cases in its cavernous boot. Before Emma could say anything, Rich climbed into the back and left the front passenger seat to her.

They picked their way through the airport traffic and out onto the main road and were soon on a modern highway heading towards the centre of the city. Emma was relieved to find that Marina didn't have the habit common to so many drivers she had come across during her time in Rome: a compulsion to drive as fast as possible at all times and with a near-Kamikaze death wish on occasions. Marina was doing just fine and Emma was able to relax and look around. The surroundings were part rural, part industrial, but certainly not by any stretch of the imagination romantic. As they went along, she and Marina talked.

'Where were you thinking of taking us tomorrow, Marina?'

'I was told you wanted to start in the mountains. Is that right?'

'Yes, the main character, Emily, and her governess have travelled down from London by train and they start their Italian tour in the high mountains just this side of the railway tunnel at, I think, Bardonecchia. Does that sound right?'

'That's right. The problem with that valley is that since then they've built a road tunnel alongside the old railway tunnel and there's now an autostrada running up the middle of the valley, so I thought we should go for somewhere a bit quieter, but still in the Alps.'

That sounded perfect to Emma. She nodded in agreement and Marina carried on.

'The valleys north of here leading into the Alps are very pretty and they're well off the normal tourist trail. I've earmarked a few places I hope you'll find suitably scenic and romantic and I've arranged for a local man to meet us up there and show us around. Is there anything specific to the plot of the movie that you need to have? I don't know... a church or a fountain or some such?'

'Let me see... the scenes in the mountains are right at the beginning of the story and the heroine, Emily, is still furious and bitterly resentful of the way she's been effectively banished from England by her domineering father. So probably not so much charming Alpine pastures and big brown-eyed cows with bells round their necks looking cute, but something a bit more stark, a bit more melancholy. Okay?'

'I'll tell Cesare, the man who's meeting us up there, and we'll see what he can come up with. As far as Turin's concerned, I haven't set anything up as I was told you weren't interested in the main cities. That is right, isn't it?'

'Absolutely.'

'Anyway, if you do decide to take a look around Turin while we're here, you'll find it's a fine historic city – and the shops are great – but I wouldn't really place it particularly high on my list of *romantic* places.'

'That's pretty much what I'd thought. As you know, our route over the next two weeks should take us down from here to the Mediterranean coast, from there into

Tuscany and then we start curling back northwards, ending up in Venice. If you can come up with some suggestions for places along the way, that'll be great.'

They chatted about the route and Emma definitely got the impression Marina knew what she was talking about. It emerged that her father had been an officer in the *Carabinieri* and so the family had moved around all over northern Italy as she was growing up. As a result, she was familiar with a lot of the areas of interest for the film. Emma nodded in silent satisfaction. It looked like Dexter had done it again. She resolved to buy him a little present when the time came to return to LA. She might even get something for Elliot if things went smoothly on the set of *Sweet Memories*.

The hotel was a very modern conversion of a fine, old building right in the heart of the city. The city itself, once they had crawled in through the very unprepossessing suburban industrial sprawl, was charming. Marina had obviously been doing her homework as she gave them a brief history of the city as they drove in.

She told them that Turin had been home to the House of Savoy and the first King of Italy and it exuded prosperity and power. The magnificent wide boulevards with their covered arcades were lined with imposing eighteenth- and nineteenth-century buildings, reflecting the wealth the city had accumulated in the wake of Italy's industrial revolution, culminating in the birth of FIAT, the *Fabbrica Italiana Automobili Torino*. Emma had never realised what the acronym stood for before and, certainly, there was no shortage of modern-day Fiats everywhere she looked.

Their hotel was set in the middle of a very classy shopping area with big-name fashion houses lining the arcaded walkways. Emma resolved to reserve a few hours for some retail therapy. She had always loved Italian shoes and she was determined to look for replacements for her scruffy, if comfortable, sandals.

Once they had checked in, Emma sat down in her room and checked her work email account. There were a couple of emails that needed urgent action for *Sweet Memories*, so she forwarded them on to Elliot with detailed instructions. It wasn't, she repeated to herself, that she didn't think him capable, but she just wanted to be sure that he would do the right thing. She almost believed herself. Once she was finally as sure as she could be that things in Hollywood were sorted, she went down to meet the other two in the stylish hotel bar. Rich looked up as she came in.

'Finally finished work for the day, boss?'

'Hopefully.'

Rich glanced across at Marina and explained. 'Emma never really stops. Every time I looked at her on the plane she was on her laptop, and not watching movies.'

Emma shook her head slowly. 'I'm not really a workaholic, but I've got another movie about to start shooting on Monday and I need to be sure everything's in order.' An image of herself, sitting at her desk in an echoing, empty building came to mind and she found herself wondering just who she was trying to fool. With her, work always had come first, to the detriment of almost anything else, starting with her personal life. Still, it had all been worthwhile, hadn't it?

Marina looked mildly surprised. 'Haven't you got an assistant?'

Rich was quick to clarify the situation. 'Emma's got a replacement covering for her and she's scared he'll screw up.'

This was a bit too close to the truth so Emma didn't comment. She just ordered herself a glass of mineral water like Rich and Marina and changed the subject to Italy, listening with interest as Marina brought them up to speed with Italy's current political and financial problems. Apparently back at the time of *Dreaming of Italy*, things hadn't been brilliant either, especially out in the country, away from big industrial hubs like Turin. Emma made a note to add this to her report. It might be worthwhile including a mention of rural poverty in the movie.

They went up to the top-floor restaurant for an early evening meal after which Emma had every intention of crashing out. Sitting down to an Italian meal brought a host of memories flooding back to her and she wondered what sort of thoughts it might awaken in Richard. He hadn't done a lot of talking downstairs in the bar and she could see he was still a bit tense. As she got to know him better, she found she liked him more and more and she resolved to be as supportive as she could. He had a long, hard road ahead of him and if she could help, she would. Hopefully, he would gradually relax more and more as he got over the jetlag.

Marina explained to them that Turin and the whole region of *Piemonte* – which meant literally 'at the foot of the mountains' – was famous for its antipasti. Apparently, meals here could consist of as many as ten or even twenty different starters, before moving on to the next courses.

After just a few small snacks on the flights, Emma was hungry, but not that hungry, and she opted to go for the antipasti first and reserve judgement on whether to have another course until she knew how much room she would have left after all the starters.

As it turned out, the answer to that was quite simple: none.

A succession of waiters began to appear at regular intervals bearing silver salvers, from which they deposited spoonfuls of food onto their plates. This entire process took almost an hour and by the end, Emma knew she was full. Finally, she sat back and tried to remember just what delicacies she had been served.

First there had been homemade Russian salad and a vast selection of salami and ham, then *crostini*: pieces of toasted bread covered with porcini mushrooms in a truffle sauce. This was followed by roast onions and slices of *cotechino* – a thick warm, boiled sausage accompanied by mashed potato – and then red peppers grilled and covered with a thick sauce made of anchovies and garlic. In spite of its potentially lethal-sounding ingredients, this sauce turned out to be exquisite. After that had come tomatoes stuffed with cheese and breadcrumbs, slices of veal in a tuna sauce, slices of tongue covered in a rich green parsley-based sauce, tiny round pieces of cheese, some topped with a spicy red sauce, others with a chunky green sauce made with parsley, garlic and olive oil and, finally, roast potatoes liberally smothered in gorgonzola.

Along with this feast, they ate the local breadsticks and she and Marina drank an amazing light red wine called *Grignolino* that fizzed as it landed in their glasses but then settled down almost immediately. Altogether, it was a wonderful introduction to the cuisine of this part of north-western Italy and Emma made a point of photographing the spread before them, determined to suggest incorporating a *Piemontese* meal in the film at some point. While anchovies and garlic maybe weren't as romantic as oysters or caviar, the end result was that Emma felt pleasantly replete, her taste buds tickled and very definitely ready for bed. It did occur to her that it was just as well she would be sleeping alone. After all the garlic, she had a fair idea that her breath would probably be able to kill at a range of several feet. One thing was for sure – there would be no vampires in her room tonight.

She was particularly pleased to see Rich gradually begin to come out of his shell and start to enjoy the meal. He refused any wine, declaring himself quite happy with cold mineral water and Emma reflected that his abstinence might be good for her, too. Last time she had been in Italy as a student, she had definitely overdone it and she knew she needed to keep a clear head this time.

In the course of the meal, it also became quite clear to Emma that Marina found the tall, taciturn American really rather appealing and Emma found herself hoping nothing would develop between them that might endanger the success of this mission. The last thing she needed was a broken-hearted guide or two members of their little group refusing to talk to each other. She had always been very much against relationships within the workplace, but she decided not to say anything to either of them for now, resolving to keep a close eye on how their relationship was developing. At least, she told herself, it didn't look as though Rich was too interested in allowing anything to develop anyway. That same rather bleak, detached air was still apparent from time to time and, while definitely sounding a bit more laid-back, he was still very reserved. Once again she resolved to do her best to help him along.

After the antipasti, she sat back and watched as tall Rich and diminutive Marina managed to put away helpings of four different types of pasta, ranging from *agnolotti* filled with mozzarella and basil to spaghetti in a rich, dark wild boar sauce. She resisted Marina's attempts to get her to try a dessert of chestnut-based *Castagnaccio* tart accompanied by the chef's homemade ice cream, but she did relent and have a couple of the silky-smooth *Gianduia* chocolates at the very end as she finished her glass of wine. She was mildly impressed to see that there was still wine left in the bottle. It looked as though Marina was also going slow on the booze which, considering she was the driver, boded well. All in all, it was an excellent first meal in Italy and she made a mental note to include some serious exercise in her daily regime or she was going to need a whole new wardrobe if she kept on eating like this.

As they were just about to head up to their rooms she remembered the historical advisor.

'Marina, we're going to need somebody who can advise on the historical aspects of all the places we're visiting. Do you know anything about that?'

Marina nodded. 'Yes, my boss called me earlier today. It's all arranged. The guy's tied up today but he'll meet up with us tomorrow or Sunday down by the coast, if that's all right with you. He'll then stay for as long as you want him.'

'That'll be fine. We don't really need a historical expert for our trip into the mountains tomorrow anyway, do we? Can you tell me anything about him?'

'All I know is that he's called Mark and he's half-English.'

'And he's an expert in Italian history?'

'Apparently. He lives here in Italy, somewhere in Tuscany, I think. Don't worry, he'll be fine, I'm sure. He's a close personal friend of my boss, Gianluca, and I know he'll vouch for him.'

'Have you worked with him before?'

'No, but he comes highly recommended.'

Emma crossed her fingers all the same.

Chapter 4

Saturday dawned bright and clear. So clear in fact that from her room on the fourth floor, Emma had an unbroken view of the stunning crescent of the Alps that ringed the city to the west and north. The distant snow-clad peaks stood out in stark contrast against the deep cerulean blue of the sky. Although a hazy cap of dirty air lay over the city itself, the sky in the distance was clear and she felt sure she should be able to get some good photos today.

Breakfast was a buffet affair, but Emma limited herself to some fresh fruit salad, a warm croissant and a wonderful cappuccino. There was just one problem: there was no sign of Richard. She and Marina waited for him until it was almost nine o'clock and then Emma went up to his room. She tapped on the door and waited for almost a minute until she heard a croaky voice from inside.

'Yes, who is it?'

'It's me... Emma. Are you up, Rich?'

There was a rattling and the door was pulled open. It was dark in his room, the curtains still drawn together, but she could clearly see that he was only wearing a pair of boxers. She took a couple of steps backwards.

'Everything okay, Rich? It's nine o'clock and we were supposed to meet up half an hour ago. Marina and I were getting worried.'

He looked shell-shocked and for a moment the thought even passed through her head that he might be stoned. But his response was heartening. He suddenly straightened up, ran his hands though his hair, and glanced back at the bedside table.

'Shit, I forgot to set the alarm on my phone.' He looked back up at her. 'Look, Emma, I'm really sorry. I'll be down in twenty, I promise. I'm so, so sorry.'

'No worries. At least you're all right. Get yourself dressed and we'll be downstairs waiting.'

He was true to his word. He arrived, still damp from the shower, water dripping off his hair, and Emma definitely felt she could detect a growl of animal attraction from their guide.

'Sorry again, boss. I promise I'll do better tomorrow.' He glanced across at Marina. 'Will we be back here in time for me to buy a few things?' He produced a shamefaced smile. 'I never was much good at packing. I think I might need more than one pair of boxers.'

'Yes, of course. The shops are open until seven or seven thirty so you should have ample time to buy all the underwear you want.'

Emma wondered if she would have time to do a bit of shoe shopping for herself as well. Shrugging that thought to one side, she switched into serious Hollywood executive mode and took the lead. 'Right, then, now that we're all here, let's get started.' She was conscious that they had a lot of Italy to cover and only just under two weeks in which to do everything. She glanced over at Marina. 'Where to?'

'Today we're going up into the Valli di Lanzo. They're a series of narrow valleys leading roughly northwards towards the high Alps. The one I've chosen ends up against the mountain range beyond which is the Val d'Isère in France. I'm sure you'll find it's a very beautiful and a relatively unknown area.'

This all sounded good. While Rich had a hasty espresso, Marina retrieved the car from the underground car park and they were soon heading north. As they drove, Marina asked for a bit more detail on the sort of locations that interested them.

'Can you give me a rough idea of the plot, if it isn't too secret? It'll just help me come up with suitable places and it might save us some time.'

This sounded like a very sensible idea to Emma. She glanced back over her shoulder and decided to give Rich a chance to show what he knew.

'Did you finish reading the screenplay last night, Rich?'

'Sort of. I actually went out like a light, but I was wide awake at about three so I sat up and finished it then.'

'And you liked it?'

'Yep, I liked it a lot.' He smiled. 'I didn't realise my old man was such a romantic.'

'Good, well, why don't you give Marina a brief summary?'

He leant forward so that his elbows were on the backs of their seats. Emma moved to one side to give him space but she noticed that Marina appeared quite happy to feel his forearm resting against her shoulder. Emma hoped this wasn't going to take her mind off the road.

'It's a love story and it takes place right before the outbreak of the First World War. There's this girl, Emily. She's English and she's been sent abroad by her father because she's got mixed up in the suffragette movement – you know, votes for women and all that. Anyway, she's travelling around Italy with her governess and she runs into this guy. It's love at first sight for her, although she struggles to come to terms with it because she's very much against all men at this point in her life. Besides, she can't work him out. He's always very reserved and… I suppose you could say he's a bit troubled. Anyway, as she travels down to Tuscany and beyond he keeps popping up all over the place and their relationship deepens.'

'So she falls in love with him, but does he fall in love with her, too?' Marina accelerated past a big truck, disdainfully ignoring the No Overtaking sign at the side of the road.

Rich nodded. 'You don't see it from his point of view but, for my money, yes. He falls head over heels in love with her. I'm sure of it.'

'So there's a happy ending?'

Emma decided it was time to interrupt the narrative. 'You'll have to wait until the movie comes out.' She grinned across at Marina. 'But if all goes well – and we've got two of the biggest stars playing the leading roles – we're hoping this particular love story will break a few box-office records.'

At that moment they drove through a dark tunnel beneath what looked like an old convent on the hill above. As they emerged on the other side, they found themselves at the entrance to a narrow valley, its steep sides reaching almost vertically upwards towards the higher mountains beyond.

'Wow, this is amazing.' Emma was impressed. 'We've only been driving for less than half an hour and we're already in the mountains.'

'Don't forget, Turin was where the Winter Olympics took place back in 2006. There are mountains all around the city. Going back to the film, would I be right in thinking it's not so much a mad passionate affair as a slow-burn "will-they, won't-they" sort of thing?'

'Exactly.' Emma nodded approvingly.

'Fine. That helps me a lot. And we aren't looking for bright, flashy places like Monte Carlo, Rome or the centre of Florence, are we? You want places with an altogether quieter, more reflective sort of feel.'

'Dead right, Marina. Our brief is to look for beauty, but off the beaten track.'

The road became ever narrower, but Marina had obviously got the measure of the big vehicle and managed to squeeze up the valley towards the solid mass of mountains in the distance. After another twenty minutes or so, the valley floor widened and they arrived at a little town. Here the houses were mostly solid structures with gently sloping roofs to catch and hold the snow as added insulation in winter, with massive slabs of stone in place of roof tiles. A river rushed down the valley through the trees below and a sturdy-looking church dominated the little main square. Marina turned right and drove up to a sign announcing the Grand Hotel.

She pulled into the near-empty car park and turned off the engine.

'I've arranged to meet the local guide here. That's probably him over there.'

Sure enough, the door of a battered 4x4 opened and an elderly gentleman climbed out. As Marina left the driving seat and went over to greet him, Emma checked out the hotel behind them. For such a tiny town in an unknown valley, it looked as grand as its name, although not in the first flush of youth. Clearly, in its day, this had been quite some place.

'*Buongiorno signori.*'

Marina led the old gentleman back to the car where he tipped his hat at them. This was a jaunty-looking green felt hat with a feather sticking up on one side. Emma later learnt from Marina that it was an army cap, showing that he had once been in the *Alpini*, Italy's elite mountain corps.

They climbed out and Marina made the introductions. The elderly man, Cesare, didn't speak any English and so Marina slipped into interpreter mode. And she was good at it. As Cesare spoke, she supplied an almost simultaneous translation. After a discussion with Marina about their requirements, Emma saw him nod decisively. She had been able to follow bits of the conversation, but the bulk of it had been too technical. Marina filled in the blanks.

'He's going to take us to a gorge with a narrow bridge over it. By the sound of it, it definitely falls into the melancholy category as well as scenic.'

This set bells ringing in Emma's head. She turned to Richard. 'Hey, Rich, you've just finished reading the screenplay. Did I dream it or isn't there a scene right back at the beginning where the old governess thinks Emily might have tried to kill herself?' In fact she already knew the answer, but it seemed like a good way of getting him involved – and checking that he really had read the thing.

He nodded. 'Yeah, quite a dramatic scene where Mrs MacDonald, the governess, goes running about wildly, looking for Emily as night's falling and then finally discovers her on top of a high cliff.'

Emma snapped her fingers. 'Bingo! Let's go and see if this narrow bridge could fit the bill instead of the cliff.' She turned back to Marina. 'Any other ideas for today?'

'Cesare suggests going right up to the top of the valley in the high mountains – there's a little restaurant there where we can have lunch. Sound good?'

'That sounds great. And it'll give us a chance to get some mountain shots for background.' Emma nodded approvingly. 'And maybe on the way back down we can check out this hotel. I think it could be right for the film. It exudes a sort of fin-de-siècle charm.' She turned to Cesare and summoned her best Italian.

'Please do you know the history of this hotel, Cesare?' Beside her she registered Marina's surprise at hearing her speak Italian.

'Yes, *signora*, it was built in about 1910 and it has had some illustrious guests over the years, from the owners of FIAT to the Italian royal family, and even Mussolini. It was ahead of its time in that it was one of the very first hotels in Italy where every bedroom had its own private bathroom.'

He was speaking slowly and Emma was delighted to find that she understood all of this, so she turned to translate it to Rich. 'That's good news. It would have been newly built only a few years before the time of our movie and was very posh in its day. We should absolutely include it. We'll take a load of shots inside and out when we come back down the valley.'

–

The gorge with the bridge was perfect and the setting, with the clear waters of the rushing river far below and the mountain peaks above was exactly the sort of place Emma felt sure would lend itself to the film. The remarkably narrow bridge was strung high above the roaring waters of the river. A fine mist of spray hung over a waterfall below and, as the rays of the sun caught it, little miniature rainbows danced in the light. Emma could almost see the hauntingly beautiful Laney Travers, wearing a long skirt, leaning against the handrail, high above the gorge, sobbing forlornly as her old governess fussed around her. She took a load of photos with the very slick camera provided by the studio and instructed Rich to do the same, just to be on the safe side.

From there they carried on up the valley, climbing steadily, until they emerged into the head of the valley. This was a wide flat-bottomed bowl ringed by walls of rock towering high above them into the snowline. A sign indicated that the altitude down here was just short of 2,000 metres and she could see the peaks above were way higher than that.

The broad floor of the plateau was covered with masses of white and pink wild flowers and a huge flock of sheep were happily filling up on the rich Alpine grass, while their shepherd and his massive shaggy hound kept watch. A river meandered through the middle, the pools of water along its banks framed by clumps of tall-stemmed yellow flowers. The road ran along one side and, following

Cesare's instructions, Marina parked among a handful of other cars and they got out. Coming from the heat of Turin, the drop in temperature was palpable, and welcome.

'We're having lunch there.' Cesare pointed up the slope to one side and they saw a fine stone and wooden chalet. 'That's the *rifugio* and it's open every day of the year – even when the only way to get up here is on skis or in a snowmobile. It's only a ten-minute walk from here and the food's good, I can assure you.'

Emma grabbed a jumper from the car just in case, but the sun and the climb soon warmed her. It was a wonderful feeling to find herself out in the clean, unpolluted mountain air, surrounded by nature rather than concrete. She had got so used to the haze of LA and the incessant growl of traffic that it came as a refreshing change to realise that all she could hear were their footsteps and distant bells. As they walked up the winding road, the view up into the high peaks grew ever more impressive and she knew this would also make a terrific backdrop to a scene in the movie.

Alongside her, Marina was keen to know more about the movie. 'So why's the main character thinking of committing suicide?'

Emma shook her head. 'She's not really. She's just so depressed that her governess fears the worst. She's unhappy to have been separated from her friends and packed off to Italy even though she's secretly been dreaming of visiting Italy all her life. As the movie progresses, she gradually gets over her depression and starts smiling again.'

'Is that because she meets a man by any chance?' Marina was grinning.

Emma smiled back. 'But of course. *Dreaming of Italy* is a romance after all.'

Over a tasty lunch of polenta with a rich game stew, Cesare told them all about the area, and Emma listened in fascination. There were paths that led from there over the mountains into France, climbing to almost three thousand metres in places. These had been used for centuries by smugglers and, as recently as the Second World War, by people trying to escape either from or into France. The area was now a National Park but, back at the start of the twentieth century it would have been popular with hunters, out to bag themselves a wild goat, or *camoscio*, or the even rarer *stambecco*, the elusive wild ibex with huge curved horns, the heads of some of which studded the walls of the *rifugio*. Emma typed a query, *Hunters?* into her phone. An image of austere gentlemen in plus-four trousers and tweed jackets accompanied by ladies in long skirts holding parasols to protect their porcelain skin came to mind and she resolved to suggest it to JM in her report.

It was a very enjoyable day and by the time they drove back down to the Grand Hotel, Emma felt confident they had made a very auspicious start. The hotel itself was duly photographed inside and out and Emma had a chat in English with the charming lady at the check-in desk, who understandably expressed considerable interest in the possibility of having her establishment featured in a blockbuster movie. Emma was able to tick the *Cooperation* box on that one and file it away for her final report.

They shook hands with Cesare and thanked him for his help before driving back down the valley once more. Marina, ever-organised, was already thinking about tomorrow.

'Have you got all the photos you need as far as the mountains are concerned, Emma?'

'Yes, I do believe I have, thanks to you and Cesare.'

'Does that mean we head for the coast tomorrow? I need to firm up the hotel bookings.'

Emma decided to involve Rich in the decision. 'What do you think, Rich? Shall we move on?'

He gave her a little grin. 'You're the boss, Emma, but I reckon we got the mountains pretty well covered today.'

'Right, then, Marina, we head for the coast tomorrow.' A thought occurred to her. 'Is there anything we should visit on the way?'

'I've been thinking about that. How does a brief detour into the vineyards around Asti sound? That's one of the main wine producing areas of Italy where they make Barolo and Barbera and many other iconic Italian wines. It would most certainly have been functioning back in the early twentieth century.'

Chapter 5

The rolling hills around Alba and Asti, covered with a regular patchwork of vines, were charming, and Emma took ever more photos, particularly when they visited an old winery which had been operating in the same charming old stone building for over two hundred years. She had spent the previous evening with Rich going through the photos they had taken and filing away the best for the final report. She had been impressed at the skill and artistic talent of his photography and she had to admit that many of his photos were better than hers. She added this observation to the confidential report she was composing on him, as she felt pretty sure his father would want to quiz her about Rich's performance. So far, so good, was her opinion at this early stage – give or take a bit of trouble getting him out of bed in the morning.

It was mid-afternoon when they reached the seaside. They drove through an unexpectedly hilly region just before the coast; the last ten or twenty kilometres on an *autostrada* that was an amazing piece of engineering, curving this way and that down the mountainside, in and out of tunnels, until it reached sea level. As it was a Sunday, there was quite a bit of traffic, presumably people from the big cities of Milan or Turin taking the opportunity to have a sunny seaside day out. They turned west and carried on along the spectacular motorway that hugged the coast, crossing valleys on scary viaducts before plunging into yet more tunnels through the headlands. The Mediterranean to their left was a deep blue, punctuated by white dots of yachts and even a large cruise liner. It was a fine view and from up here it was easy to make out the old road far below, based upon the ancient Roman Via Aurelia, with the railway alongside it that the characters in the movie would have taken.

Around mid-afternoon they came to the stylish seaside resort of Bordighera, not far from the French border, a stone's throw from Monte Carlo. As they drove down the narrow, winding road into the town centre, they began to see spectacular villas on either side of the road, surrounded by luxuriant gardens. Clearly these had been the homes of the very rich.

Emma queried this with Marina. 'These villas look pretty old. Do you think Bordighera was already a seaside resort back at the start of the twentieth century? Would these places have existed before the First World War?'

Marina shook her head. 'Probably, but I honestly don't know. We can ask Mark, the historian. He's arriving by train in half an hour or so. Is a villa important for the movie?'

'Sort of. Here on the coast's the spot where the heroine, Emily, first catches sight of Robert, the army officer. They've just travelled down from the mountains, like we've done, and they're staying in a hotel, but in my mind's eye I imagine the hotel to look like one of these villas. It would be good to find an old-fashioned-looking one.'

Marina grinned. 'Hold that thought. I think you might be interested to see where we're staying tonight.'

The hotel turned out to be exactly what Emma had in mind. It was a large cream-coloured villa set back from the promenade and immersed in wonderful subtropical gardens that reminded Emma of JM's place back in LA. The garden walls were covered in deep purple bougainvillea, and palm trees towered above a mass of shrubs and colourful flower beds. Marina told them it even had its own private stretch of beach a few hundred yards away for the use of guests. It was warmer today and Emma decided to go for a swim in the sea later on, once they had met up with Mark.

The girl at the front desk told them that the fine old hotel had started life as the private summer residence of one of the senior aides to the King of Savoy, whose wife had had her own villa just a few hundred metres along from there. It had already been turned into a hotel by the end of the nineteenth century so Emma was able to tick this off as a possible stopping point for Emily and her governess in *Dreaming of Italy*. She happily added it to her list of locations and thanked Marina most warmly for finding it.

It was certainly atmospheric and the gardens added a romantic air to the place. She promised herself she would come out into the park at twilight so as to take a few more photos. This might well be the place where Emily would first set eyes on the male lead played by Emma's friend, the screen idol, Ethan Dukes, and she knew she owed it to him to find the perfect spot.

While Emma and Rich sat down under a parasol on the terrace in front of the hotel, Marina went off to collect

Mark from the station. Emma phoned Elliot back in LA to check that everything was still on target for tomorrow when the cameras would start rolling on *Sweet Memories*. He sounded a bit miffed at her constant surveillance, particularly on a Sunday, but she wasn't sorry. Ever since childhood, she had been a perfectionist and she wanted to ensure the movie was as good as it could be. Besides, it was her head that would be on the block if it all started to unravel, so she was as nice to him as she could be, but she made sure he was firmly on the case.

Finally reassured, she ordered an ice cream and a glass of mineral water while Rich opted for an ice coffee. Together, they reviewed the photos of the vineyards and, once again, his were generally better than hers and she told him so. He looked pleased to receive the compliment.

'Make sure you tell my old man. At least it'll show him I can do something right.'

'I certainly will. Tell me, Rich, what did you do at university? Film studies?'

He smiled. 'You'd think, wouldn't you, but no, I did economics. I quite like figures and my father didn't object. I guess he thought it might make me more useful to the business.'

'And this is what you want to do as a career, to go into JMGP?'

He gave her a little smile. 'What would you do in my place? It's not every guy who can walk into a senior management position in a big company at the age of twenty-seven. I just hope I'm going to be up to it.'

'You'll do just fine, Rich, I'm sure. I like the fact that your father's trying to get you to learn about it from the bottom up.'

'You trying to tell me this is the bottom? From what my father says, you're on the fast track to the top.'

This sounded very good, but Emma was quick to play down any developing importance she might have in the company. 'First, we've got to help make *Dreaming of Italy* into next year's blockbuster. Easier said than done.'

Just at that moment the familiar people carrier with Marina at the wheel appeared on the drive and drew up just below them. Emma's eyes tracked the car's movements and she watched as the car door opened and a man stepped out.

As Emma's eyes alighted on his face, the weirdest sensation went through her. For a moment she thought it might be the cold ice cream on a warm, empty stomach, but as the man walked up the steps to their table, carrying a holdall in one hand, she got a better look at him and it happened again. This time she couldn't ignore the fact that the cause of it somehow had to be down to him. And if it was, it had to be the first time in a long, long while that a man, any man, had affected her this way. She took a hasty mouthful of cold water and stood up to greet him.

'Hi, Mark? I'm Emma and this is Richard. You've met Marina already.'

To complicate things further, as he shook her outstretched hand, another pulse of electricity went through her body. She waved him to a vacant seat and sat down herself, actually quite glad of the support, as her knees were feeling decidedly jelly-like. If he noticed anything, he was diplomatic enough not to comment.

'Hello, good afternoon, Emma. Sorry I couldn't join you in Turin, but something came up. I'm at your disposal from now on though, for as long as you need me.' He had an educated British accent, but without any noticeable regional inflection.

'Thanks a lot. I imagine you know what we're in Italy for, don't you?' She was relieved to hear her voice sounding pretty normal, although she could still feel where his hand had touched hers.

'My friend Gianluca told me you're scouting locations for a new movie. And he said it's to be set around the beginning of the twentieth century. Is that right?'

'Pretty much. We're actually looking at the days immediately before the outbreak of World War I – June 1914.'

He nodded again. 'Ah, yes, the end of the *Belle Époque*, one of my favourites. That was the time when everybody thought everything was going right for the world, while the spectre of what would be the bloodiest war in history loomed before them. My period's pretty much any time between the *Risorgimento* – that's the unification of Italy in the mid-eighteen-hundreds – and the Second World War.'

'Your period? Are you a teacher?'

'No, but I did a degree in history and that period was my favourite. I've kept up an interest in it ever since. You maybe know I'm part-Italian, so I've always been fascinated by the history of this country.' He gave her a gentle smile. 'And, boy, does Italy have a lot of history!'

As he was speaking, Emma found herself surreptitiously checking him out. He was tall – not as tall as Rich or his father, but over six feet. He looked as if he was around her age or maybe a year or two older, maybe even nudging forty. His hair was light brown and cropped fairly short. His eyes were an unusual blue-grey colour and he looked as though he had been out in the sun. His face and his strong forearms were tanned a light golden colour which contrasted well against the crumpled white linen shirt he was wearing. His shoulders were broad and he appeared fit and healthy. There was no doubt about it, he was a very good-looking man, and Emma couldn't deny the annoying feeling of attraction building inside her.

It was annoying because this sort of thing just didn't happen to her.

After years without any but the most casual – mainly just physical – interest in men, she couldn't understand why her brain had suddenly reacted like this, and before he had even spoken to her. She did her best to ignore the confusion in her head, but it was far from easy. Taking a firm grip on her emotions, she waved to the waitress to order a drink as a distraction from the turmoil swirling inside her after her reaction to meeting this man. As the waitress arrived at their table, the girl gave him a far broader smile of welcome than she had given Emma. Clearly, Emma wasn't the only one to find this man attractive.

Shrugging off what could only be explained as a spark of jealousy, Emma waited until he had ordered a cold beer in perfect Italian and the girl had retired before asking about the history of Bordighera. His reply confirmed that he knew what he was talking about.

'This part of the coast was pretty much invented, or at least discovered, by the English. In the late eighteen hundreds, the railway finally linked this part of the coast to Paris and then, in 1885, to London. Instead of weeks bumping about in a horse-drawn carriage, people could travel from London to Bordighera in comfort in less than twenty-four hours. As word got out of the mild winters down here, more and more wealthy Englishmen started building villas here. Up until then, there had been little more than fishing villages along this coast, but within a few years, around the turn of the century, they were transformed into chic watering holes for the very well off.'

'So the villas we saw on our way into town would have already been here in 1910?'

He nodded. 'Many of them, yes. Like this place.' The waitress returned with his beer and he rewarded her with a smile that actually made the girl blush. He, however, appeared totally unaware of her reaction and turned back to Emma, raising the beer bottle before putting it to his lips and taking a sip. 'Cheers. I needed that. It's taken me six hours to get here, and the trains were crowded.'

'Where've you come from?'

'Umbria.' Seeing the expression on her face, he elaborated. 'The most beautiful region in Italy – well, in my humble opinion anyway. It's to the south and east of Florence. You must have heard of places like Assisi and Perugia. And then, of course, there's Orvieto.'

Emma nodded. 'And you live in Umbria?'

He nodded. 'I do now. As of a year ago.'

'And you say it's very beautiful. Maybe we should swing through there as part of this tour.' At that moment Marina reappeared and Emma turned the question to her. 'What do you think, Marina? Mark says Umbria's gorgeous. Could we add a visit to that region or is it out of our way?'

Marina sat down and nodded. 'Of course we can. In fact, it's already on my list with a question mark alongside it. Mark's right about it being very, very lovely.'

As Marina spoke his name, that same ridiculous sensation of jealousy struck Emma once more. What on earth was going on? She was jealous of another woman saying his *name*? Without thinking, she took a big spoonful of ice cream, followed by an even larger mouthful of sparkling water and only then realised this had been a serious mistake. As the freezing cold mixture in her mouth fizzed and bubbled and threatened to go up her nose, she had a horrible feeling she might be about to spit it out across the table and the result of that was too awful to contemplate. She was reaching for a handful of paper napkins from the chrome dispenser on the table when she heard Mark's voice, his question directed at her, apparently unaware of her agitation.

'Can you tell me a bit about the movie, Emma, or is it a secret?'

One thing was for sure: speaking was out of the question for now, unless she wanted to sandblast everybody around the table. Holding the napkins to her mouth, she looked desperately towards Rich and was mightily relieved to see him realise she was in difficulty and pick up the gauntlet. He gave Mark a sketchy outline of the plot and Emma had time to collect herself and finally clear her mouth. As the ice cream disappeared down her throat, she took a couple of big breaths and a much smaller sip of water, gradually recovering her composure. When Rich came to the end of his exposé, she shot him a grateful look and picked up the conversation.

'The girl in the movie, Emily, has been involved with the suffragette movement and she's here not because she wants to be, but because her father said so.'

'Fascinating.' He sounded as if he meant it. 'Who came up with that idea?'

'My boss, Rich's father.'

Mark nodded across the table at Rich. 'Great idea.' He returned his attention towards Emma. 'I'd better read up on the suffragette movement, I think.'

'You do that.' Emma did her best to sound like a Hollywood executive after her moments of unexpected disorientation. 'Anyway, I'm delighted we're going to visit Umbria after what you've said. That sounds great. It's not such a big name as Tuscany and that's what we're looking for. Our brief is to find beautiful places that aren't as familiar as more famous ones.' She caught Marina's eye. 'What about tomorrow? Can you think of anywhere around here that's a bit off the grid, but beautiful?'

Marina nodded. It didn't surprise Emma to hear she had already thought about this. 'Yes, I have something in mind that I believe would suit, but can you remind me where we're at in the movie?'

'Emily's either just met or she's about to meet Robert, the young British army officer she falls in love with.'

'So it needs to be somewhere particularly romantic. Unless you find somewhere here in Bordighera that particularly appeals to you, I think we could take a trip inland to the little town of Dolceacqua. It's only ten kilometres or so from here and it looks very historic, very scenic and, although I've never been there, very romantic with its narrow, winding streets, old buildings, a medieval castle on the hill, that sort of thing.' She glanced across at Mark. 'Do you know it?'

He shook his head. 'Like you I've heard about it and it sounds like the sort of place you're looking for, and it was certainly there in 1914. I look forward to seeing it.'

'And then, if there's time, I thought we could drop into the Hanbury Gardens in the afternoon.' Marina was checking details on her phone. 'It's the same kind of distance from here as well.'

'Hanbury? That doesn't sound like an Italian name.'

Emma was pleasantly surprised to hear Rich speaking up and sounding interested. Although gradually loosening up, he still had a tendency to be quiet and reserved and it was good to see him getting involved.

Marina gave him a smile. 'It isn't. He was another Englishman. He built a villa right on the coast along to the west of here and he laid out some lovely subtropical gardens. They're open to the public.' She stopped. 'Assuming they were there in 1914, of course.'

Mark was quick to confirm this. 'I think I'm right in saying that Sir Thomas Hanbury built the gardens in the last half of the nineteenth century, so they would indeed have been in existence in time for the events of your movie. Not necessarily open to the public back then, but a bit of poetic licence would get your Emily and Robert in there, I'm sure.'

Emma sat back contentedly. 'Great. That's tomorrow planned.' She glanced at her watch. It was almost six o'clock. 'I don't know about anybody else, but I'm going down to the beach for a swim.'

Whether the idea of seeing Mark with his shirt off was in any way responsible for her opening up the idea to the group was something she was not prepared to debate at this point.

As it turned out, she did not, after all, have that experience. She and Rich went swimming by themselves and she couldn't help a feeling of disappointment as she floated about, checking the beach in vain for any sign of Mark. After a while, she deliberately ducked her head into the cold water and shook it. She had only just met this man, so why was she letting him mess with her head? Besides, as she had told herself many times, she had no interest in finding herself a man. For now, work had to come first. Hadn't it?

Chapter 6

That evening they went out to a fish restaurant in the centre of town and afterwards Emma and Mark went for a stroll along the promenade in the fading light. Rich and Marina disappeared back to the hotel and Emma found herself wondering whether they might end up together, but she decided to ignore that relationship for now while she tried to work out what was happening inside her own head.

The railway line that Mark had mentioned ran along parallel with the coast directly behind the promenade, and from time to time they heard trains coming past. It was a warm evening without a breath of wind, and the tiny waves barely sighed as they brushed against the shore. The beach itself was made up of pebbles rather than sand, but the water that afternoon had been crystal clear and just about an acceptable temperature; certainly a lot cooler than the temperature of the average California pool, but all the more refreshing as a result. Presumably the water temperature in the Mediterranean would rise as the summer wore on.

As they walked along, they chatted about inconsequential matters like the meal, the weather and the sea temperature, while at the back of her mind, Emma found herself wondering what was happening to her. Finding herself so struck by a man was so unusual and unexpected to be almost worrying. What on earth was going on? And the other thought running through her head was whether Mark felt the same spark. For his part, he showed no sign of developing anything but a working relationship with her and the others, and there certainly hadn't been anything remotely flirtatious in his behaviour over dinner. Doing her best – at least for now – to banish any further conjecture, she asked how he had come to live in Italy.

He told her his parents had been killed in a car crash when he was still just a little boy and he had been brought up partly in Umbria and partly in the UK by the two sets of grandparents. As a result, he was effectively bilingual. He was clearly intelligent as he had won a bursary to Oxford University and, from there, he had moved on to working for the British government. Now, after the recent death of his Italian grandfather, he had given up his job in Britain and had returned to Italy where he was currently living in the house he had inherited from him.

'So you aren't working at the moment?'

'I've been pretty busy supervising the renovations and alterations at my grandfather's place but, apart from this interlude with you guys, I'm not doing anything else of a historical nature.'

'Can I ask why you left the old job?'

'I was invalided out.' He gave her a slightly odd smile. 'Repetitive Strain Injury – from typing in too many thousands when doing the MP's expenses.'

She didn't comment. He was clearly joking, but it did make her wonder just what might have happened; however, that was his business. 'So what would you like to do? You're a bit young for retirement.'

'I'm thirty-eight, which makes me about ten years older than you.' Emma liked the sound of that and didn't disabuse him for now. 'As for work, I don't know, really. As I say, I've been fairly busy tying up granddad's affairs and sorting out his old house, but I've been thinking about maybe going back to university in a couple of years to do a doctorate. Something'll come up. I'm in no hurry.' He glanced across at her as they walked along the promenade. 'And what about you? Gianluca said you're a high flier.'

'People keep telling me that, but I'm not sure. What I do know is that there's a lot riding on the success or failure of this trip. If we can find the right locations, it'll do wonders for the movie's chances. If I screw up, there could be serious consequences.'

'For you or for the company?'

'For everybody.'

'Are you telling me your job's on the line?'

She shook her head. 'I don't think anybody would fire me, but let's just say it wouldn't do a lot for my chances of promotion.'

'And that's what you want – promotion?'

'I love my job, Mark, and I'm good at it. At least, that's what people keep telling me. I've been working really hard for the company and it would be good to rise up the food chain – not least as the movie business is still very much a man's world.'

'Sounds like a situation the heroine of *Dreaming of Italy* would have recognised. That's what the suffragettes were all about, after all.'

'Things have moved on a lot since 1900, but there's still some way to go.'

'Do you think you'd have been a suffragette if you'd been around way back then?'

'I'm not sure I'd have been brave enough. They got themselves beaten up and arrested, you know, but I'd like to think that even back then I would have felt as I do now – women are equal to men. That's why I work hard and want to do my best. Don't get me wrong, Mark, I do it because I love it. In spite of what some people might think, I'm not really a workaholic. Yes, I do work hard, but it's because I enjoy my job. You've got to understand that I was dreaming about Hollywood when I was still in my teens. To find myself part of it now is awesome.'

'And how about your personal life? All work and no play makes Jack a dull boy, after all.'

'I play. A bit. I've never been that interested in going out just for the hell of it. My parents taught me to work hard and find my reward in that. All right, I took that with a pinch of salt growing up, but I do see what they were talking about now. Like I say, I wouldn't do it if I didn't enjoy it.'

She waited for him to ask her about any men in her life but he said nothing. She wasn't sure whether to be relieved or disappointed. The plain fact was that over the years she had consistently put her career first and in so doing had probably missed out on numerous opportunities to meet new people and forge new relationships but, like she had told him, it had been her choice and she didn't regret it. Or did she? If she had been asked that question just twenty-four hours earlier, she wouldn't have hesitated but now, ever since meeting this man, she suddenly didn't feel so sure. For somebody usually so clear in her thinking and decision-making, it felt weird.

Her musings were interrupted as he changed the subject.

'And what's the deal with Richard? I gather he's the boss's son, but he doesn't act like the next in line to the throne. In fact it's quite clear you're his boss here.'

Emma wasn't going to mention Rich's drug problem, so she improvised. 'He had some health problems in the past and dropped out of college, I believe, and he's only just graduated at the age of twenty-seven. I think the trouble now is he's a bit low on confidence. Hopefully he'll get himself together and I can see a definite improvement already. His father wants him to experience all branches of the business, so that's why he's here with me.' She decided it was better to get off the subject of the boss's son. 'So why did you decide to come on this trip?'

'I'm doing a favour for a friend and I liked the sound of it. I'm not really employed by them. I was at university with the guy who set the whole thing up and we've stayed in touch. Gianluca's very bright. He's a hundred percent Italian but I sometimes think he speaks better English than I do. He came back to Italy after Oxford and opened his agency. He spotted a gap in the market and he makes a good living supplying logistical support to people like yourselves, or international firms thinking of setting up in Italy and so on. He's built himself a great reputation and he employs really good people.' He stopped and glanced across at her in the dwindling light of the setting sun. 'Sorry, I wasn't referring to myself. I was thinking of Marina. She's very smart. Like I say, I'm not really a proper employee, but I can tell you this, I'm glad I decided to come along.'

Annoyingly, she immediately found herself wondering what he meant by that remark. Was he glad he had come for her sake, for the sake of the food, the surroundings, the historical element, or what? A few hours earlier, Hollywood exec Emma would have asked him straight out but not this new, uncertain Emma. She suppressed a little snort of frustration. What on earth was happening to her?

They talked some more about the film industry in general and how it worked – at times walking so close to each other that their hands almost brushed. Every time it happened, a small thrill went through Emma and she found herself peeking up at Mark to look for a sign of reaction, but his face remained infuriatingly neutral.

By the time they got back up to the hotel, the sun had almost disappeared behind the hills but there was still a delightful pinkish light all around them. Remembering her promise to Ethan back in Hollywood, Emma decided to get some shots of a suitably romantic part of the garden before it got too dark. When she explained this to Mark, he immediately offered to help.

'What're you looking for? A bench in a rose arbour or something of the sort?'

'That would be perfect. Somewhere romantic, shaded, and away from prying eyes.'

'Okay, well, why don't you go left and I'll go right and we'll meet up in the middle? As far as I can see, the garden stretches all the way round the hotel.'

Emma slowly made her way through the grounds of the hotel, stopping every now and then to check out suitable spots. It was cooler now that the sun had almost disappeared and she had to weave about to avoid the sprinklers busily watering the well-tended lawns. As the bushes gave way to a flat open space, she found what she had been looking for, but she wasn't the first to get there.

'How about this place for a romantic setting, Emma?'

A single antique lamp illuminated a circular pond with a fine statue of a seahorse in the middle, a gentle stream of water trickling from its mouth. The sound of the fountain effectively drowned out any residual noise of traffic on the road beyond the walls and an old wooden bench positioned nearby made a perfect resting place. Sitting on the bench was Mark, looking relaxed and way too handsome surrounded by roses. He gave her a warm smile.

'Come and see if it feels idyllic enough.'

She went across and joined him on the bench which was still warm from the last rays of the dying sun. Behind her was the hotel, ahead of her the garden with its lush vegetation and, beyond that, the flickering lights of houses dotted across the steep hillside leading inland. She leant back and exhaled.

'This'll do just fine. I can just imagine Emily and Robert having their very first clandestine meeting out here in the twilight, out of sight of her stern old governess.'

'They're the main protagonists, right? Can you tell me who's going to be playing them in the movie?'

'Yes, I'm not sure if it's common knowledge yet, but they'll be played by Ethan Dukes and Laney Travers.'

'Wow! Big names. You guys are certainly pulling out all the stops on this one.'

'Like I said, there's a lot riding on this movie.'

She settled back and closed her eyes, savouring the sweet scent of roses wafting over her shoulder from the bed behind them. Yes, she thought to herself, this place certainly had romance written all over it. For a moment she fantasised about what she would do if Mark were to slip his arm behind her and lean across to kiss her, but he didn't make a move. She sat there and mulled it over in her head. The fact that she was even taking the time to consider her reaction spoke volumes. With any other man it would have been simple. She would have told him in no uncertain terms to keep his hands to himself and that would have been that. But, for some weird reason, with Mark here tonight it was different, though she couldn't work out why. As it was, she had to settle for his shoulder lightly brushing against hers, but even this minimal contact was enough to give her goose pimples.

'There's a place rather like this in my grandfather's garden.' His voice sounded dreamy and far away. 'The difference is that from there you can see down across the valley to the distant lights of Gubbio on the hill on the other side. It's a wonderful place by day and by night.' She opened her eyes and saw him looking at her and that same inexplicable shudder went through her yet again.

'It sounds delightful.' For some reason she had to clear her throat before she could get her words out. Fortunately he didn't appear to notice.

'If our trip takes us anywhere near there, I'd like to show you that spot.'

She found herself smiling and, although he might not be able to see the smile in the darkness, she thought he should be able to hear it in her voice as she replied.

'I'd like that, Mark. Very much.'

Chapter 7

When Emma came down for breakfast the next morning she was surprised, and impressed, to find Rich already sitting there with a coffee in front of him.

'Hi, Rich, good night?'

'I slept like a log. And you?'

He was definitely looking brighter and more cheerful. Whether this was just the result of a good night's sleep or some other night-time activity was something upon which she didn't feel like fixating. For now. Instead, she gave him a contented smile as she ordered a cappuccino and sat down.

'Same as me, the first full night's sleep since I arrived in Italy.'

In fact that wasn't completely true. It had taken her quite some time to get off to sleep last night, her head filled with thoughts of the new arrival and still churning over just how he had managed to make such an impression upon her in such a short time.

She could honestly say that she had never been in love before. Yes, she had had boyfriends, yes, she had had a few flings, but there had never been any great depth to the emotions aroused by these liaisons. Although her industry revolved around the idea of romance, to her love was just as foreign as zombie invasions or gruesome murders – something that might happen to other people, but not to her. Somehow, she had always been able to look on with the eyes of a researcher or a scientist, trying to understand, but never empathising with, the complications love brought to the lives of others. And now this…?

'Hi, guys. All well?'

Mark's voice roused her from her reverie. She looked up to find him standing by the table in shorts and a very sweaty T-shirt, obviously just back from a run. His T-shirt clung tightly enough to his body to confirm the impression she had already gained the night before that he looked after himself. Swallowing hard, she gave him a bright smile.

'Not as well as you, by the look of it. You're putting us all to shame. And I was just saying to myself the other day that I had to start getting some serious exercise before all these Italian delicacies turn me into a big fat blob.'

'Somehow I can't imagine you ever turning into a blob.' He was smiling back at her. 'Well, I try to go for a run every morning. If you feel like joining me, I'd enjoy the company.' Just as she was debating whether this constituted a sort of date, he transferred his attention to Rich and repeated the invitation. 'And you, Rich, you look like a fit guy. Care to join us tomorrow?'

'You know something, Mark, I reckon I will. Just come and bang on my door.'

Clearly this had not in any way been anything more than an offer to get some shared exercise, but, in spite of feeling what might have been disappointment, she was delighted to hear Rich sounding so bright. Certainly the idea of getting some exercise sounded very good, so she agreed. Besides, she told herself, romance – particularly if unrequited – was unlikely to make her lose anything like as much weight as a good run every morning.

After breakfast Marina drove them up a broad river valley away from the sea towards Dolceacqua. As she had told them, it was a short trip and they soon reached the little town. They approached it from the opposite bank of the river and saw the old town on the far side, with a mass of red-roofed houses covering the steep slopes leading up to a kind of promontory protruding from the wooded hills that surrounded the town. On top of the pyramid-shaped outcrop was a fine old castle, its twin towers gleaming in the morning sunlight. Skilfully, Marina squeezed the big vehicle across a narrow bridge over the river and found a parking space.

Together, they walked up through the tortuous lanes, lined with shops – most of them catering to the tourist trade – until they reached a small piazza below the castle. As they walked, Mark pointed out that the labyrinthine layout of the roads and alleys would have worked as a defensive measure to help protect the town against marauding bands of North African pirates who preyed on the coast in the early Middle Ages. The panorama over the town from high up was charming and the view from the castle itself even better. Although it had clearly been restored not many years earlier, a lot of the medieval fortress was open to the elements and the tourists.

Even at this time on a Monday morning in June, there were already numerous tourists about, and Emma could imagine how busy it was likely to get as the summer wore on. As they sat on the old castle wall, looking down onto the town and up the valley to their right towards the higher hills, they discussed the town's merits and disadvantages. In the end, they decided that, nice as it was, the logistics of getting access to the town for a full film crew without modern-day references like road furniture or shop signs was going to be just too complicated, so, regretfully, Emma scrubbed Dolceacqua off her list.

The Hanbury Gardens, on the other hand, were charming and full of little romantic hideaways and Emma immediately recognised it as a possible location. They entered from the top, leaving the car by the side of the old Via Aurelia heading towards France, and slowly followed the winding paths down through amazing vegetation to sea level. There were cactus plants as tall as houses, sweet-scented exotic bushes, insect-eating plants, palms and numerous little pools and fountains along the way.

At one of these fountains, Emma got a surprise. As she was standing, chatting to Mark, looking at a strange, irregular statue on a plinth in the middle of the water-lily covered pool, he suddenly caught hold of her forearm. For a moment she had no idea what was happening but then she saw him point at the statue with his other hand. She followed the direction of his finger and suddenly part of the statue moved. To her amazement, she realised that what she had interpreted as a statue was in fact a cluster of terrapins, basking in the afternoon sunshine somehow perched on top of each other, and she gave a delighted laugh. If this was strange, so was the involuntary thrill Mark's brief touch of her arm had aroused in her. Doing her best to concentrate on the matter in hand, she took some photos, made a note of the place for her report, and tried not to think of Mark and just what on earth was going on inside her head.

Just then her phone started ringing and she saw that it was Elliot, calling from the first day on the set of *Sweet Memories*. Her heart sank.

'Hi, Elliot, what's happened?'

'Hi, Emma, I just thought you'd like to know that it's all going fine. The director's been here since about dawn and he says he's very happy with everything. The set's fully up and running, and none of the actors have baled on us. It's all good.'

Emma heaved a massive sigh of relief, still trying to come to terms with the fact that she had completely forgotten about *Sweet Memories*. This was so unlike her as to be seriously disturbing. Still, all was well. 'That's really great to know. When I saw your number, I thought something awful had happened.'

'I can imagine.' She could hear what might have been sympathy in his voice. 'Don't worry, Emma, it's going great. All your planning's worked out just fine. I'm on it now, so just relax and enjoy your Italian holiday.'

'Holiday?' For a moment she was about to snap at him that this was very much a work trip, but then her eyes focused on the shimmering blue Mediterranean through the trees below them and the tall handsome man beside her, a gentle smile on his face. She felt her frown melt away and when she resumed the telephone conversation, her tone was far less aggressive. 'Well, the sun's shining and the sky's blue here on the coast. For a work trip, it's pretty damn good.'

Elliot must have noted her change of tone. 'That's the spirit, Emma, and listen, I got it here. You can relax.'

'You know something, Elliot, I really think I can. I know you'll be just fine. Thanks for the call. I mean that – thanks a lot.'

'You're very welcome.' He sounded as relieved as she felt. As she slipped the phone back in her pocket she caught Mark's eye. The little smile was still on his face as she walked over to him.

'That was my replacement back in LA. Things are okay with the new movie.'

'Were you in any doubt?'

She shrugged. 'No... well, yes, maybe a bit. You know, stuff happens.'

'But it hasn't.'

She smiled back at him. 'No, it hasn't, so I'm a happy girl.'

'I'm delighted for you. All your efforts paid off.' As he spoke, he gently nudged her with his elbow.

She could still feel his touch several minutes later; it hadn't lasted more than a second or two.

In the middle of the gardens was a fine ochre-coloured villa with blue-green shutters at the windows. Huge purple garlands of wisteria swathed the walls and the whole building was surrounded by exotic plants. A sign told them that this had been the home of Sir Thomas Hanbury over a century ago and it didn't take much imagination to picture horse-drawn carriages passing though the arched entrance and depositing elegant ladies and gentlemen at the front door, where liveried footmen would have been waiting to usher them in for afternoon tea. This, too, made it into Emma's report.

The views as they walked down to the sea were splendid. The sea itself was clear and transparent – light blue at the beach and darker further out. Marina pointed out that Monte Carlo was just around the next couple of headlands and, to prove her point, a series of ostentatious multi-million-dollar yachts came cruising by, their fortunate owners sunning themselves on deck as they did so. One was so large it even had its own swimming pool and helipad. There was little doubt that they were in the realm of the super-rich here. Somehow, Emma had the feeling Ethan and Laney were going to fit in just fine and enjoy themselves here.

They paused for coffee down by the shore. This part of the coast where Italy joined France was made up of inhospitable cliffs and rough, inaccessible beaches. It was virtually unpopulated, compared to Bordighera, Sanremo and the line of resorts stretching off into Italy to the east and large conurbations like Nice and Cannes on the French Côte d'Azur to the west. Down here the only engines they could hear were those of the distant luxury yachts, and the only voices were those of the visitors to the gardens. In fact, this area had clearly remained substantially unaltered since the days of Sir Thomas Hanbury and, of course, *Dreaming of Italy*. Emma shot off a bit of video to show just how tranquil it was and added this waterside location to her list.

As they sipped their cold drinks, they had a little council of war. Marina was keen to know where Emma wanted to head next. Emma had been flicking through the screenplay in the car and she outlined what was happening at this stage of the plot.

'Emily's still trying to come to terms with the fact that she feels attracted to Robert, this man she's only just met, but her governess smells a rat and thinks it best to separate them. They take the train eastwards and somewhere along the coast they stop off at a hotel. Two or three days later they find Robert and his group of friends on a yacht in the very bay where they're staying. So we're going to be looking for somewhere by the water. Any ideas?'

Marina's head tilted to the side in thought. 'How about the Cinque Terre? Ever heard of that area?'

Emma shook her head. The translation was easy enough: Five Lands. But she had no idea where these five lands were. Mark, on the other hand, knew the area well.

'If Italy's shaped like a boot, the Cinque Terre region's on the left hand side, right near the top. It's a series of little fishing villages on a very rocky bit of coast below Genoa and there's virtually no access by road. It's a UNESCO World Heritage site and the whole area is gorgeous. Marina's right, it's exactly the sort of romantic place you want for your movie.'

'So if there's no access by road, how do we get there? Swim?' Rich was looking puzzled.

Marina laughed. 'The railway runs right around the coast so there's access that way or, of course, by ferry boat or, like in the movie, by private yacht. In fact, I believe it's now actually possible to get to most of the villages by car, but it's a struggle and parking's a nightmare. I think it's best if we stay a bit further up the coast in Rapallo or Santa Margherita where there are lots of hotels, and take the train along to the Cinque Terre. I've been to a rather nice hotel there in the past and I can check to see if they've got space if you like the idea. And then the following day we can head down to Tuscany.'

Emma had no hesitation. 'Brilliant, Marina — that sounds perfect.' She glanced across at Rich. 'Okay with you, Rich?'

'Fine by me, boss.'

An hour or two later, just as they were getting out of the car back at the hotel in Bordighera, Emma got another call. As she glanced at the caller ID, she was surprised to see it was none other than Ethan.

Feeling more than a little curious — they were good friends but casual phone calls weren't really their thing — she answered the call. 'Hi, Ethan.'

'Oh, good, Emma, hi.'

He sounded unusually flustered and the fact that he had used her real name, rather than just calling her 'English', was suspicious. She decided to try to keep it light.

'So, how you doin'?' Ethan did the Joey accent much better than her but, even so, she saw Mark's eyebrows raise.

'Me, yeah, fine... Well, no, not really. Not so good.'

'What's the problem?' She shot an apologetic look at the others and headed for the privacy of the hotel garden. If the world's handsomest man was about to pour his heart out to her, she knew she had to keep it confidential. As she reached the safety of the wide front lawn, she asked him again. 'What's bothering you, big guy?'

'It's Laney...'

'Laney Travers? What about her?'

'I don't think she likes me.' He sounded like a little boy and Emma pursed her lips to keep a laugh from escaping. It was hard to remember that she was talking to a hunky Hollywood star.

'What makes you say that? Have you seen her?'

'Yes, she's over here in London, just finishing filming a romcom – something to do with the royal family, I think she said.'

'You're in London now?'

'Yeah, I flew over yesterday to have a chat with her about working together. You know, break the ice sort of thing...'

'And she told you she doesn't like you?'

'No... not in so many words, but it was pretty clear.'

Emma's mind was racing. If the off-screen chemistry between these two titans wasn't perfect, *Dreaming of Italy* could be heading for disaster before filming even started. She wondered if he had talked this over with anybody else. Did JM know?

'How clear, Ethan? Tell me what happened.'

She sat down on the low stone wall of a flower bed filled with sweet-scented little pink flowers and listened intently as he told her about the dinner he and Laney had had together the previous night. Apparently Laney hadn't said very much and had appeared bored and disinterested. And, the final nail in the coffin, at the end of the evening she hadn't kissed him goodbye. This worried Emma, so she thought she had better check exactly what he was talking about.

'When you say "kiss", you didn't try to snog her, did you?'

'Oh, Jesus, no. I mean just a peck on the cheek... or not even that. She just...' She heard him hesitate before spitting out the ultimate insult. '...she just shook my hand.'

This sounded serious and definitely way above her pay grade. She racked her brains as to what to do. To give herself time to think, she tried to make more neutral conversation.

'So, how long are you staying in London?'

'I was thinking of staying, like, a few days, maybe a week, but now...'

She had never heard him so down, so she tried to think of something to cheer him up. Suddenly, mercifully, it came to her.

'Why don't you come over here to Italy for a day or two and we can talk about it? I can show you some of the gorgeous locations we've found for *Dreaming of Italy*! What do you say?'

'Italy... well, I love the food, and I have to go to Naples for an award ceremony. That's on Thursday, I think.' She heard him call out to Sinclair, his personal assistant and constant companion. 'Naples is Thursday, isn't it, Sinc?' The reply was affirmative. 'Yeah, English, it's Thursday.'

This was a good start, so Emma went in for the kill. 'Well, tomorrow or Wednesday we're going to be in a place where I've heard that the food's the best in Italy.' In fact she hadn't heard anything of the sort, but she knew how much he liked his food.

'Is that right?'

She could hear definite interest in his voice now, so she reeled him in.

'We're going to be staying close by what's reckoned to be the best restaurant in Italy.'

This, too, was pure invention, but she knew she needed to paint as rosy a picture as possible. Besides, going by her track record so far, surely Marina would be able to arrange it.

'I can't make it tomorrow, but I might be able to come over on Wednesday, before going on to Naples. Where's this restaurant?'

Bugger, Emma thought to herself, where had Marina said they were going? The Cinque Terre, that was it, but that was tomorrow. After that it was going to be...? It came to her at the last moment.

'Tuscany.' A hazy image of a map of Italy appeared before her eyes and she took a stab. 'I don't know the name of the place, but it's near Pisa. You know... the Leaning Tower of Pisa and all that?'

'I've always wanted to see that. Yeah, why not? I'll come and join you for a day on Wednesday. Thanks, English. I look forward to it.'

He sounded a bit brighter and Emma breathed a tiny sigh of relief. 'So what are you going to be doing tomorrow? Trying to get together with Laney again?'

His answer was reassuring. 'No, I'm on my way to the airport right now. I'm flying up to Scotland for a family wedding, so I won't see Laney for a while.'

As far as Emma was concerned, the later the better so she could have time to relay this information up the line and somebody could decide what to do to resolve it.

'Well, you get yourself a flight into Pisa on Wednesday and we'll pick you up. All right? Text me when you've got your arrival time.'

'I can come any time to suit you guys. I'll use a Learjet.'

For a moment there, Emma had forgotten she wasn't speaking to a normal mortal who relied upon public transport. Of course he would just rent an aircraft. 'How about mid- to late-afternoon? That'll give us time to show you the Leaning Tower and then we can head off to the restaurant.'

As soon as he had rung off, she dived into her purse and located the card with Dexter's phone number. She called him immediately, even though it was no doubt a busy Monday morning over there in California. Somehow she didn't think he would mind. He answered straight away.

'Yes.' His voice was non-committal. Clearly, he didn't recognise her number. She was quick to tell him.

'Hi, Dexter, it's me, Emma, calling from Italy.'

'Hi, Emma. Trouble with Richard?' She could hear immediate concern in his voice.

'No, Rich is fine. In fact, he's doing really well. No, it's Ethan. He's just called me.'

She went on to relay the conversation she had just had and what she had suggested as a temporary solution. When he responded, she was delighted to hear approval, maybe even admiration in his voice.

'Terrific, Emma, that's a great idea. Get him out of her way and over to Italy.' There was a slight pause for thought before he resumed. 'Right, so that gives us almost forty-eight hours to sort out what we're going to do. Leave it with me and I'll take it straight to JM. And thanks a lot, Emma. Full marks for thinking on your feet.'

She hurried back into the hotel and found Marina sitting on the terrace with Mark. Rich had presumably gone up to his room. She sat down to talk it through but, first, she reminded them of their responsibilities.

'I've got something to tell you, but it's really confidential. I want you to promise not to breathe a word of it to anybody else. All right?'

They both nodded and Mark added some extra reassurance. 'We've both signed non-disclosure agreements so you don't need to worry.' Seeing her expression, he explained. 'Didn't you know? Before taking us on, a guy called Dexter made Gianluca sign an NDA and we, in turn, had to do the same for him. So we won't tell.'

Emma smiled back, greatly relieved. 'That's great. Thanks.' Yes, Dexter really did think of everything. 'Well, look, it's about Ethan Dukes...'

By the time she had finished, she could see that they were impressed – not necessarily by her ability to think on her feet as by the prospect of meeting a Hollywood legend. Marina, in particular, was looking positively starstruck.

'So you want me to find a hotel near Pisa for us four plus just about the biggest film star on the planet? Will he be travelling on his own or will he have an entourage of minders and bodyguards?'

'I'm not sure. He'll definitely be with his minder, Sinclair, but I'll try to find out if there's anyone else travelling with him. Probably best to work on the assumption of at least one extra person, maybe two. Remember, above all, make sure you find somewhere very discreet. And what about the restaurant?'

Marina gave her a reassuring smile. 'That won't be a problem. Tuscany's full of wonderful restaurants. I'll tell Gianluca and he'll find somewhere good. Don't worry, we'll blow Ethan's mind as far as the food's concerned.'

'And the hotel?'

'We'll find somewhere. Would I be right in thinking that cost isn't a factor?'

Emma nodded decisively. 'Forget the cost. Just find somewhere really good.'

Chapter 8

They checked into a hotel on the hill overlooking the sea in Rapallo just before lunchtime on Tuesday. This was a fairly large seaside resort not far from the iconic jet-set hangout of Portofino which Marina and Emma had already discounted as too well known. After an unexpectedly good snack lunch at the station buffet, they caught a local train along the coast. The rugged coastline of the Cinque Terre was gorgeous and they snatched tantalising glimpses of it as the train ran in and out of the countless tunnels as it twisted and turned hugging the seashore.

Monterosso was a charming little village built right by the sea, its narrow streets curling steeply up the valley into the hills behind it. The railway itself barely emerged from a tunnel before the station and then disappeared into another tunnel through yet another rocky headland straight afterwards. The little town, with its pink, yellow and orange houses with their green shutters was picturesque and atmospheric but the problem was that it was jam-packed with people. It was immediately evident that to try to take the place over with a film crew, possibly for several days, was going to be next to impossible; even assuming the inevitable convoy of vans and trucks containing all the equipment could make it down there on the narrow mountain roads in the first place.

Regretfully, Emma had to scrub Monterosso from the 'possibles' list.

However, what they did next was much more promising. Marina had organised for them to take a boat trip along the coast and Emma immediately recognised an opportunity. As they sat on the deck of the little ferry, she explained.

'We could incorporate a boat trip in the movie, maybe get Emily onto the yacht with Robert. That would be pretty romantic, wouldn't it? She and he are getting ever closer now and a scene on board the yacht, looking back at the coastline here would be great, I'm sure. The coast here surely looks exactly the same as it did a hundred years ago, apart from the occasional modern bridge or building high up on the hillside.'

The green hills, covered with a mix of bushes, scrub and pine trees, sloped steeply down to the sea with barely any sign of human activity. Deserted coves and beaches dotted the coastline and the only people visible were walkers on the tortuous coastal footpath that linked the little communities. It would be easy enough to get permission to close that off for an hour or two while shooting or, Emma thought to herself, if the film crew came past in a boat very early in the morning they could probably get more than enough footage even without stopping the walkers. She knew full well that the editors back in Hollywood would easily be able to blank out any odd people in modern dress. So a coastal sequence went onto the list and she asked Rich to shoot two minutes of video to support it.

The boat trip took less than an hour and dropped them at the little town of Riomaggiore, from where they would take the train back to their hotel later on. It had been a very scenic trip and a very hot afternoon. Most of the men on the boat had stripped to their shorts, but, to Emma's inexplicable frustration, Mark stubbornly kept his T-shirt on. The sense of attraction she felt for him was showing no signs of diminishing as the days went by – in fact, the opposite seemed to be happening. Although he hadn't shown even the slightest hint of attraction towards her, the same couldn't be said about her.

In spite of her best intentions, in spite of her reluctance to shack up with any man, she was finding herself drawn to him like a moth to a flame and this was causing her no end of exasperating self-analysis. Suddenly, here she was, prey to emotions she genuinely had thought completely missing from her make-up. Instead, it was now patently clear that this was not the case at all. After years of total conviction that she was a sensible, dedicated career woman, intent upon rising up to a position of importance in a multi-million-dollar corporation, she now found herself as confused as a lovelorn teenager. It was as frustrating as it was inexplicable.

The only consolation was the lack of spots on her face.

Marina also stripped off to reveal the top half of a fairly minimal bikini and Emma saw undeniable interest on Rich's face. He was looking even more relaxed today and he had a bit more colour in his face. On their inaugural run this morning he had proved to be well able to keep up with Mark, although she had had the suspicion that Mark might have been throttling back for her sake. Unfortunately, Emma hadn't thought ahead and had left her bikini in her suitcase so she had to sit alongside Mark, both of them covered up and, at least in her case, feeling decidedly clammy.

Back on shore, they were sitting under a parasol outside a little *gelateria* eating ice cream when Emma's phone rang. It was Dexter.

'Hi, Emma. Listen, I've talked it through with JM. By the way, he sends his best wishes and says thanks. Anyway, the plan of action is like this.'

He went on to tell her that he had already spoken to Laney in London and had arranged that they would fly her over to Italy at the weekend for a briefing and an introduction to the locations for the movie. The film director, Erasmus Delgado was in Europe and would also be jetting in from wherever he had been. Ethan would of course be invited as well and it would then be up to Erasmus to 'bang their heads together'. It was down to Emma and her team to find a suitably 'secure and discreet' hotel where the presence of these three well-known faces together would not leak out.

Emma heaved an internal sigh. Easier said than done.

Dexter then went on to make it clear that it would also be greatly appreciated if Emma could lend a hand in greasing the wheels of the superstars' relationship.

By the time he rang off, Emma was even hotter and more bothered than she had been on the boat. But this time the sun had nothing to do with it. Things were getting complicated, fast. She took a deep breath and broke the news to the others.

'So, guys, it's like this. Tomorrow, we've got Ethan pitching up for a quick look at the Leaning Tower and then the best dinner he's ever had.' She caught Marina's eye and managed a grin. 'No pressure there, Marina.

Then he's apparently heading off to Naples for some award ceremony or other but coming back up to join us for the weekend, as are Laney Travers and Erasmus Delgado, the film's director.'

She glanced around at their faces. Even Rich looked shell-shocked. She did her best to sound encouraging.

'Hopefully Laney and Ethan'll be able to settle their differences and it'll be all systems go for the movie.' She read considerable scepticism on the faces opposite her, but she kept going. 'First, we need to find a suitable hotel. According to our schedule, where are we going to be by the weekend, Marina?'

Marina nodded and consulted her phone. 'Today's Tuesday and we're here on the coast. Tomorrow it's Pisa, Ethan Dukes, the Leaning Tower and the big meal. I know you said to leave out famous cities, but we have no option, seeing as you mentioned Pisa to him. How does the next leg of our journey tie into the plot – what happens next for Emily?'

'She's finally given in and admitted to herself that she's attracted to Robert, even though she still mistrusts men and hates living in a man's world. However, Mrs MacDonald, the governess, doesn't want her getting involved with any man. She bundles Emily up and they head away from the coast and on down into Tuscany. Seeing as we're committed to going to Pisa with Ethan, we might be able to include at least a cameo of the Leaning Tower, but I think we'd better avoid Florence at all costs. It's just going to be impossibly crowded there. What do you think, Marina?'

'I'm sure it would be.' Marina was checking her phone. 'So Wednesday's Pisa and we can use Thursday to see a few fine historic places around Florence, but not the city itself, and we can spend Thursday night somewhere in rural Tuscany. Then on Friday we head via Siena over the hills into Umbria. I'd been planning on finding a comfortable hotel with a pool for the weekend somewhere out in the country for a bit of relaxation. Now that I know we've got all these famous people coming to join us I'll have to add top secret and private to the specification. Then next Monday we travel north from there to Bologna and onwards to Venice.' She looked up from the screen. 'How does that sound?'

Emma gave her a big smile. 'That all sounds great. The problem, as you say, is that we need somewhere in Umbria for the weekend that's comfortable, luxurious but above all very, very secluded and discreet. If the media get a sniff of Ethan, Laney and Erasmus holed up together, we'll find ourselves with paparazzi crawling all over us.'

Marina nodded slowly, returning her attention to her phone. 'Well, the good news is that for tomorrow Gianluca's found us a little place near Pisa which should be fine. It's a boutique hotel with only eight rooms and he's been able to persuade the owner to give us the whole place, so Ethan Dukes's presence should be safeguarded – as long as he doesn't get recognised at the Leaning Tower. I suppose we could curl back round on Friday and go there again, as long as the hotel isn't already booked up. It'd be a few hours' detour, but it could be feasible.'

Rich was nodding approvingly. 'I like that idea of taking over a place just for ourselves. That's surely the best way to keep everything under wraps. Marina, could your boss find us somewhere similar in Umbria, maybe?' He glanced across at Mark. 'Umbria's where you live, isn't it, Mark? Can you think of anywhere that might be suitable?'

All eyes turned to Mark, who was looking contemplative and didn't respond for a few long seconds. Emma was about to prompt him when he suddenly appeared to come to a decision. Reaching into his pocket, he pulled out his phone. After scrolling through his photos, he found what he wanted and handed it across to her.

'Might this sort of place be suitable?'

Emma took the phone from him and squinted at the screen. It was a photo of a stunning old villa, almost like a castle, nestled among cypress trees, partway up a wooded hillside. It was big, redolent with history, and it was gorgeous. She passed the phone round the table and looked across at Mark.

'Wow, what a place. It's amazing and, by the look of it, there isn't another house for miles. It's exactly the sort of thing we need. But is it likely to be available? It is nearly high season, after all.'

She heard the other two murmuring appreciatively as they checked out the photo. Mark's answer, when it came, caused considerable surprise.

'It's available.' He produced a little smile. 'This is my grandfather's old house, near Gubbio. That's where I've been living for the past year. He always said he wanted me to transform it into a hotel after his death. Even though I don't... didn't know the first thing about hotels, that's what I've been doing over the last few months. The builders finished a few weeks ago. I've engaged a really good manager and a brilliant chef, and we've been taking bookings from the first of July. That's only a couple of weeks away now and most of the staff are already in place so I'm pretty sure it should be possible to open it up this weekend for you guys.'

Marina, ever practical, started asking him about rooms, facilities and location. As he explained all of this, Emma had a sudden thought. This could really work!

'Listen, guys, there's something else. In *Dreaming of Italy*, the female lead, Emily, gets very sick partway through the movie. She contracts a bad fever and they take refuge for a week in a Tuscan villa while she gets over it. Mark's place looks gorgeous and it doesn't matter a jot to the movie whether Emily's bed rest is in Tuscany or Umbria. Not only would this solve the problem of Ethan and Laney, but it would also tick off another important location for us. Mark, if we were to come and film for a few days at your place this autumn, would that be all right?' She placed a hand on his arm and did her best to ignore the tingle this caused. 'I realise this is a huge ask, especially as you're just getting the hotel off the ground.'

He grinned, capturing her hand and giving a light squeeze of reassurance. 'All right? For somebody new to the whole hotel business, even I can see how amazing it would be for us to appear in a blockbuster movie. Of course we'd be delighted.'

Emma was well pleased – and not just with the touch of his hand on hers. Hopefully this would mean they could kill two birds with one stone, although she wasn't looking forward to having to act as go-between in the megastar showdown to come this weekend. Meanwhile, Mark was thinking along strictly practical lines.

'I'll call Claudio, the manager, and ask him to set it up. Marina, can you ask Gianluca to send over copies of the non-disclosure agreement for our staff to sign, please?

So, just checking, this means we should be arriving there this Friday night, leaving on Monday morning?' Emma smiled and nodded. Then the smile was wiped off her face by what he said next. 'That's really good. That means I get to see Carmen again sooner than I thought. I've been missing her these past few days.'

'Come on, guys, we've got a train to catch.'

Marina's voice prevented Emma from dwelling any further on the implications of what she had just heard. She handed a twenty euro note to a passing waitress and stood up, wondering if Carmen was of Spanish extraction and, more importantly, whether she was Mark's girlfriend, fiancée or wife. Not that it mattered. It should have been pretty obvious that a good-looking, intelligent guy like Mark would already be taken. Besides, she had her career to consider. There would never have been a future for her with a man who lived six thousand miles away. She sighed to herself as she collected her change and the obligatory receipt and followed the others down to the station.

Chapter 9

When Ethan appeared through the anonymous side exit of Pisa airport – the one reserved for special passengers arriving in their own aircraft – Emma almost didn't recognise him at first. In fact, it was only the sight of his minder/bodyguard/PA, Sinclair, that gave away the identity of the long-haired tramp in the crumpled Metallica T-shirt and torn jeans beside him: the sexiest man in the world. Clearly, Ethan was doing his best to remain incognito. His efforts at concealment would however have been more effective if Sinclair hadn't been wearing his usual dark suit and shades and looking like something out of *The Godfather.*

The two together made a seriously odd couple but, so far, none of the people wandering about with bags and trolleys appeared to have noticed anything untoward, so Emma hurried across and escorted the two of them into the waiting car. Marina was at the wheel; they had left Rich and Mark at the charming little hotel Marina's boss had found for them in the hills above the historic old city of Lucca, less than half an hour from Pisa. It was another very hot day and the two men were no doubt sunning themselves at the hotel pool by now.

Sinclair slid into the front seat and Emma found herself alongside Ethan in the back.

'Welcome to Italy, Ethan.'

In response he leant towards her and gave her a hug, kissing her warmly on the cheek. She kissed him back and caught Marina's eyes in the rear-view mirror. The expression on her face was not dissimilar to the way her family's old spaniel used to look every time he smelt sausages grilling. Emma almost erupted in a fit of giggles.

'Hi, English. It's great to see you again.' He took a good long look at her. 'And you're looking good, really good.'

'That's more than I can say for you, Ethan. You look as if you've just crawled out of a ditch.'

He grinned. 'This is my "low-down bum" outfit. Works every time. People don't look at me too closely for fear that I might spit at them or punch them.' He glanced out of the window at the suburban sprawl through which they were driving. 'So, where's this tower, then?'

Marina glanced back over her shoulder and answered. 'Ten minutes or so and we should be in the city centre. I'll drop you guys right beside the Campo dei Miracoli. Just call me when you want picking up again.'

Emma translated the name for Ethan's benefit. 'The Field of Miracles is where the Leaning Tower is located. I suggest we just stroll about there, rather than try to climb the tower. I was checking it out on Google last night and it all looks very claustrophobic. The staircase is really narrow and I fear it would be all too easy for somebody to recognise you and then if that happened, God forbid, there could be a riot.' She gave him a wink. 'If too many women jump on you, the tower might even topple over.'

Ethan nodded in agreement. 'Good thought. To be honest, I'm not that fond of heights anyway. Yeah, let's just look at it from the ground.'

Marina dropped them off near the grassy piazza with its iconic tower and the equally stunning cathedral and baptistery. All around were stalls selling souvenirs and fast food and the place was heaving with visitors. Emma and Ethan, with Sinclair a few paces behind them, joined the hundreds upon hundreds of tourists milling about there and this just confirmed what she had feared. As far as the movie was concerned, the Leaning Tower was best avoided. Trying to get permission to film here and to restrict access to tourists for as much as a whole day would be almost impossible. For very practical reasons, JM had been right. Big-name places weren't what they needed.

They were there for about half an hour, and Emma took advantage of being alone with Ethan to talk to him about his concerns with regard to relations with his co-star-to-be. She relayed the message she had received from Dexter.

'Apparently Laney's been in a foul mood for the past couple of weeks. The word is that she's split up from that French guy she was dating – you know, the tennis star?'

'Tall black guy. Yeah, I know the one you mean.' He glanced across at her. 'So that's finished, has it?'

'Yes, and it would appear she was pretty fond of him so that would explain why she was so sniffy with you. It wasn't you, Ethan. It was just because she was pissed off with life. She'll snap out of it, you'll see.'

'I hope you're right. Shooting a romance with some-body who isn't into romance is going to be hard, hard work.'

'It'll be fine. You'll see. Just work some of that Ethan magic...' She gave him a playful nudge and was pleased to see him smile in response.

After circling the tower – which really did lean alarmingly – they headed for the cathedral. This was a magnificent structure built of the same white marble as the tower, and Emma was fascinated. Beside her, she got the impression that even Ethan – who wasn't known for his interest in architecture – appeared to enjoy it. There was just one tricky moment right at the end of their visit. As she and Ethan were standing just outside the main exit, looking at the intricate carvings around the doors, with Sinclair lurking a few paces away, they heard the unmistakable sound of American voices. Emma glanced round to find a whole coach load of American tourists descending upon them. Even with his disguise, there was a very real risk of Ethan being recognised. Making a split-second decision, she reached up with her arms and threw them around his neck, turning his face towards hers and pulling him down towards her. As she did so, she hissed out a command.

'Keep your head down and don't look up.'

She tugged his shoulders towards her until his cheek was resting against hers and wrapped one hand across the side of his face in mock passion to add extra camouflage. They stayed like this until the wave of tourists had disappeared into the cathedral, and then she relaxed. As he straightened up again, he gave her a peck on the cheek and a wink.

'Quick thinking, English. By the way, did anybody ever tell you, you smell really good?'

She grinned, caught him by the arm and marched him away from the doors towards the open grassy field surrounding the monuments. Once safely away from possible eavesdroppers, she pulled out her phone and called Marina.

'Time to go, Marina, please. We've just had a close call.'

'I found a parking space just along the road and I was coming over to the cathedral to meet you. I saw what just happened.' There was a cheeky note in Marina's voice, but she didn't comment further. 'Anyway, two minutes and I'll pick you up from where I dropped you off.'

In the car on the way back to the hotel, Ethan removed the wig, ran his hands through his hair and relaxed. 'Great, well, that's two things ticked off my bucket list – I've seen the Leaning Tower of Pisa and I've ended up in the arms of the most desirable woman in Hollywood.'

Emma could feel her cheeks burning. 'Ever considered getting your eyes tested?' She took a deep breath and steered the conversation back to practical matters. 'So have you got the message about the weekend? We're all meeting up in a lovely remote hotel in Umbria the day after tomorrow where you'll have the opportunity to make friends with Laney and Erasmus Delgado.'

He nodded. 'Yeah, got it. I know Razzy Delgado already. I've been in a couple of his movies. He's a bit eccentric, but he's a great director. Here's hoping Laney decides she likes me after all.'

'When you say eccentric…?' Emma had never worked with the famous director, but she had heard a few stories and wasn't sure what to believe. 'How eccentric are we talking?'

'Very. Where do I start? He eats everything with a spoon. Doesn't trust forks. Seriously, you should see him with steak. He drinks half a pint of black coffee for breakfast out of an old tooth mug that's rumoured never to have been washed. He carries the mug around with him hooked to his belt wherever he goes. They say he meditates for ten minutes before and after every bowel movement. He never wears green. I forget the rest, but you'll love him. He's a hoot.'

Emma rolled her eyes. It looked like it was going to be a surreal weekend.

Meanwhile, Ethan leant forward and tapped Sinclair on his powerful shoulder. 'When we come back from Naples, what airport are we flying into on Friday, Sinc?'

'Perugia airport. Flight plans have been filed for the late afternoon.' Sinclair swivelled round so he was looking at Emma. 'I'll find out the exact ETA and let you know.'

'Great, thanks, Sinclair. I believe Laney and Erasmus are arriving on Saturday morning. Anyway, Marina'll come and pick you guys up on Friday afternoon.' She exchanged glances with Marina in the mirror. 'You wouldn't mind picking Ethan up again on Friday, would you?' As she saw Marina's eyes and smile widen, she reflected that it was without doubt a rhetorical question.

Back at the hotel, Ethan disappeared up to his room and Emma was about to go out and look for Mark and Rich to tell them that their illustrious guest had arrived when it occurred to her that today was the third day of filming of *Sweet Memories* back in Hollywood and she hadn't spoken to Elliot since Monday. Yesterday she hadn't even thought about the new film. Was her Italian 'holiday' taking the edge off her Hollywood executive persona? And if so, was that a good thing? She looked down at the phone in her hand and mulled it over for a few moments before deciding to leave well alone. He hadn't called, so that meant everything was fine. It was his responsibility now, not hers. A weight had been lifted from her shoulders. She returned the phone to her pocket and went down to the pool.

As she had expected, Mark and Rich were by the very secluded pool, but once again, Mark had eschewed the water and was lying in the shade, still wearing a T-shirt. Rich on the other hand had obviously just come out of the water as he was still dripping when he addressed her.

'Tell Ethan to come down for a swim. The water temperature's perfect. And why don't you have a swim as well, boss?'

Emma glanced at the water and thought about how inviting it looked. She had been planning on going back to her room to spend an hour on the internet checking out the locations Marina had earmarked for tomorrow, but she could do with a little break after the crowds and hustle of the Leaning Tower of Pisa.

'I think I'll do just that, Rich.'

Back home in LA she would never have dreamt of skipping work for the sake of a swim but this wasn't LA. All right, she wasn't on 'holiday', but she knew there was no real reason why she couldn't have a dip in the pool and do her work later on.

Mark looked up from his book. 'Did the great man arrive safely?'

'Yes, and we've done the whole Leaning Tower thing with him.' Then, out of what the rational part of her brain clearly identified as sheer mischief, she chose to elaborate. 'A whole bunch of American tourists turned up at one point and I had to take him in my arms and kiss him until they passed.' She gave them both a grin. 'I love my job.'

By the time she had changed into a bikini, wrapped herself in a towel dressing gown from the back of the bathroom door, and made her way back out to the pool again, she found Ethan and Marina already there. He was fooling about with Richard, trying to push him into the water while Marina, now wearing an even smaller bikini, stood by and watched the show wide-eyed. There was no doubt about it. Ethan had an amazing body, although Emma knew more than most the extent of the relentless hours of hard work and discipline that went into keeping him looking so good. For a moment or two, Emma also allowed herself the treat of seeing two good-looking men grappling hand-to-hand. Then, as they both finally toppled sideways into the water, she slipped off her robe and turned to set it down on a sunbed next to the other good-looking man around here. As she did so, she distinctly caught Mark's eyes on her body and she gave him her biggest smile.

'Not coming in, Mark?'

Was he blushing? Surely not. When he replied, however, he sounded quite relaxed, so maybe her eyes had been deceiving her.

'No, thanks, I'm happy as I am. Enjoy your swim.'

She toyed with the idea of diving in, but the memory of her embarrassment some years previously when she had done just that at a friend's house, only to resurface without the top half of her bikini, persuaded her to be more cautious. While she rather liked the thought of having Mark's eyes on her, that might be too much, too soon. Instead, she walked carefully down the tiled steps at the shallow end and slowly sank down until the water covered her shoulders. Only then did she lie back and let her feet float to the surface, her eyes trained on the cloudless blue of the sky above and the tops of three majestic palm trees that leant over the pool. It felt wonderful and she couldn't remember the last time she had felt so relaxed. The last holiday she had taken had been almost two years ago and that had been a mad rush back to the UK to see her parents, coupled with two days in London meeting people for work. It had rained all week and she had returned to LA feeling little fresher than when she had left. Now, a happy smile on her face, she floated and swam about in the water for a good long while before climbing back out again.

By now Marina had joined the two men at the far end of the pool and Emma had no doubt she would be enjoying herself immensely. After all, how many girls could say they'd been swimming with a Hollywood A-lister? And, for that matter, with the man who might become the next king of Hollywood?

Emma went over to a shower in the corner and washed the pool water off her body and rinsed her hair. Then, returning to the sunbed where she had left her robe, she dabbed herself reasonably dry before stretching out on top of it and lying back. The sun was pleasantly warm on her body, the air filled with the heady perfume of the lavender and broom plants that surrounded the pool, and she was very aware that she was lying, half-naked, alongside a man whose very presence gave her goosebumps. It felt really good and she found herself smiling, although she had to remind herself that he was already taken.

'So, are you happy with the way things are working out so far?'

She rolled her head towards the sound of Mark's voice. 'So far, so good, thanks. We've found some great locations, Rich is sounding good, Marina's a treasure, and I've got my very own history expert at my side. What more could a girl want?'

His eyes flicked towards where Ethan was still swimming. 'Maybe a Hollywood megastar at your other side?'

His voice was so studiously neutral it screamed curiosity, and she had a little smile to herself. Maybe he was interested after all. Mind you, she reminded herself, she had better restrict herself to just flirting with him. He already had a wife or girlfriend waiting for him back in Umbria, so maybe enough was enough now. The last thing she wanted to do was to annoy him or to cause any kind of friction within the group. He had been a mine of useful information so far and she knew his knowledge would be even more helpful from tomorrow when they hit the real historical heart of Tuscany. There was no way she wanted him to feel left out or miffed in any way. She rolled onto her side and propped herself on one elbow as she replied, but only after taking a quick look down the pool to be sure the others were still well out of earshot.

'Not this megastar. In fact, no megastars. Ethan's a sweetie. I've known him for quite a few years now and we get on well together but, and I know this is going to sound ridiculous seeing as he's a Hollywood idol and all that, but I've only ever thought of him as a friend, more like a sweet little brother really. Underneath that hunky exterior, he's remarkably insecure. I'm sort of his shoulder to cry on.'

'Well, we all need a shoulder to cry on from time to time. He's a lucky man to have you as a friend.'

There was something in his voice that cut straight to her heart and she couldn't help herself. Stretching out her free arm, she caught him briefly on the forearm with her hand. She gave him a reassuring squeeze before releasing him again.

'Any time you need a shoulder to cry on… or a friend, I'm here, Mark.'

Chapter 10

Dinner that night was amazing. Marina drove them further up into the hills until they came to a tiny village – little more than just a collection of a dozen or so houses at the side of the road. A wonky wooden arrow pointed off to the right with just two words on it: *La Luna*. Marina turned off and they headed up a very bumpy track further into the tree-covered hills. Finally, just as Emma was beginning to wonder if they had somehow got lost, they arrived at their destination. Another even more precarious-looking wooden sign on the gatepost indicated that this rambling old stone building was indeed called *La Luna* or The Moon.

Marina swung the big vehicle in through the ancient arched gateway and drew up in what was quite evidently a farmyard. Just in case they might have had any doubts on that score, a noisy collection of ducks and chickens scattered at their approach, clucking and quacking in protest at being disturbed. Emma, quite happily seated beside Mark, with Rich and Sinclair behind them in the back, exchanged uncertain glances with the others. Marina caught her eye in the mirror and grinned.

'It's all right, this really is the place.'

'You're telling me this is the best restaurant in Italy?' Ethan in the front seat didn't sound convinced. Marina did her best to reassure him.

'That's what they say. Gianluca, my boss, told me the owner of this place used to be the head chef at the swankiest restaurant in Rome, one of only a handful of restaurants in the whole country with three Michelin stars. He retired up here a few years ago and he only comes out of retirement for a very few, very select customers.'

'I see. Well, hey, that sounds great. I'm honoured.'

Emma could hear that this had got Ethan intrigued. In fact, from what Marina had told her, the chef was only doing this tonight as a favour to her boss. The fact that he would be catering for a Hollywood great hadn't cut any ice with him at all. Suppressing a smile, she turned to Mark alongside her.

'Shall we go? I'm feeling quite hungry.'

As they climbed out, a massive shaggy dog appeared in front of them and stood there immobile, staring at them, clearly suspicious. From the look of it, its pedigree most probably had to include wolf as well as maybe even grizzly bear. It was enormous and it was sporting an impressive set of gleaming white teeth. For a moment, Emma had a sudden horrific image of the world-famous actor alongside her being assaulted and scarred for life by this giant hound. She was just about to risk throwing herself between Ethan and the beast when she felt Mark push past her and walk over to the dog. As he approached it, he dropped to one knee and held out his hand.

'*Ciao, bello.* Who's a very good dog, then?'

To Emma's relief, the mixture of languages appeared to work. Reassured, the dog took a step forward and buried his head in Mark's chest, his tail beginning to wag. While the beast was otherwise engaged, Emma took Ethan by the arm and hurried him across to the front door. As they got there, it opened and a matronly lady appeared, wiping her hands on her apron. Seeing the dog, she addressed him in firm tones.

'Rocky, leave the guests alone. Go off back to your bed, or you won't get any leftovers.'

This threat worked wonders and the dog trotted off round towards the rear of the house without a backward glance. The lady transferred her attention to her guests.

'*Buonasera, signori*. Welcome to *La Luna*. How very kind of you to choose to come and dine with us.'

She shook hands with each of them in turn. If she recognised Ethan – no longer in his heavy-metal aficionado disguise – she gave no sign of it.

'Do come in please.'

She ushered them along a corridor and into a fine old dining room. There was only one table in there, and it was set for six people. One wall was covered with framed certificates and awards of the highest order for services to Italian cuisine, all in the name of their host. A massive old dresser held row upon row of cups, shields, bowls and statuettes, commemorating his achievements. Emma caught Ethan's eye. Clearly, they were in the presence of culinary greatness.

The high ceiling was supported by massive wooden beams with ancient red bricks between them. The floor was paved with lovely old terracotta tiles, worn down by the passage of countless feet over the centuries, and a glazed arch in the end wall provided a stunning view out over the wooded hillside back down to the valley below.

The sun was low in the sky and its rays had turned the distant hills a ruby red colour. It was an enchanting place with an inspiring view and Emma had her camera out in an instant.

As they stood there, admiring the view, another door opened and the chef appeared. He was a jovial-looking man with an impressive paunch and a moustache worthy of a Mexican bandido. He was wearing a pristine white chef's jacket with his initials embroidered onto the left breast. He smiled as he saw them.

'*Signori, buonasera. Mi chiamo Rodolfo. Benvenuti alla Luna.*'

He came round, shaking their hands and slipped seamlessly into excellent English as he told them the history of this place. To Emma's amazement it was almost six hundred years old and had been in his family for as long as anybody could remember. As he was circulating, his wife appeared with a magnum of Tuscan sparkling wine. The chef informed them that this rosé wine came from Radda in Chianti, just below Florence, and was, in his opinion the best sparkling wine in Italy. When Emma had the temerity to query where Prosecco figured in his estimation he only rolled his eyes and handed her a glass of the rosé. She took a sip and had to admit that it was excellent.

After the introductions had been completed, Rodolfo turned to the main point of the evening: the meal.

'Do any of you have any allergies? Anything you particularly like or dislike? Vegetarians, maybe?' Nobody said a word so he continued. 'Excellent. Well, I hope you enjoy the dinner I have planned for you. When I worked in Rome, my team and I used to go out of our way to produce dishes of almost impossible refinement and novelty. It became a competition, an obsession, to see who could come up with the most bizarre combination of ingredients. I grilled cauliflower and served it with caviar, roasted red peppers and stuffed them with scallops. I cooked pigeon in straw, scampi with aniseed jelly and all manner of other dishes designed to catch the eye of a certain type of diner.

'Now that I've returned to my native Tuscany, I've come full circle and I let the quality of the raw materials speak for themselves without all the excess. This is food the way it's been cooked in this part of Tuscany for centuries. Everything you will eat tonight was grown or reared within walking distance of this place, just like it would have been once upon a time. The fish is the exception, but it only comes from the nearby coast and I can guarantee you there are no chemicals, additives or other artificial enhancements in anything on your table tonight. My menu changes according to the seasons and I can promise that what I offer you is genuine, real food.'

There was a murmur of approval all round. Emma was particularly pleased to see Ethan nodding enthusiastically.

'Tonight, if you're agreeable, I thought I would prepare some local specialities as a starter, followed by home-made pasta. Tonight I've made *pappardelle*.' Seeing the expressions on some of the faces – including Emma's – he explained. 'These are broad strips of homemade pasta which I propose serving with a sauce made from smoked ham, porcini mushrooms and truffles from our very own woods.' He gave them a broad grin. 'I'm afraid I can't tell you the exact location where we find these treasures or you would never be allowed to leave here alive.'

Emma shot another glance across at Ethan to see how this was going down with him. By the look of anticipation on his face, he was impressed.

'And then for the main course, I would propose a mixed platter of grilled meats. I have some particularly good steak, fine little lamb chops and, of course, local Tuscan sausage made by my friend Armando, the finest butcher in this part of Italy. And for any of you who don't want too much meat, I will grill some seasoned pecorino cheese as well.' He beamed at them. 'How does that sound?'

Unsurprisingly, there was general approval and Rodolfo bowed and withdrew, leaving his wife to top up their glasses, after which she disappeared only to return with a tempting platter of canapés. These varied from tiny toasted squares of the lovely Tuscan unsalted bread topped with homemade wild boar pâté and soft goat's cheese, to delicious marinated prawns on cocktail sticks and tiny spicy sausages that tasted of rosemary. As they stood there, savouring the food and enjoying the view, Emma found herself next to Mark, so close, she could feel the hairs on his bare forearm against her skin. She took a hasty sip of cold wine and transferred her attention to Ethan.

'Not a bad view, eh, Ethan?'

He turned back from the window and smiled at her. 'It's amazing. The whole place's amazing. And I love the fact that the chef's going to give us real food, rather than the airy-fairy crap that turns up all too often when I go out to eat. Did you know? In a restaurant in London the other day they tried to tell me it was forbidden to drink beer with their *refined* food. That's what the pretentious little cock of a headwaiter called it. Refined my ass!'

Emma giggled. 'And how did that end up?'

'We left. Sinc and I got a takeaway and a six pack. Had it in my hotel room and loved every minute of it.'

A few minutes later, the antipasti arrived and they all sat down. Emma put Ethan at the head of the table and she sat on one side of him, Marina on the other. Rich sat down next to Marina with Sinclair alongside him and this rather neatly meant that Mark ended up next to Emma.

The first dish to arrive was a massive wooden board bearing slices of freshly hand-carved cured ham, surrounded by apricots that had been gently cooked in some sort of sweet wine. The combination of tastes was amazing. Alongside this was a selection of local salami, among which Emma particularly loved the *finocchiona*, a cured sausage flavoured with fennel. There were dishes containing olives, little onions and baby mushrooms in thick, green, aromatic olive oil. There was also Rodolfo's take on the traditional Tuscan bruschetta. Instead of slices of bread, he used grilled polenta and topped the slices variously with mushrooms, tomatoes, chicken livers, goat's cheese and pâté.

To drink, they were given bottled water and two anonymous straw-covered flasks of red wine. There were no labels and when asked, Rodolfo's wife just winked, tapped the side of her nose with a finger and told them it was made by a friend of Rodolfo's. It was absolutely exquisite.

As they moved onto the pasta course, which was sublime, Emma decided to slow down and try to fight the temptation to have a second helping. She felt pretty sure there would be a mountain of grilled meat on its way very soon. Instead, she glanced sideways to see how Mark was doing. He and Rich had been chatting across the table and she listened in. They were talking about Mark's home in Umbria.

'Yes, it's old all right, Rich. The tower's medieval although the rest of the villa was built at the end of the seventeen hundreds, but underneath are the foundations of an eleventh-century fortress with walls over two metres thick. Probably just as well as we're in a seismic zone in Umbria and there are regular tremors. You maybe heard of the big one back in 1997 which caused a load of damage around Assisi. Hopefully the villa's solid enough to withstand a quake.'

'Wow! And that's where you're going to spend the rest of your life?'

'I honestly don't know. I've turned it into a hotel, just like my granddad wanted, but I've kept the old stables for myself. I'm going to have to be involved with the hotel at least for the first few years until everything's bedded in. I've employed some good people, so hopefully they'll soon be up to speed. So theoretically, in a few years' time, I could move anywhere.'

Emma decided to join it. 'What about going back to the UK? Is that an option?'

He turned towards her and she felt those blue-grey eyes lock onto hers. 'Maybe, but I'm in no hurry. If I decide to become a student all over again, I'd probably see if my old college at Oxford might want me. Otherwise, there are some very good universities here in Italy. We'll see.'

Emma took a mouthful of wine before risking her next question.

'And what would Carmen think about relocating to England?'

He laughed. 'She wouldn't mind, I'm sure. But I'd need to get her a passport first.'

'Really, she doesn't have a passport?' So, presumably Carmen wasn't Spanish, but home-grown in Italy. 'Hasn't she been outside Italy?'

'She hasn't been outside of Umbria.' Seeing the expression on Emma's face, he went on to explain. 'She comes from just a couple of kilometres away in Gubbio. She belonged to my grandfather and now I've inherited her.'

Emma couldn't believe what she was hearing. 'You inherited her?'

'That's right. He died quite unexpectedly and she was left all alone at the age of five.' He picked up his glass. 'Now she's mine and I love her to bits. Granddad was a great opera fan. That's why he called her Carmen. She's a very, very good dog.'

'Dog...?' The penny was taking an inordinately long time to drop.

'She's a Labrador, a black Labrador. I'm sure she'll like you. She's got a thing for pretty girls.'

'Haven't we all?' Rich glanced sideways at Marina. 'What about you and dogs, Marina? Like them?'

'Definitely, although I prefer ones that are a good bit smaller than Rocky the giant beast out there.' She glanced over at Emma who had just about recovered from the shock of discovering that the love of Mark's life had four legs and a tail. 'What about you, Emma? Are you a dog person?'

'I love them. We always had a dog at home, but since moving to the US I haven't been able to get one.'

Marina leaned towards Emma. 'Why's that? Doesn't your partner like them?'

'Partner?' Ethan joined in with a broad grin on his face. 'Marina, this is the ice maiden you're talking to here.'

As Emma felt her cheeks flush, Ethan elaborated for the benefit of the whole table. 'Back in LA there's a queue a mile long of hopefuls who'd just love to take her out, but all she thinks of is work.' He gave Emma a little wink. 'I've been at the head of the queue for years.'

Emma felt sure this wasn't true, although it was nice of him to suggest it. She knew her relationship with him didn't go beyond friendship but as for the 'ice maiden' thing, this came as a bolt from the blue. Surely people didn't really think she was that cold and unemotional. She took a swig of cold water and queried it with him.

'Ice maiden? Really? Who says that?'

He was still grinning, but now he even managed to look a little bit embarrassed – he was a very good actor after all. 'Oh, just people. No, of course you aren't icy. Everybody loves you. I love you but, let's face it, the job comes first with you.'

'Well, maybe that's because I like my job so much.' She glanced across at Rich and summoned a grin. 'Now, don't you go telling your father that or he'll make me work even harder. But I'm not really one of those boring people who just lives for her work... am I?' The idea that her colleagues thought of her as distant and aloof was disconcerting.

Rich grinned back at her and, at her side, she heard Mark's voice.

'There's more to life than work. That's personal experience talking. Trust me.'

As she returned her attention to him, another thought crossed her mind. Yes, he had revealed that Carmen was a dog, but that didn't necessarily mean that there wasn't a special someone waiting for him back in Umbria. She took another sip of red wine and decided she had to know.

'So, what about you, Mark? Did you manage to balance your private life and your work? Did you find your Mrs Right?'

In an instant, a cloud flashed across his face and his eyes suddenly dropped to the table top. She could have kicked herself. This had obviously been a question too far. Then, while she was desperately trying to think of a way out of the mess she had just created, he looked up again with those hypnotic eyes, the upset in them all too visible.

'I thought I had, Emma, I thought I had.' She saw him take a deep breath and she very nearly reached out to offer him a consoling hug, but she restrained herself as he added in clipped tones. 'But I'm afraid it ended in tears.'

Fortunately, at that moment, Rodolfo's wife appeared bearing a huge terracotta dish piled high with grilled meat, cheese and snake-like coils of sausage, all surrounded by what looked like thick, multi-coloured crisps. These turned out to be slices of potatoes, sweet potatoes, carrots, beetroot and some sort of turnips, quickly fried so the outside was crispy, while the inside remained soft and very, very tasty. Everybody started speaking at once, blown away by the sight and scent of the feast before them, and the moment passed. Emma slipped a glance sideways towards Mark and saw him smiling once more as he explained to Ethan just what delicacies were before them.

She drained her glass and reached for the Chianti. Rich got there first and filled her glass for her. He gave her a little, wry smile and she had a feeling he must have realised what had been going through her head. He topped up his own glass and clinked it against hers and then Marina's.

'It's been a lovely evening. In fact, speaking personally, these have been the best few days I've had in years and it's down to you and, of course, Marina. Thanks, boss.'

Ethan was quick to reach over and bang his glass against theirs and then Sinclair and Mark followed suit. As Mark's glass clinked against Emma's she heard him repeat Rich's words. 'Thanks, boss.' There was a pause and then he added five little words so very quietly only she could hear. 'I'm glad I've met you.'

Chapter 11

Next morning they all went for a run along a track though the woods above the hotel. Ethan and Sinclair soon accelerated away, leaving the others in their wake. Emma had a shrewd idea that Mark could have gone with them, but had chosen to stay behind and run alongside her. Behind them, Marina and Rich gradually slowed to a trot and receded into the distance. Soon all Emma could hear was the rhythmic pounding of her own feet as they scuffed through the dry leaves and twigs on the track. Everywhere was terribly dry and notices on gates and fences warned against starting fires. Last night Rodolfo and his wife, who had joined them for a glass of his home-distilled grappa, had told them about the great fire, the previous August, which had come within a hundred metres of *La Luna*. It was barely mid-June now and the grass was already turning brown. By August, it would be tinder dry.

Although it was still early, the temperature was already high and Emma was soon sweating profusely. As the track emerged from the trees onto a sort of headland overlooking the valley below, she spotted a fallen tree and glanced across at Mark.

'Feel like taking a break for a minute or two? I'm still burping grappa.'

He grinned back at her and they slowed to a stop. She sat down on the big, old, tree trunk and he took a seat beside her. Stretching her back, Emma surveyed the view as her heart rate slowed once more.

It was a charming scene, looking down the hillside and out across the wide valley floor as far as Pisa and the coast beyond it to the right. It was too far for her to make out the Leaning Tower, but she felt pretty sure she could see the huge white bulk of the cathedral. The distant Mediterranean was shimmering in the morning sunshine and the air was full of the perfume of wild thyme and rosemary. She ran her hands through her hair and glanced across at him. He was sitting quite still, his eyes far away, his expression difficult to interpret. It wasn't really happy and it certainly wasn't really sad. In the end she settled for troubled. He must have felt her eyes on him as he suddenly turned towards her.

'Look at you. You're barely panting. Do you run every day back in Hollywood?'

'Not every day, but when I can. I play tennis at least once a week as well and I live in a complex with a pool, so I get a fair amount of exercise.' A thought occurred to her. 'So, is there a pool at your lovely hotel in Umbria?'

He nodded. 'It was only finished and filled a couple of weeks ago, but the water temperature's been climbing steadily. Hopefully by the weekend it won't be too chilly.' His face broke into a little smile. 'Our main problem at the moment is keeping Carmen out of it. Like all Labs, she loves the water. The trouble is that filtration systems and dog hair don't mix.'

'I look forward to meeting the love of your life.'

She smiled back at him, but his smile had gone now. He turned his face sharply away from her and gazed out over the valley before them once more. She sat there, wondering if she should say anything, but uncertain how to begin. In the end, he was the first to speak.

'They're wonderful things, dogs. Pure, unadulterated love is what they give you. When I was growing up, after the death of my parents, it was my granddad's old dog, Tosca – he always named them after characters in opera – who kept me going. I'm sure she realised I was grieving and she stuck by my side like glue. She slept beside my bed – and on it when grandma wasn't looking – and she accompanied me everywhere.' He turned his head and caught Emma's eye for a few seconds. 'I'm not sure how I'd have coped without old Tosca.'

There was a catch in his voice and Emma couldn't resist reaching out and resting her hand on his wrist. 'It must have been so, so tough to lose your parents. How old were you?'

'Five, coincidentally the same age as Carmen the dog was last year when my grandfather died.'

His eyes were trained on her hand on his arm. She didn't make a move, waiting for him to say more, but she had to wait a good long while. In the end, when he finally looked back up, the pained expression had cleared from his face.

'Thanks, Emma. Now, shall we head back to the hotel?'

She wasn't sure what he was thanking her for, so she just nodded.

–

They left the hotel at just before ten and dropped Ethan, now wearing his wig and a White Snake T-shirt, back at the airport along with Sinclair. Ethan gave her a big hug before climbing out of the car.

'Thanks, English, that was fun. And thanks for listening.'

'I'll always be here for you, Ethan. You know that.' She and he had spent an hour the previous evening just talking and she got the impression it had helped him work through the remaining doubts he had about his working relationship with Laney. She kissed him on the cheek. 'See you guys tomorrow. Enjoy Naples.'

As Marina drove out of the airport complex once more, Emma queried her on the day's plans – more for the sake of Rich and Mark, seeing as she and Marina had already discussed this at breakfast.

'First stop, Lucca. It's smaller and a bit less well known than Pisa or Florence, but it's a lovely historic town all the same.'

'And it would almost certainly have been on the route of the Grand Tour a hundred years ago.' Mark clearly approved of the choice.

'And we're really not going to Florence?' Rich was sitting alongside Marina, but he screwed his head round and directed his query to Emma.

She shook her head. 'Sorry, no, we're going to give Florence a miss. Too big, too busy, too well known. But, don't worry, you'll see it. Marina's found a little road that winds through the hills outside Florence and from there we should have a pretty good panoramic view of the city.' She turned to Mark beside her on the back seat. 'You happy with that, Mark?'

'You're the boss, but, yes, I'm sure you're right. You need quieter places. Tell me, where are you planning on going this afternoon?'

'We were wondering about San Gimignano, but Marina's afraid that's going to be equally crowded.'

'And she'd be right. As an alternative, we could go to Certaldo. Ever heard of it?' All three shook their heads. 'It's a sort of a poor man's San Gimignano. Not so many towers, definitely not so many tourists, but a fine old castle and the higher part of town, Certaldo Alto, is an authentic medieval township. And the views out over the hills are spectacular.'

—

Lucca was, indeed, a lovely historic town. They parked outside the massive stone and brick walls, clearly built to withstand cannon fire, and walked into the town through a narrow arched gateway. Much of the centre of town was a pedestrians-only area, although they soon learnt to beware of bikes and scooters rattling past over the uneven flagstones that paved the narrow lanes. Mark pointed out that the architecture was a mixture of styles and eras from the Middle Ages to the present day. The road wound in and out among the buildings, opening up from time to time into tiny squares, some punctuated by trees, until they emerged into Piazza dell'Anfiteatro, ringed with mainly cream-coloured three- and four-storey buildings with green louvred shutters. All around were cafes and restaurants with tables out on the square and here they stopped for coffee under a large parasol.

It was almost midday by now and a digital thermometer outside a chemist's shop was indicating it was twenty-eight degrees. Emma wondered how much hotter it would get in high summer. She ordered a cappuccino and sat back to enjoy the view. On the way there, she had taken a load of photos and she felt sure the narrow lanes, brick archways leading to hidden courtyards, medieval churches and amazing Renaissance palaces would be well worth including in the movie. Lucca was definitely making it onto the list.

She cast a glance across at Mark who was looking quite relaxed again. They hadn't spoken much since their run, but she was beginning to get the feeling that maybe she might end up acting as a shoulder to cry on not only for the Hollywood megastar, but also for this man who had suffered a terrible blow as a child which still resonated today. And there was also the matter of how he had reacted last night to her question about finding Mrs Right. Quite clearly, he was still hurting from whatever had happened there. She resolved to do her very best to help him – for his sake but also, maybe, for hers.

After last night's feast, they just opted for a light lunch. The men bought focaccia sandwiches while Emma and Marina just settled for ice cream cones, and they continued their walking tour of Lucca, returning to the car around mid-afternoon. From there, it took less than an hour to get to Certaldo, which was situated in the first rows of hills rising up on the southern side of the valley of the River Arno. The hills themselves were dotted with olive groves, vineyards and the ubiquitous Tuscan mix of umbrella pines and tall, slim cypress trees. At first Certaldo didn't seem like it was anything special, until they turned off the main road and made their way up to the old part of town that Mark had described; up at the top, it was charming.

Leaving the car by the side of the road, they walked around the little hilltop township, admiring the ancient buildings, mostly constructed of wonderful old rose-tinted bricks, some with the render peeling off the walls. Beneath their feet, the narrow roads were paved with red bricks laid in herringbone fashion, giving the place an almost magical feel. They looked into the castle, admired the medieval town hall and stopped at an observation point to look out at the view. As Mark had said, it was terrific from up here and they gazed in wonder over the red roofs of the town below and beyond them up across vineyards, olive groves and fields towards San Gimignano itself, clearly visible on top of the distant hill. The silhouette of the iconic towers was unmistakable and Emma had no hesitation in adding Certaldo to the growing list of suitable locations on her phone.

Rich and Marina went off to get drinks while Emma and Mark sat down on a bench shaded from the sun by a massive old tree, and gazed at the view. After a minute or two of silence, he turned towards her with a raised eyebrow.

'So, the ice maiden, eh? Are you really so wedded to your work?'

She gave him a wry smile. Ever since Ethan had used the expression she had been asking herself if she really was that cold, that aloof. She certainly didn't want to give anybody that impression, but she knew she could sometimes be a bit single-minded, a bit dismissive.

'I must admit I didn't know they called me that – mind you, that might just be what Ethan calls me – but I suppose there's some truth to it.' She paused to shoot him a cheeky glance. 'For the sake of accuracy, not the "maiden" part, but I've been in the company for twelve years now and I can honestly say I've enjoyed virtually all of it. They work me hard and I suppose I have to hold my hand up and add that I work myself hard, maybe to the detriment of my personal life.' She turned more fully towards him. 'But I only do it because I enjoy it. As for the "ice" thing, I really try not to be cold towards anybody, but I must admit that dating's been pretty low on my agenda for a good long while now. As for the queue of men all round Hollywood, that's just Ethan. You know what they're like, these film stars – always exaggerating.'

Mark held her eye for a moment before looking away. 'You want to know something? I reckon he was serious when he said he was in the queue... at the head of the queue even.'

Emma stared at him blankly. 'You're joking, surely? Yes, I see Ethan often. He's contracted to our studio. We talk and spend time together, but there's no way he'd ever be interested in somebody like me, not when he's got millions of women all over the world just dying to jump into his arms, not to mention his bed.' The more she thought about it, the more ridiculous it sounded.

'Don't you believe it? You're beautiful, you're very bright and you're a genuinely nice person. Any man would be lucky to have you.'

For a moment she thought about querying his use of the term 'any man'. Might that also include him? But, instead, she found herself taking issue with his choice of vocabulary.

'That's the point, really. I don't want to be "had" by any man. I'm my own woman and I choose my own partners.'

'Sorry, of course I didn't mean "have" in the sense of "possession". Anyway, apologies again, I didn't want to intrude. It just interested me that you appeared to be rejecting a Hollywood heart-throb.'

'There's no need to apologise, but I think you've misread the signs. My relationship with Ethan isn't like that.' She looked him square in the eye. 'And it never will be.'

'Message received loud and clear, boss. Okay. So, if you're turning down the sexiest man on the planet, then that means there's no hope left for any other man on the planet. We're all doomed.'

She rather liked the fact that he had used the pronoun 'we' and she rather regretted being quite so sharp with him. But then, she told herself, maybe it was for the best: there was no future for her with Mark, given that they would soon be on opposite sides of the globe, and the sooner her heart and her brain started operating on the same wavelength, the better. She gave him a smile.

'Nobody's doomed, Mark. Right now, the fact is that my job means more to me than any man.'

'Any man?'

'That's the way it's been so far.'

At that moment, Marina and Rich returned with bottles of water and the conversation turned to more practical matters. Emma wasn't sure if she should be sorry or relieved.

'Our hotel for tonight's right in the heart of the Chianti region, south of Florence.' Marina glanced across at Rich. 'But I promise you'll get a good view of Florence on the way there. The hotel's actually an *agriturismo* on a working wine estate. Have you come across those?'

Mark was quick to explain. 'Think bed and breakfast, often very upmarket bed and breakfast, sometimes with dinner, but on a farm, or at least out in the countryside.'

This sounded rather good to Emma and she realised it might work for the movie as well. 'In the movie, as they're on their way from Florence to Siena by road, the car taking Emily and her governess breaks down and they have to spend the night in a rat-infested country inn. This *agriturismo* should fit in fine.'

If there were any rats in the *agriturismo* where Emma and company spent the night, they were without doubt some of the luckiest rats in Italy. The place was very luxurious, very comfortable, scrupulously clean and in a delightful position, their bedroom windows looking right out over the rolling Chianti hills. On the way there, Marina had been true to her word and had taken them along a series of narrow roads through olive groves and vineyards to the south of Florence, driving right in towards the city as far as the hills directly above the River Arno. They saw the roofs, cupolas, towers and domes of Florence, laid out like a model below them, but didn't venture any further into town. More photos were added to the pile but Emma had no regrets at leaving out this internationally recognised World Heritage site which, she knew, would be even more crowded than Pisa.

The hotel had a swimming pool and Emma spent a happy hour there before going inside for a wonderful long bath, emerging feeling energised and refreshed. She met up with the others in the bar downstairs before dinner for a glass of the excellent wine produced here on the estate.

The walls were covered in old black-and-white photos of men and women harvesting the grapes onto horse-drawn carts. Rich suggested taking photos of some of these photos to help the costume department. Emma was impressed and told him to go ahead, mentally adding this little sign of initiative to the secret report she was preparing for his father.

That evening, after an excellent dinner, Marina and Rich stayed inside to chat to the owner, while Emma and Mark went for a little walk along a track at the rear of the hotel. From there they had a wonderful view down over the rows of vines, laid out with mathematical precision, clearly visible in the light of an almost full moon. Night had fallen by now and as they strolled along, Emma started to see little flashes of yellow light in the darkness, where fireflies flew among the vines. Above them somewhere an owl hooted, close enough to startle her, and she instinctively reached out and grabbed Mark's arm. As she realised what had caused the noise she hastily removed her hand and apologised. He turned towards her and chuckled.

'Any time you want me to defend you from an owl, just say so. But if it's a wild boar, I may not be so obliging. I was talking to the owner and he told me they've had a lot of trouble with them. They dig up the vines and cause a lot of damage and, if you get in their way, they can be dangerous. We've had them around the villa too.'

'And I thought knights in shining armour were fear-less.'

'Not this knight. I pick my battles.' There was a momentary pause before he added something that puzzled her. 'At least I do nowadays.'

'You used to be fearless?'

'I think the word you're looking for is reckless. But I learnt my lesson. Anyway, enough about me, what are you afraid of? Not a lot, I would guess.'

She thought about probing him on what he had meant, but decided against it. He had obviously decided to change the subject. She did her best to answer his question honestly.

'Oh, I get scared all right. I'm terrified of snakes. Believe it or not, a rattlesnake even got into one of the studio lots a few years back. The security guys shot it and hung it on the gate. Although it was as dead as a dodo, it still frightened the life out of me. Otherwise, I'm okay with most animals and I'm reasonably okay with heights. I suppose if I'm totally honest, the thing that frightens me most is the idea of getting shot in some random attack or at the hands of some madman. There are an awful lot of guns in the US. Give me a good old English Bobby with his truncheon any day.'

'But you've been living in the US for years and, presumably, you intend to stay there at least until you're running JMGP, so you can't be that scared.'

'I suppose not, but it's absolutely terrifying having a gun pointed at you. It happened to me once and the pistol was in the hand of a cop, but it frightened the life out of me all the same.' She turned her head towards him. 'Have you ever had a gun pointed at you?'

'Afraid so. You're right. It's definitely very scary.' He didn't go into any detail as to the circumstances under which the weapon had been pointed at him and she didn't press him. Instead, she turned the conversation to happier matters.

'Less than a day to wait until you're reunited with Carmen. I'm looking forward to meeting her. Have you got a photo?'

He reached into his pocket and pulled out his phone. He scrolled through until he found what he wanted. He held the phone out towards her and she caught hold of his hand to look at the photo of a very happy-looking black Labrador with a huge branch in her mouth.

'If you scroll back, you'll see a few more.'

She did so and found many more pictures of the dog. Clearly, he thought a lot of her but then, of course, Carmen was effectively the last remaining memory of his grandfather. Finally she released his hand and saw him return the phone to his pocket. It had felt good to touch him. Disturbingly good. She glanced at her watch and saw that it was almost eleven o'clock, so she decided to get away while the going was good. There's a limit to the amount of willpower a woman can summon up, and her hand was itching to grab onto his once more.

'She's a lovely dog. And I'll tell her that myself when I see her. Now, I'd better go up to my room. I've got to check in with my boss and see if there any messages. Are you coming in?'

To her surprise, and no little pleasure, his hand found hers in the darkness and caught hold of it for a second or two. She felt a little squeeze and then heard his voice.

'I think I'll stay out and stare at the moon for a bit. Goodnight, boss, and remember what I said about not working too hard.'

'I'll remember. Goodnight, Mark.'

Chapter 12

Next morning there were grey clouds in the sky and a hint of drizzle in the air. The people in the winery informed them with barely concealed delight that rainstorms were predicted for later on in the day. Although Emma would have preferred wall-to-wall sunshine during her stay in Italy, she didn't blame them. Anybody could see that the dusty earth and the tiny young grapes were crying out for a good soaking.

They drove down to Siena on the back roads, stopping off en route to visit a wonderful old fortress in a little place called Staggia. This imposing stone castle with its massive defensive walls dating back to the first millennium appeared to be a bit off the normal tourist trail and they were the only visitors there that morning. A chatty guide showed them round and encouraged them to climb to the battlements at the top of the imposing tower from where they had a lovely view out over the fields and hills of Tuscany and down onto the remnants of the medieval walls surrounding the little town below.

There was a very old and very quiet feel to the place and Emma had absolutely no hesitation in adding it to her list, as the spot where in the movie Robert and Emily would meet up again after losing contact when her car broke down. By this time in *Dreaming of Italy* Emily knew she was falling in love with Robert, but he remained impossible to read. Emma found herself sympathising with the Emily character. In her own case, though she knew it was futile, it would have been good to find out Mark's true feelings towards her. He remained stubbornly hard to fathom. It was as if a veil shrouded his feelings and it was exasperating. Suppressing a little snort, she did her best to dismiss such thoughts and focused on adding peaceful Staggia to her list of locations.

From there, they drove to the beautiful city of Siena. Here, however, things were anything but quiet and peaceful. As they walked from the car park to the gateway leading into the old walled city, the sight of a line of coaches disgorging hordes of tourists gave them a foretaste of what they were to find inside. Sure enough, the narrow roads were filled with people, and even the magnificent sloping main square, the Piazza del Campo, was crowded. They toured the city, taking lots of photos, but Emma was already mentally adding *unsuitable* alongside the name of Siena on her list when Rich made a sensible suggestion. He had been looking and sounding brighter and brighter over the past few days and Emma was delighted to hear him getting more and more interested in *Dreaming of Italy* as they went along.

'Why not shoot a scene way up on top of one of the towers with just glimpses of the city over the rooftops? It should be easy to keep the hordes of modern-day tourists down below out of shot and we could even build a mock-up back in the studios for the close-ups or if the scene needs to be longer.'

Emma agreed enthusiastically and added his suggestion to her list. She also made a note that Rich had come up with it in her confidential report for his father.

After a light lunch they returned to the car and followed a series of scenic, winding roads through the hills towards the east. Sinister dark grey clouds were gathering more and more as the day progressed and Emma had no doubt the weathermen had got it right.

As they approached the border between Tuscany and Umbria, Mark took over from Marina as their local guide, pointing out the beautiful town of Cortona high above them, a mass of red roofs sprawling up the hillside. Then, a few kilometres later, they came to the vast open expanse of water of Lake Trasimeno and he told them all about it, such as the fact that the lake had numerous rivers and streams running into it, but none running out. As a result, the water levels could vary considerably from one season, or one year, to another and it had gained a reputation over the centuries for its vicious mosquitoes and, not that long ago, malaria. They stopped for coffee overlooking the lake and, as they did so, the rain started: shower clouds swept across the now steely grey surface of the lake as the winds picked up.

They had to make a run for the car as the rain became torrential. Fortunately, it didn't last too long, but they were continually driving in and out of ever-longer showers as they headed up into the tree-covered hills of Umbria. The scenery here was altogether a bit wilder and less cultivated than Tuscany had been, although the stone and sun-bleached brick farmhouses dotting the hillsides looked very similar. Mark assured them that on a clear day they would have been able to see right across to the peaks of the Apennines, but the horizon was swathed in clouds today. Emma hoped it would clear over the weekend so they could get some good photos of what promised to be a very scenic area.

It was just after four when they finally arrived at Mark's home. Marina had been following the signs to Gubbio for some time now, down through the hills and into the wide river valley, and it was only when the old town was already in sight on the hillside opposite them that that they turned off onto a much narrower country road leading back up the hill directly opposite. Through the rain it was hard to make out much of the town on the other side of the valley, but Mark assured them it would be well worth a visit when the skies cleared. After five minutes of hard climbing up a winding lane that got progressively narrower, they came to a fine pair of stone gateposts set in a solid ancient perimeter wall made of the local red brick.

'We're here. Welcome to Villa Graziella.' Mark sounded glad to be home.

As Marina turned in through the gateway, they saw a smart new sign advertising that they had arrived at what was billed as a luxury boutique hotel. Emma glanced across at Mark.

'Looks good. So, tell me, who is or was Graziella?' Although she felt sure it couldn't be, an obstinate part of her brain waited apprehensively for him to announce that it was the name of his fiancée, wife or mistress. Silly as the idea had been, she couldn't help a sensation of relief when he explained.

'She was my great, great, great, and a lot more greats, grandmother. From what the history books say, she was quite a lady, with a terrific depth of culture at a time when women who could read might have been suspected of witchcraft. Some say she was the secret advisor to the Duke of Urbino who was responsible for much of the grand architecture in Gubbio way back in the fourteenth century. Anyway, whether she was or not, she still managed to produce no fewer than eleven children and, if she hadn't done that, I wouldn't be here today.'

Rich turned around and surveyed Mark with renewed interest. 'You can trace your ancestry back seven hundred years? Wow, all I know is that my father's grandfather was a wool merchant in Kiev at the time of the Russian Revolution and his name was Miroshnychenko. When he and his family emigrated to New York, the immigration official at Ellis Island shortened it to Miros, but that's as far as it goes.'

Emma was equally awed by Mark's story. 'And you wouldn't believe how many Taylors there are in England. So does this mean you're of noble blood, Mark? Should I be curtsying every time we meet?'

He gave her a broad grin. 'That's all in the past. Italians don't do noble titles any more. We're a republic, and republics and nobles are mutually exclusive. No, I'm just plain old me.'

While they were chatting, Marina was following the gravel track as it wound its way through a dense wood composed of a spectacular variety of trees, from oaks to umbrella pines, hollies to palms, as they gradually gained even more height. Finally, after at least several hundred metres, they emerged from the wood and found themselves in a wide, open, nearly flat, parking area overlooking the valley below. A massive sweeping stone staircase led up from there to one of the most beautiful houses Emma had ever seen. The photos on Mark's phone hadn't done it justice. This place was stunning.

As Marina turned off the engine, all they could hear was the drumming of the rain on the roof of the car, and they all just sat and stared.

It was built in three distinct layers on the sloping hillside. The first layer was a terrace, surrounded by decorative balustrades and classical style statues. No doubt from there, guests would have a spectacular panorama across the valley towards Gubbio, which clung to the steep slope on the opposite side. Leading off this terrace was the entrance to the ground floor. This whole part of the structure was made of light-coloured stone and composed of a mixture of arches and pillars. The doors themselves – tall enough and wide enough to get a coach and horses through – were adorned with masterful whirls and curls of carved and gilded wood, with modern glass doors fitted inside.

Above this was the main body of the house, arranged over two floors and covered in gorgeous ochre-coloured render, the windows highlighted by aquamarine, louvred shutters. Finally, from the very centre of the building rose a massive tower, built of wonderfully weathered ancient bricks. This was clearly very old and had almost certainly performed a defensive function back in the Middle Ages. The lower windows were little more than arrow slits, with larger, arched windows up on the top floor from where the views must have been amazing.

Emma gaped at it in awe.

'Will it do?' Mark's voice sounded maybe just a little bit hesitant and she was quick to reassure him.

'Will it do? It's perfect. I don't think I've ever seen anything quite like it. And to think we're going to be staying here…'

'I'm glad you like the look of it. The interior's been completely revamped so hopefully you'll find that to your liking as well.' He looked relieved. 'So, remind me, what happens here in the movie? Didn't you say the heroine gets sick?'

Emma nodded. 'She develops a raging fever and they fear for her life. Don't forget this would have been before Alexander Fleming and the discovery of penicillin. People really did die of a high temperature back then. The old governess also contracts it and it falls to Robert, who's a friend of the marquis who owns the place, to help look after both of them. There's what should be a real tear-jerker of a scene, where he believes Emily has died and this, more than anything else, makes him realise the depth of his feelings for her.' She gave Mark a smile. 'Fortunately she gets better very quickly and they're ready to move on after a week.'

'And the governess?'

'She survives as well and she now understands that Robert isn't an evil gold-digger or a rapscallion just trying to have his wicked way with Emily, and her whole attitude towards him changes for the better, so that when they leave, it's with a smile on their faces.'

'So this is the place that puts a smile on everyone's face. Well, let's hope it does the same to you guys and to your famous guests. Look, here's Claudio.'

He pointed through the windscreen and they saw three figures hurrying down the steps towards the car, carrying umbrellas. The first to reach them was a tall man in a very smart dark suit. Claudio the manager certainly looked the part. Beside him were two staff members, also immaculately turned out. All of them were smiling.

'*Ciao Claudio.*'

Mark jumped out and shook him warmly by the hand. As the others followed, they were handed umbrellas and shepherded up the steps towards the terrace and the shelter of the front door. As Emma handed her soaking umbrella to another smiling staff member and went in through the glass doors, she saw Mark suddenly fall to his knees in front of her and she rushed forward in concern.

She needn't have been concerned.

'*Ciao bella gioia. Come stai? Ciao Carmen*, it's good to see you.' As Emma's eyes focused, she realised that he was hugging a very happy – and presumably bilingual – black Labrador; the dog's whole body wagging along with her tail while she nuzzled into her master's armpit, emitting contented little canine whines as she did so.

'Emma, Rich, Marina, come and meet Carmen.'

Mark glanced up over his shoulder and Emma could see his eyes gleaming. She hadn't seen him with such an expression of happiness before and, if anything, it made him look even more desirable – and for the first time in her life she felt jealous of a Labrador.

They were introduced to the dog who was very pleased to meet them, but it was clear where her main affections lay.

Emma couldn't fault the dog's taste.

After saying hello to Carmen, Emma stood up and took a good look around. They were standing in what was now the main lobby of the hotel. The floor was made up of slabs of polished marble, alternating red, white and black, in a sort of checkerboard pattern, and the walls were hung with mirrors in ornate gilt frames. Over to one side was the reception desk with, behind it, another welcoming face, this time a very pretty dark-haired woman probably still in her twenties.

'Would you like me to show you to your rooms?' Claudio picked a handful of keys off the desk. 'Or would you prefer a cup of tea first?' His English was excellent and his smile was infectious as he caught Emma's eye. 'You are English after all, and tea *is* traditional, isn't it?'

Emma smiled back at him. 'Could I do both? Maybe see my room and then come back downstairs for a cup of tea?'

'Of course, Signora Taylor. And your colleagues?'

Emma looked across at the others. 'Marina, what time's Ethan due in?'

'Six thirty. And it's barely half an hour from here to Perugia airport, so I don't need to leave until six, or a bit before. Do you want to come with me?'

Emma would have been quite happy not to go out in the car again, but she wondered if Ethan might be expecting her to be at the airport to greet him. At the same time, she couldn't help remembering Mark's conviction that Ethan might even have a thing for her. Maybe she should let Marina go on her own, so as not to give the actor the wrong idea. For the first time in ages, she found herself really stumped. Normally she was very logical in her decision-making. Suddenly, since she had arrived in Italy, she was a different person. No, she immediately reminded herself, like it or lump it, the fact was that this new uncertain Emma hadn't started upon arrival in Italy. It had started upon meeting Mark for the first time when her knees had turned to jelly. As she was still trying to work out what to do, Rich gave her a helping hand.

'Why don't you take it easy, boss? I'll go with Marina.' He grinned as he switched into his English accent. 'When one is English, one normally does like a cup of tea in the afternoon, doesn't one, what?'

Emma couldn't help laughing out loud. 'One certainly does, Rich. All right then, if you're sure, I'll take it easy.' For Ethan, being met by the son of the big boss, who would in all probability become the future head of the studios in his turn, would surely more than compensate for her absence at the airport. She checked her watch. 'Anyway, it's only half past four now so we can all take it easy for a while. Marina, are you sure you're okay to drive? Not too tired?'

'I'm fine, thanks, but I might have a little lie down for half an hour.'

Emma turned back to the manager. 'Then it's settled. If we could see our rooms, please, and then those who feel like a cup of tea, or whatever, can meet me back down here. Those that want a rest, please do, and we'll meet up when Ethan gets here.' Somehow she didn't expect to see Marina or Rich again until later on. Although they were being very discreet, she had little doubt that there was something going on there. From the smiles on both their faces, it wasn't doing either of them any harm, so Emma kept on turning a Nelsonian blind eye.

Claudio gave a little nod of agreement. 'Certainly, signora. And we'll send your luggage up directly.'

'I'll show you to your room, Emma, if you like.' Mark glanced across at Claudio. 'She's in the Verdi suite, isn't she?' The manager nodded again and handed Mark the key. Emma smiled.

'You've given the rooms operatic names?'

'Yes, as a little salute to my grandfather. He was a lovely man.' There was a touch of sorrow in his voice, but the smile returned almost immediately. 'You're on the top floor, so we'll take the lift.'

Emma's room was enormous and delightful. In fact it was effectively two rooms, divided by a charming Japanese-style screen. In the main part there was an elegant modern sofa and two armchairs, a massive television, and picture windows looking out over the park. Emma followed Carmen the dog over to the window, which was streaming with water as the rainstorm outside intensified. As she stood there, she heard Mark's voice at her ear.

'You'll have to take my word for it that there's a terrific view right across the valley to Gubbio and onwards towards the peaks of the Apennines beyond.'

'It's amazing as it is.' In spite of the torrential rain, Emma found herself gazing down onto a pastoral scene with meadows sloping towards an ornamental lake with what looked like a couple of ducks or geese bobbing happily up and down in it. She turned back to face him. 'It's charming.'

'Come and see if you approve of the rest of the room. I need your honest opinion. You are a guinea pig, after all.'

Emma walked past the screen into the sleeping area. There was an enormous king-size bed, a clearly antique dresser and matching wardrobe, and a door through which she could see a pristine all-white bathroom.

'It's beautiful, Mark. I love it, although I'll probably get lost in this enormous bed.'

And then, suddenly, an all-consuming vision of the two of them lying naked across the bed, entwined in each other's arms, filled her head and she even felt her cheeks begin to colour. Once again she did her best to give herself a stern talking-to. She was a thirty-five-year-old woman, not a giddy teenager, for God's sake.

'I'm glad you like it. You deserve it. Nothing but the best for you...' His tone was warm and caring and she felt her heart begin to melt. But then he added a single word that dampened her ardour. '...boss.'

He turned and headed for the door, leaving her still struggling to recover from the wave of emotion – or, more accurately, lust – that had swept over her. As he reached it, he looked round.

'After you've had your tea, if you'd like to come over to my house, I could offer you a glass of wine, maybe?' She nodded mutely. 'Claudio will show you where it is.'

He and the dog were already halfway through the door when she finally gathered her wits enough to say thank you.

Chapter 13

A few minutes after Mark had left her room, there was a tap at the door and her luggage arrived. She was still wondering whether to tip the porter when he gave her a smile and left again before she had a chance. She took her laptop from her bag, sat down on the sofa, and tried to do some work. It wasn't easy. Her mind and, if she was honest, her whole body were still recovering from the thrill of attraction and plain unadulterated lust that had shot through her. And, she repeated to herself over and over again, it wasn't as if Mark had done anything to set her off. In fact, he probably hadn't been aware of anything. She rather hoped he hadn't. Simply his presence beside her and that enormous bed had been enough to reduce her from an intelligent, efficient, switched-on Hollywood executive to a pathetic, helpless wreck, incapable of rational thought.

The logic of her position was inescapable, so why wouldn't her brain just accept it? He had displayed no interest in her, apart from general friendship. He hadn't made any suggestive remarks or thinly veiled hints. He was clearly still trying to come to terms with the loss of the love of his life, whoever that had been, and, besides, the unavoidable fact was that he and she would soon be on opposite sides of the globe. It would be highly unprofessional, and frankly crazy, for her to give in to her base animal desires. Mind you, the fact was that she hadn't given in to her base animal desires for quite a while now and there was no doubt her body knew what it wanted, even if her brain was trying to think otherwise.

She went into the bathroom and ran herself a bath. As she lay in the soapy water, she turned over and over in her head just what she should do. Yes – she was now prepared to admit it to herself – the idea of jumping into bed with Mark was very, very inviting, even though the relationship would inevitably be brief and destined for disaster. She had never before been of the 'better to have loved and lost than never to have loved at all' mindset, but maybe she should rethink that and throw caution to the wind. No sooner did that thought cross her mind than she realised it was just plain crazy.

First, he probably wouldn't be interested, and she would just make a fool of herself if she flung herself at him. Second, as he had underlined a few minutes ago, she was sort of his boss, albeit temporarily. And, third, promotion and a massive step up in her career rested upon her completing this location-scouting trip success-fully and without any hiccups. Propositioning one of her staff would certainly fall into the serious hiccup category – if not the projectile vomiting category – if he took it the wrong way. Regretfully, she climbed out of the bath and towelled herself down before changing into a smart dress – not, she told herself firmly, for Mark's benefit, but simply as this villa was a very smart sort of place. After a quick glance in the mirror, she went down for tea in the orangery. Not surprised in the least to find herself all on her own, she spent an inordinate amount of time trying not to feel jealous of Marina and Rich. She hoped they were enjoying their 'rest'.

By the time she had finished her tea, limiting herself to just one small piece of the enticing freshly baked sponge cake offered to her, Emma was pleased to see that the rain had stopped. She checked her watch and was mildly surprised to see that it was already half past five. As she did so, she heard voices and saw Marina and Rich come into the orangery looking full of beans. Emma did her very best to produce a warm smile without a hint of jealousy.

'Hi, guys, the rain's stopped.'

'Yes, we saw that, the sky's clearing. At least that means Ethan shouldn't have any trouble landing in Perugia.'

Marina cast a covetous eye at the sponge cake and, as she did so, the waitress appeared and offered tea or coffee and, of course, cake. They both chose coffee and big pieces of cake and were out of there within ten minutes. Marina clearly wasn't taking any chances with traffic hold-ups. She knew better than to keep a Hollywood heart-throb waiting.

Not long after they left, Emma went out to the lobby, and the porter pointed out the way to Mark's house. He gave her an umbrella, 'just in case', but there were already big blue patches in the sky above and the clouds were rapidly changing from grey to white. After the rain, the countryside was already getting back to normal and swallows were wheeling high above her. The sound of water dripping around her was all-pervasive and she wondered how long it would take the ground to soak it up and return to its former arid state.

To get to Mark's house, she followed a stone-paved path around the side of the villa to the rear where an enclosed courtyard had obviously once been home to horses and carriages. Now there were just a handful of cars, presumably belonging to the staff, and a lovely old red sports car in the far corner alongside a far scruffier little Fiat. Just behind this was the door that the porter had indicated. There was an anonymous bell alongside it, so she pressed it and hoped. A second later, she heard a single woof and then the sound of footsteps running down the stairs towards the door.

'Hi, Emma. Thanks for coming. Carmen, be a good girl and leave Emma alone. She's wearing a smart dress.' Mark glanced at Emma and grinned. 'In fact, a very smart dress. You look great. Is this for the benefit of the Hollywood star?'

Emma was very pleased he liked it, but she didn't want him to think she had put it on for Ethan – or indeed for his sake. Instead, she bent down to pet the dog and just produced a throwaway line. 'I always dress like this in five-star hotels.'

'Well, my house isn't exactly five star, I'm afraid. All our energies have been directed at renovating the villa so far this year. This place is next on the list, but it'll do for now. Come on up. It's not luxurious, but I like it, and it already feels like my home.'

As Emma emerged from the top of the old staircase, she immediately fell in love with Mark's house. It might not have been five-star luxury, but it was absolutely charming and redolent with history. The ceiling was supported by big wooden beams and the floor was covered in old terracotta tiles, so ancient in fact that the joists supporting it had clearly sagged over the years and the floor now undulated in gentle waves. The stairway emerged into a huge open-plan living space with a kitchen area to one side incorporating a farmhouse table, and a large lounge on the opposite side with sofas and armchairs. A door at the far end presumably led to Mark's bedroom but Emma was under no illusions that it would be very, very risky to go in there – not because of Mark, but because of her.

Clearing her suddenly dry throat, she turned to Mark. 'I love it. What a lovely big open space.' She indicated the kitchen. 'Do you cook?'

He nodded. 'Yes, more than you'd think. Claudio keeps telling me I should go and eat over at the hotel, but I know that would be a slippery slope. I've managed to lure a terrific chef away from Perugia to come and work here, and the stuff he prepares in amazing. Hopefully you'll agree when you sample dinner tonight. A few months or years of eating like that and I'd end up looking like the Michelin man. No, I do a lot of my own stuff, mainly salads at this time of year. When the weather dries up, I'll show you our walled vegetable garden. We grow as much of the produce we use as we can, and it's good, with no nasty chemicals. As the Italians say, it's *genuino*.'

While he was talking, Carmen came across and leant against Emma's bare legs. She bent down to ruffle the dog's fur and, in response, the Labrador slowly slid down until she was lying stretched out on the floor, tail beating softly on the tiles. This did not go unnoticed by her master.

'I told you she liked pretty girls.'

'She's a very pretty girl herself.'

'What can I get you to drink? Cold beer? Or maybe you'd like a gin and tonic? Or there's wine, made here on the estate. The cold rosé's really pretty good.'

Although a gin and tonic sounded appealing, Emma knew there was only one answer to an offer like that, so she opted for the local wine. As he went over to the kitchen to open a bottle, she left the dog sprawled on the floor and wandered round the room, looking at paintings on the walls and photos in frames. There were several of an elderly couple, presumably Mark's grandparents; a touching one of a young couple with a little boy who had to be his poor dead parents with a very young Mark, but no sign of anybody who could be described as the love of his life. Maybe he kept her photos – if he had any – in his bedroom or just on his phone.

'Here, cheers, and thanks for coming.'

She took the glass from him and clinked it against his. 'Cheers and thank *you*.' She tasted the wine and gave him a thumbs up. 'That's excellent. I love it. And I also love your Alfa Romeo out there – I presume it's yours. I've always had a thing for classic cars but I've never been able to afford one. Have you had it long?'

'Me personally, only since my granddad died. He left it to me along with the villa. He bought it new almost fifty years ago and it was his pride and joy. I don't use it that often as I'm scared of scratching it. I'm sure he'd never forgive me. I tend to use the little Fiat Panda out there.'

Emma rolled her eyes. 'You have a classic sports car and you don't use it. Shame on you.'

He grinned. 'I tell you what, let's you and I go out in it sometime this weekend.'

She grinned back. 'It's a deal.' And the idea of going off alone with him was definitely alluring.

As she spoke, a ray of evening sunshine cut across the room as the clouds continued to retreat. Seeing it, Mark made a suggestion.

'It's pretty warm in here, isn't it? I could switch on the aircon or, if you like, we could go out onto the loggia.'

'The loggia?'

'Very traditional around here and in Tuscany. Many of the old houses have them. It's a covered terrace where there's normally a bit of a breeze, but it provides shelter from the sun.'

'Sounds great. Lead on.'

To her perturbation, he led her down the room to the door at the far end. This opened into a corridor and the first door they passed was unquestionably his bedroom. His bag was resting on the big double bed and a towel was hanging on the window handle. She took a deep breath and told her body to keep walking. Thankfully, her legs obeyed.

At the end of the corridor was a glazed door and through it they stepped out into the loggia. The roof with its massive timber trusses was supported by hefty brick pillars, and there was a table and chairs in the middle. The view was stunning. As the rain clouds rolled away, the panorama down and across the valley had suddenly opened up. Gubbio was now laid out quite clearly in all its glory as a mass of red roofs hugging the hillside and Emma's eyes were immediately drawn to what looked like a huge square castle with crenellated battlements quite high up the slope, alongside an open piazza. Mark came up beside her and followed the direction of her eyes.

'That's the Palazzo dei Consoli, built at the time of my ancestor Graziella. As I told you, she was a very erudite woman. I would love to think she had a hand in designing it.' He was so close that Emma could hear him breathing. The effect this had on her was to make her stop breathing entirely and it came as a considerable relief when he stepped back and pointed to the chairs. 'Do sit down, please.'

Inhaling gratefully, she sat down opposite him and took a big mouthful of wine. She felt a movement under the table and then a warm, hairy body plonked itself down on her feet. She reached down to scratch Carmen's ears, glad to have something else upon which to concentrate her attention.

'Looks like you've definitely made a friend there, Emma. Carmen doesn't often take to people so quickly. She can obviously tell you're special.'

Emma glanced up. This sounded almost like flirting and another surge of longing flowed through her. She very nearly downed the remains of her glass of wine in one, but her brain finally came to the rescue in the nick of time. Alcohol would only make matters worse... much worse. She did her best to sound normal as she replied.

'We always had dogs at home. Maybe she senses something. Mind you, she might just like the smell of my new shoes. I bought them in Turin.'

'And very smart they are, too.'

This time he sounded just a bit too formal and she found herself wondering if he, too, was affected by the intimacy of the two of them being alone together only a few steps from his big double bed. She took another sip of wine and decided to steer the conversation onto less charged matters.

'You're a very lucky man to be able to live here. This house is gorgeous, the villa's amazing and from what I've seen of Umbria so far, it's a delightful area.'

As he answered, he sounded almost relieved to be back to small talk. 'If you feel like it, we can do a little tour of places like Urbino and Assisi, or even drive down to Orvieto one of these days before we head off northwards to Bologna.'

'That sounds lovely.' A thought struck her. 'Although our illustrious guests may prefer to keep a low profile. We'll have to ask them.'

'If they want to stay here, there's plenty to do on the estate. There's the pool and a tennis court, as well as walks and a good run around the perimeter. You said you played tennis, didn't you?' Emma nodded. 'Well, you and I must have a game some time. I'm getting very rusty.'

At that moment, Emma's phone beeped. It was a text from Marina.

> Plane just landed. We should be back in half
> an hour. M

As Emma relayed the message to Mark, she found herself thinking of ways to while away thirty minutes in Mark's company. The possibilities were stimulating and her throat turned dry again. However, as it turned out, he had another suggestion which was far less tantalising, but no doubt much more sensible.

'As we've got a little spare time, why don't we take Carmen for W-A-L-K?' He grinned at her over the rim of his glass. 'She understands the word in both languages. And don't worry about your shoes. We can stay on the paths where it won't be muddy.'

Swallowing a feeling of disappointment, followed by the rest of the wine in her glass, Emma stood up and collected the empty glasses to take them back to the kitchen. As she did so, the rational portion of her brain – which appeared to be shrinking at every encounter with Mark – was telling her that a walk was a very sensible course of action. Her body, however, was telling her the exact opposite.

—

Although the evening was fast approaching, the sun had already raised the temperature significantly and they hugged the shade of the trees as they followed a gravel path around the edge of the woods. From time to time Carmen the dog disappeared into the undergrowth where they could hear her snuffling about happily in the wet leaves.

'This is a wonderful place for a Labrador, isn't it?'

Mark smiled back. 'Yes, she's a lucky dog, all right, even if she isn't allowed to go swimming in the pool. By the way, seeing as we're out here, shall I show you where it is? That way you'll know where to come if you feel like a midnight swim.'

Banishing the thought that instantly sprang to her mind of skinny-dipping with Mark, she gave him a smile and a nod. 'That's a good idea. But what about Carmen?'

'Don't worry, Claudio tells me the carpenter was here yesterday and he's put in a gate. That should keep her out.'

Leaving the visibly miffed dog on the other side of the smart new gate, Mark led Emma through a stone archway and down to the pool. This was set low down, protected from the wind and prying eyes by high banks on all sides.

Palm trees and large cacti had been planted all around and Emma could well imagine it looking like an oasis in a year or two. The water was crystal clear and very inviting and she could see why the dog might be feeling miffed. As she stood by the side of the pool looking on, Mark crouched down to test the temperature of the water with his hand. It was at this moment, that disaster in the shape of an enthusiastic water-obsessed Labrador struck.

Somehow, Carmen must have been able to open the gate or circumvent it. Hearing a noise, Emma turned in time to see the dog charging down the path at speed, her nose headed inexorably for the pool. Unfortunately, as she launched herself bodily towards the water and her master, Mark also turned to see what was going on. Momentarily off balance, he didn't have a chance as sixty or seventy pounds of joyful Labrador cannoned into his side. Man and dog both tumbled into the pool with a tremendous splash as Emma looked on, trying not to burst out laughing.

'You stupid mutt, how did you get in here?' Mark's head, and then his body, appeared above the surface, his T-shirt riding up to his shoulders, exposing his whole torso. He was at no risk of drowning, since Emma could see the water barely reached his waist as he stood up staring accusingly at the dog. 'Come on, Carmen, get the hell out of here. You know you aren't supposed to be in here. *Via, via, cagnaccia della miseria!*'

Carmen's head also emerged from the water and Emma couldn't miss the big canine grin on her hairy black face. However, it wasn't this that kept Emma there, rooted to the spot. Her eyes had locked onto Mark's naked back. She found herself staring, not at the V-shaped muscles, nor at his broad shoulders, but at three ragged white scars in a vertical line directly behind his right shoulder blade that stood out in stark contrast with the honey colour of the rest of his skin. As he caught hold of the dog and turned towards the side of the pool, pulling her by the collar, Emma's eyes alighted upon three neat little round scars on the front of his chest directly in line with those on his back. Whatever had gone in had come out again, making one hell of a mess. Such a mess in fact that Emma could hardly believe he had survived.

Reaching up with his free hand, Mark pulled his T-shirt down again until the scars were hidden from view. When he glanced up, Emma did her best to show no sign of having noticed anything untoward. Suddenly his reluctance to expose his torso was explained and she felt a wave of sympathy for him. Wounds like this must have been life-threatening and she could only imagine the trauma he had suffered. Luckily he appeared unaware that she had seen the signs of his injury. He caught her eye and grinned.

'Bloody dog. I wonder how she managed to get in.'

Emma smiled back at him. 'You might need to rename her Houdini.'

Mark cast an affectionate look down at the dog and released his hold on her collar. 'Well, all right then, Carmen. Seeing as we're both in, we might as well have a swim.' As Carmen paddled happily away, he glanced back up at Emma. 'The good news is that the water temperature's risen a quite a bit over the past few days and it's really very pleasant in here. The bad news is that I've got my phone in my pocket. Anyway, if you feel like joining us, Carmen and I will avert our eyes.'

For a moment Emma was sorely tempted to slip out of her dress and join them, but then common sense kicked in. Regretfully, she shook her head.

'I'm very tempted, but I think I'll just stand and see which of you is the better swimmer.'

She settled back on a bench and looked on as Mark demonstrated that he swam very well indeed, even fully clothed, putting his head down and setting off on a dozen lengths, before finally shepherding the Labrador back towards the steps at the shallow end. With a bit of pushing and shoving, he managed to eject her and then waited as she shook herself energetically. Carmen then trotted across to say hello to Emma who took immediate evasive action to avoid being soaked as the dog shook herself again. While this was happening, Mark climbed out of the pool and stood there dripping. He reached into his pocket and brought out his phone.

'Well, I'll be…! It really is waterproof. Remind me to write to Apple to congratulate them.' He squelched across towards Emma. His clothes were plastered tightly across his body and he looked even more appealing, if that was possible. She swallowed hard and gave him a smile.

'Somehow I think you might need to change before dinner.'

Chapter 14

Marina and Rich arrived at the villa with Ethan and Sinclair bang on seven o'clock. Mark was back at his house reprimanding his dog and changing his clothes; Emma was waiting on the steps to meet Ethan as he emerged from the car.

'Hi, guys. Welcome to Villa Graziella. Good flight?'

Ethan came across to her, caught hold of her affectionately round the waist and lifted her easily into the air.

'Hello, gorgeous. The villa looks as stunning as you do.'

As he set her down again, Emma smoothed her dress and grinned at him. 'I bet you say that to all the villas you meet. How did the award ceremony go?'

'I won Best Male Actor in a Horror Movie. Mind you, there wasn't much competition – most of the others didn't need any make-up to turn them into zombies.'

'Ouch, that's a bit catty! Didn't your mummy tell you to be nice? Anyway, congratulations on yet another trophy. Your collection must be enormous by now.'

'You should come over to my place and check them out some time. Sinc keeps telling me I should store them in a vault somewhere, but I get a kick out of looking at them from time to time.'

Sinclair shook his head in resignation. 'One of these days the bad guys are going to come looking for your stash of trophies and then you'll wish you'd followed my advice.'

Emma led them into the hotel and handed them over to Claudio and his team who were doing a masterful job of trying to look as if the arrival of a global megastar was an everyday event. As they escorted him to the lift, Emma gave him a little wave.

'Once you've freshened up, we'll be in the orangery if you want to come down for a drink.'

As the lift doors closed, Emma turned towards Marina and Rich and noticed the same odd expression on both faces.

'What's up, guys? Something happen out on the road?'

Marina glanced across at Rich and then answered for both of them.

'No, the trip was fine. It's just something Ethan said in the car.' Emma saw her searching for the right words. 'He was asking us about you, you see.'

'About me...?'

'We think he's interested in you.' Rich sounded unusually hesitant and Marina took over.

'What he actually asked was whether you were seeing anybody... you know, a boyfriend.'

Emma took a few calming breaths, trying not to panic. Maybe Mark had been right after all. 'Ah, okay, and what did you tell him?'

'The truth – we don't know.' Marina gave her a nervous little smile. 'Did we do the right thing?'

Emma did her best to smile back, although her mind was whirling with the possible complications this could cause. 'Of course you did and thank you both for telling me.' She reinforced her smile. 'Leave it with me. I'll sort it out. I'm sure he was just curious. He and I go way back and he was probably only being nosey. And, seriously, thanks for coming to me with this. I appreciate it.'

As Marina and Rich set off up the stairs, she saw relief on both their faces. As for her, things had potentially got a lot more complicated. She walked back to the orangery and ordered a double espresso. She needed her brain to be sharp this evening. If it was true that Ethan was interested in her, how should she react? The last thing she wanted to do was to rebuff him and maybe even piss him off so seriously that he might throw a tantrum and storm off. The alternative would be to play along with him for now and then let him down gently when they were back in Hollywood. She immediately discounted this idea. First, she had never been the sort of woman to use sexual favours to get ahead and second, there was Mark.

'*Ecco, signora.*'

The waitress set the little cup down in front of her and Emma reached for it immediately, shooting the girl a little smile and murmuring *grazie*. It was boiling hot, so she just took a sip as she returned to her internal debate.

She was under no illusions that she had developed a deep attraction to Mark in such an incredibly short space of time. Never in her life had she been so immediately swept away by a man. Whether this overwhelming sense of attraction was in any way reciprocated by him remained uncertain, but she potentially now found herself in the sights of one of the most familiar, and desirable, faces on the planet and she knew that getting together with Ethan would totally change her life forever: overnight she would be catapulted into the limelight and she had enough experience of what media hounding could do to people to want to stay well clear of that, even if she were interested in Ethan in that way, which she just wasn't. Crazy as it would, undoubtedly, sound to a lot of the female population of the globe, she just didn't feel physically attracted to the sexiest man on earth.

It was very, very annoying.

Her musings were interrupted by the arrival of Claudio, who also had an odd expression on his face. For a moment, Emma wondered whether Ethan had been quizzing him about her relationship status as well. 'Signora…'

'Emma, please.'

'Signora Emma, your guest has arrived.'

'My guest?' Had Laney Travers arrived a day early? 'What's her name?'

'*His* name. It's a… gentleman.' There was a slight moment of hesitation before he decided on the correct nomenclature. 'His name is Delgado, Erasmus Delgado.'

Comprehension dawned in Emma's head. 'Oh, right, good. How did he get here? We were expecting to pick him up from the airport tomorrow.'

'I believe he was driven here by his personal assistant. She is here with him.'

By this time Emma was on her feet. She swallowed the rest of her espresso and braced herself for action.

'Right, thanks, Claudio. Please lead me to him.'

Erasmus Delgado was standing with his back to the reception desk, while a tall woman with very short-cropped hair completed the formalities. Erasmus Delgado's hair, on the other hand, was anything but short. It hung in long, straggly grey cascades onto his shoulders and reminded Emma of stained-glass images of biblical prophets in St Martin's church back home in Norfolk. His attention was directed at a gorgeous display of roses of all colours from deepest dark red to purest virgin white in a crystal vase on a delightful antique table, their perfume filling the air of the lobby. Emma went up to his side and did her best to attract his attention. It wasn't easy.

'Mr Delgado, good evening and welcome. My name's Emma Taylor and I work for JMGP. It's wonderful to meet you.'

His gaze never wavered from the roses as he answered. 'I imagine it is.'

Clearly this particular film director wasn't of the modest, self-effacing variety – not that there were a lot of them about. Emma had met his sort before so she just bolted on an even broader smile and tried again.

'We're so glad you could come here to meet up with Ethan and Laney. I'm sure they'll be so happy to meet you.'

'Yes.'

Emma waited for more, but nothing was forthcoming. Instead, she felt a touch on her arm and turned to see the lady with the urchin haircut. The smile still on her face, Emma introduced herself. The woman, who was probably in her forties or even early fifties, didn't smile back, but she replied cordially enough.

'I'm pleased to meet you. My name is Katya. I am Mr Delgado's personal assistant.' The accent was mid-European, her attitude brusque.

As they shook hands, Katya almost broke Emma's fingers. Surreptitiously nursing them behind her back, Emma continued with her charm offensive.

'I hope you had a good journey. We would have been very happy to meet you and drive you here from the airport.'

'Mr Delgado prefers to avoid air travel where possible, so we drove up from Rome, stopping off in Orvieto on the way as he was keen to see the town. His carbon footprint causes him sleepless nights.' Emma nodded, vaguely wondering how he had managed to get to Europe from the USA, but Katya hadn't finished. 'Mr Delgado has a deep and lasting respect for the planet.'

'I see. That's good to know. Well, at least you've arrived safely.' Emma turned her attention back to the director and for the first time she noticed a lump at his waist, concealed beneath his crumpled Hawaiian shirt. Might this be the famous tooth mug Ethan had mentioned? Clearing her throat, she had another go at establishing communication with him. 'Is there anything we can do for you, Mr Delgado? Something to eat or drink, maybe, or would you like to see your rooms?'

To her surprise, this elicited a response, but it wasn't exactly what she had been expecting.

'So sad, so very sad…' His voice tailed off and his eyes never strayed from the roses. Fortunately, Katya was there to interpret.

'Mr Delgado hates to see dead things. These flowers have been cut, so they are dead. This saddens him.'

'Ah, yes, of course.' Emma was beginning to feel she was in one of those dreams where you are trying to run through quicksand but it just drags you down and down. Fortunately, help in the shape of a Hollywood hunk arrived to save her.

'Razzy, my man, it's great to see you again.' Ethan enveloped Erasmus in a bear hug and then transferred his attention to Katya, giving her one of his broadest and most beguiling smiles that would have had the knees of millions of women around the globe trembling in response. 'Katya, my darling, you look just as gorgeous as ever. What happened to all the hair? The plaits?'

As he said it, an image crossed Emma's mind of Katya with blonde plaits, dressed in a dirndl, running across an Alpine meadow singing about the hills being alive with the sound of music. However, Ethan's greeting brought no more than a token polite reply. Emma found herself wondering if the woman ever smiled. Mind you, from what she had seen of Erasmus so far, working for him was unlikely to be a bundle of laughs.

'Good evening, Ethan.'

Katya held out her hand towards him and it was on the tip of Emma's tongue to warn him to beware of the vicelike grip but she decided to keep her mouth closed; however, she felt sure she saw him wince at the contact. Whipping his hand away again, Ethan turned to Emma and repeated his warm smile. Her knees didn't tremble, but she definitely found herself smiling back.

'Hi again, English. Who does a man have to kill around here to get a cold beer?' He glanced over his shoulder at the monolithic figure of Sinclair who had materialised behind him, arms crossed. 'Two beers?'

Sinclair nodded at his boss and then shot a hint of a smile at Emma who immediately pointed in the direction of the orangery.

'No need to kill anybody. Come on through and let's have a beer.'

To her surprise, Katya took Erasmus by the arm and led him firmly, but not unkindly, away from the roses in the direction of Emma's pointing hand. He obeyed meekly and Emma was impressed. However unapproachable she might appear, Katya did at least know how to deal with her eccentric employer and this boded well for the success of the weekend.

They ordered drinks and then took up places on two comfortable leather sofas facing each other across a glass-topped coffee table, Katya at her boss's right hand and Ethan beside Emma. Sinclair perched on a bar stool a few feet away and kept a weather eye open. Ethan tapped Emma's arm.

'So, how's it been going? Found any other romantic places for us?'

Emma was happy to be able to launch into a detailed description of the places they had visited since they had said goodbye in Pisa. Gradually, as she did so, she spotted more than a glimmer of interest on the face of the director and a hint of a smile, although this might have been simply as a result of tasting one of the villa's special apple, kiwi and passion fruit smoothies. Katya, Emma noticed, drank nothing. By the end of her exposé, during which she also gave Erasmus a quick outline of the locations they had found up north, she definitely got the impression that he had been listening. Clearly he was already familiar with the screenplay and he proceeded to ask a number of questions about the different locations, culminating with Villa Graziella itself. Emma told him about her idea.

'I thought this might be an ideal location for the point in the movie when Emily and her governess have the fever.

I know it's Umbria, rather than Tuscany, but I don't see that as a problem. Do you?'

Erasmus shook his head. 'Absolutely no problem at all. I think it would be perfect.' Then, to Emma's total surprise, he actually paid her a compliment. 'JM was right – you know what you're doing.'

From the expression on Katya's face, she was equally surprised and maybe even a bit miffed. Maybe even jealous? However, before she could chime in, Erasmus swallowed the last of his smoothie and jumped remarkably nimbly to his feet. 'And now I have to meditate.'

Remembering what Ethan had said about the link between meditation and bowel movements, Emma had a shrewd idea what this might portend, so she stood up hastily and ushered him to the lift. As they got there, Katya reaffirmed her authority, pressing the call button before Emma had a chance.

'Thank you, Emma, I'll take it from here.' She shepherded Erasmus into the lift and as the doors hissed shut, Emma felt a wave of relief.

'Hey, boss, is it safe to come out now? We've been hiding.' She turned to see Rich peeking out from behind a lemon tree in a terracotta pot in one corner of the lobby. Marina's head emerged alongside him, a broad grin on her face. Rich was also grinning by now. 'I was terrified I'd burst out laughing. My father told me some stuff about Erasmus, but I had no idea he was quite so wacky.'

Emma laughed out loud and the release of pent-up tension felt good. 'He's a hoot, all right, but there's no doubt he's one of the best in the business. After all, they say the dividing line between genius and madness is a very fine one. I remember reading that back in the Forties,

Howard Hughes locked himself in his screening room for four whole months, living off nothing but milk and chocolate bars and peeing into bottles. Erasmus is a little weird, but not that weird, and he's very good at his job.'

Just then the glass doors hissed open and Mark appeared. If Emma had had any doubts about the depth of feeling building up inside her, the involuntary warm glow his arrival spread throughout her body provided all the proof she needed.

'What's the joke?' He walked across to them.

Emma and Rich gave him a brief thumbnail sketch of Erasmus and he shook his head in disbelief. 'This I've got to see.'

Together, they walked back into the orangery where Ethan was already on his second beer. Sinclair, on the other hand, was still nursing his first bottle.

'Hey, Mark, how's it hanging?' Ethan sounded in good spirits.

'I'm fine thanks. Apart from being pushed into the pool by my dog.' Naturally he then had to recount what had happened and they all had a good laugh at his expense.

Ethan was sitting alongside Emma, while Mark had opted for an armchair nearby. She was secretly relieved, fearing that she might find herself squeezed between two men, one of whom she fancied, and one who allegedly fancied her. That could have been complicated. The conversation flowed and any fears she might have harboured that Ethan was about to get a bit more familiar were soon allayed. He kept a discreet distance and behaved impeccably. She began to relax, starting to believe that maybe his query in the car about her love life had just been nothing more than curiosity.

Dinner, as promised by Mark, was excellent and it was also hilarious. They took their places in the dining room and there was an immediate hiccup, before they'd even sat down, when Katya took Emma to one side to whisper sternly in her ear.

'We have a problem, Emma. The napkins are green.'

In fact, the napkins were white with just a narrow green border, but Emma remembered what Ethan had said about Erasmus never wearing green. Without batting an eyelid, Emma immediately took the matter in hand.

'Of course, leave it to me, Katya.'

She went over to where Claudio and his staff were hovering and outlined the problem. He went up considerably in her estimation as he managed to keep a perfectly straight face, while issuing orders for the offending napkins to be replaced by plain white ones. Emma gave him a little wink, returned to the others, and invited them to be seated at the large round table in the centre of the room. She decided to put Erasmus on one side of her with Ethan on the other. The others then settled down so that Mark was alongside Katya – Emma had whispered a warning to him to be wary of her handshake – with Marina, Rich and Sinclair completing the circle.

It soon transpired that Erasmus's dislike of dead things didn't extend to food and Emma breathed a sigh of relief. Although Claudio had assured her that they had a vegan plan B up their sleeves, it was going to make life much easier for everybody if they all could all eat the same thing. What she hadn't bargained for was his preference to start the meal with a short bout of meditation. As they all sat silently, trying to avoid looking at him as he clasped his palms together and muttered to himself, Emma found herself hoping that this meditation would not spark off any bodily functions. She hastily identified the location of the door marked *Servizi* to one side of the room, just in case.

During the meal they chatted and Emma was delighted to find Erasmus, once he had completed his meditation, actually joining in almost like a normal human being, and she heaved a silent sigh of relief. As Ethan had warned her, he ate the whole meal with a spoon and his fingers, and his white napkin was soon far from pristine. One unexpected discovery came when Katya changed during the course of the meal from cold and impassive to positively jovial. The reason for this can't have been alcohol, as there was only water in her glass. Instead, it appeared to be the fact that in Mark she had found somebody who spoke her native language remarkably fluently. As the two of them chatted animatedly in what might have been Polish or Czech – Emma had no idea really – she had to come to terms with the fact that there was a lot she still didn't know about this man. Somehow this mystery rendered him even more appealing – if such a thing was even possible.

At the end of the meal, they all separated and Emma invented a headache in order to disappear up to her room to get some work done and avoid any kind of embarrassing confrontation with a potentially amorous Ethan. As she did so, she caught a glimpse of the expression on Mark's face. It was definitely one of concern for her well-being and she shot him a reassuring little smile. Whether this concern was just out of simple friendship or a sign of something deeper was a question that occupied her for much of the rest of the night, but without any kind of answer.

Chapter 15

Next morning dawned bright and sunny, the sky once more a clear cloudless blue. As she was just debating what to do, her phone beeped. It was a message from Mark.

> Feeling better? Coming for a run? M

Using the excuse of the aftermath of last night's fictitious headache, she declined the invitation, but suggested he might like to take the others out for a jog around the estate. She then checked her emails and found the one she had been waiting for. It was from Dexter, informing her that Laney and her minder would be arriving at Perugia in a private jet at eleven o'clock that morning. He didn't ask how things were going, but when she replied to confirm they would be at the airport to greet her, she added a couple of lines.

> Ethan's already here and Erasmus arrived unexpectedly last night. After a tricky start (he is a little quirky), all went well and he seems genuinely pleased with what we've managed to find so far. All good with Richard. All well with Sweet Memories?

By the time she returned from the shower with a towel wrapped around her, there was a reply already waiting. She checked her watch. It was almost eight o'clock. That meant it was one o'clock in the morning in LA. Did he ever sleep? She laughed out loud when she read what he had written.

> A little quirky?? You really like understatements, don't you? Erasmus is looking at quirky in the rear-view mirror. I've got a poodle that's saner than he is. But the fact is that he's the best in the business so humour him. Capeesh? Dex. PS. Sweet Memories all good.

She was impressed that he had resorted to an Italian conclusion, even if the spelling was American. She was also moderately surprised that he had a pet and she was delighted all appeared to be going well with the new film. In response she sent him just one word.

> Capito.

As she pressed 'Send', there was a tap at the door. Tugging the towel more tightly around her, rather wishing it were a bit longer, she went over to see who it was. She opened the door to find Ethan standing there in his running kit, sweat dripping from his brow.

'Hi, English, I came to see how you're doing.' She saw his eyes flick down across the towel before returning to her bare shoulders again. She struggled hard to avoid blushing under his scrutiny.

'Hi, Ethan, I'm fine now, thanks. I think I was just a bit tired last night.'

'Working too hard again. You gotta learn to relax.' He grinned at her. 'Why not take up meditation like Erasmus?' He glanced over his shoulder and lowered his voice to a conspiratorial whisper. 'When we were out running with Mark, we found Erasmus on his knees under a tree, like he was in a trance. He didn't open his eyes as we went past, not even when Mark's dog went over and stuck its nose up his butt.'

Emma giggled at the thought. 'Well, I hope you enjoyed your run and he enjoyed whatever he was doing.'

'So, what's the deal today? When's Laney getting here?' That same apprehensive expression was back in his eyes.

'We're picking her up from the airport at eleven. Why don't you come with us? That way you can sit in the back alongside her and try to make a bit of small talk.'

'Do you think that's a good idea?' He was still sounding very uncertain.

'Definitely. And Sinclair can sit in the back row with her minder.'

Ethan's expression lightened. 'Have you met her minder?' Emma shook her head. 'Her name's Marylou and she looks and sounds like a younger Dolly Parton, but Sinc tells me she used to be a pro wrestler. She's a real tough cookie.'

Emma smiled at the thought. It promised to be an even more bizarre weekend than she had expected. 'Well, the more the merrier. So are you coming with us?'

'If you're going to be there, I'll come. I'd go anywhere with you.' For a moment it looked as though he might be about give the conversation a more intimate turn, so she was quick to take evasive action.

'Great. Now, if you don't mind, I'm in the middle of an email to Dexter and I've got to get dressed. See you downstairs for breakfast?'

As he nodded hesitantly, she gave him a big smile and closed the door, reflecting, yet again, that the queue of women who would give their eye teeth to take her place, wrapped only in a towel in the presence of Ethan Dukes, would no doubt span the equator.

–

Breakfast was an amazing spread including everything from fresh fruit salad to pickled herring and from home-made cake to bacon and egg. As Emma walked in, she was pleased to see Marina and Rich already there and, alongside them, Mark, freshly showered after his run, his hair still damp. He looked fit, healthy and very, very desirable. Now, she reflected, if *he* had appeared at her door in place of Ethan, there would have been a very real chance of her towel falling off. Taking a deep breath, she walked over to greet them.

'Morning, team, how are we?'

'More importantly, how are you, boss?' Mark's concern for her well-being would have been more touching if he had omitted the final word.

Emma gave them all a smile. 'I'm fine, thanks. I think I was just a bit tired last night. You guys been for a run?'

Marina shook her head. 'They did, I didn't. So, what's the plan for today? Have you got an arrival time for Laney Travers?'

Emma outlined what she and Ethan had decided and Marina nodded, before making a suggestion. 'Assisi and Perugia are both stunning and they're barely a handful of kilometres from the airport. Should we take them there on the way back, maybe?'

Just at that moment, Ethan and Sinclair arrived – Ethan in shorts and T-shirt, Sinclair in a dark suit as always. Ethan came in at the end of Marina's suggestion and shook his head.

'Laney won't go for it. She was telling me how frustrating she found it in London, being followed everywhere by the paparazzi. She'll want to hole up here and keep her head down.' He caught Emma's eye. 'To be honest, I feel pretty much the same way.'

She nodded in response. 'Fine, we'll just make it a straight airport transfer. I remember reading that she plays tennis. Maybe we could all have a game this afternoon.'

When they set off to collect Laney and her ex-wrestler minder Marylou, Mark and Rich were left at the villa with strict instructions to keep an eye on Erasmus. Rich was clearly disappointed not to be with Marina, and Emma could see that their relationship was advancing steadily – a hell of a lot faster than any relationship she might have hoped to have with Mark. Ignoring her own frustrations, she gave him an encouraging smile.

'We'll be back in an hour or so. Just make sure Erasmus doesn't go walkabout or start operating heavy machinery.'

–

Laney Travers arrived just after eleven and they saw her come down the steps of the private jet with a face like thunder. As this was an internal flight and a private plane, Marina had been able to drive right onto the tarmac. Apart from two men in reflective jackets, there was nobody else around so at least Laney was able to get from the aircraft to the car without being recognised. As she ushered the megastar into the rear seat alongside Ethan, Emma made the introductions but got nothing back. Marylou, the minder, hefted the two large suitcases into the boot as if they weighed nothing and then took her place alongside Sinclair behind them, while Emma slid into the front passenger seat and listened carefully, her fingers firmly crossed. It took several minutes before she heard Ethan's voice, sounding decidedly tentative.

'So, Laney, good trip?'

'No.'

A further pause ensued and Emma was about to wade in to see if she could help Ethan's cause when Marylou from the back of the vehicle added an explanation. Not only did she look like Dolly Parton on steroids, she sounded just like her too.

'Laney got mobbed at Milan. Somebody must have got wind of her departure time and the airport was crawling with fans, paparazzi, and God knows who else. Even the police were taking photos.'

'Oh, Christ, Laney, that's terrible. I just hate it when that happens.' Ethan sounded genuinely sorry for her and maybe it was this that finally broke the ice. A few seconds later, Emma heard Laney start to speak.

'You know something, Ethan? I was scared. Genuinely scared that something was going to happen. You should have seen the way they were pushing and crowding round.'

'Tell me about it. It frightens the crap out of me too sometimes. They just don't get it. We're people, just like them, but when a crowd gets excited, it's like a bunch of wild animals.'

The conversation continued in a similar vein for several more minutes before gradually becoming lighter and turning to more pleasant matters. Ethan gave her a glowing description of the villa and by the time they got back, the atmosphere in the car had thawed considerably. Emma gave a surreptitious sigh of relief. So far, so good.

As they accompanied Laney up the steps to the terrace, Rich and Mark appeared at the door. As Laney caught sight of them, the troubled expression on her face morphed into something much brighter. Emma watched as the movie star walked across to the two men and held out her hand, a real smile appearing on her face. Emma was just wondering if she maybe already knew Rich, via his father, when the actress's hand reached for and caught hold of the hand of Mark, not Rich.

'Hi, I'm Laney. It's good to meet you.'

'Hi, Laney. I'm Mark, and this is Rich.' He was looking vaguely puzzled and a bit overcome.

From the expression on Laney's face, it was clear which of the two men interested her, so Emma hurried across to make sure she knew just whose hand she was shaking – and maybe to wrestle her away from Mark.

'Richard is JM's son from JMGP.' This elicited a bit more interest and a smile aimed at Rich.

Ethan made his way over and joined in the conversation. 'And Mark owns this place.'

Laney's eyes lit up. 'Wow, you lucky man, Mark. It's delightful.' By now Laney had moved on from gracious diva mode to flirty diva mode, and she even reached over and patted him on the arm. 'I look forward to getting to know your beautiful house, and you, a lot better.'

Emma could feel a rising sense of what could only be explained as jealousy and she fought hard to dominate it. Fortunately at that moment Erasmus appeared, trailed, as ever, by Katya who was wearing a purple caftan and oriental headdress. Erasmus looked as if he was wearing the exact same clothes as last night: a crumpled Hawaiian shirt, the breast pockets bulging with all manner of junk, and the scruffiest pair of jeans Emma had ever seen outside of a rodeo. On his feet, as a nod to the sunny weather, he was wearing sandals today, rather than last night's battered deck shoes, and it looked suspiciously as though his big toenails had been painted bright orange.

'Laney, my dear, how wonderful to see you and how outstandingly beautiful you look, as always. A delight for the eyes.'

'Erasmus, darling, long time no see. I'm so, so excited to be working with you once more. I can't imagine anyone better.' Abandoning Mark, Laney walked across and air-kissed him noisily. He beamed back at her.

'The pleasure will be all mine. It's a real privilege to work with the very best.'

Emma and Mark exchanged glances. He was looking askance, but Emma knew that this was tame by Holly-wood standards. She knew lots of people for whom these effusive compliments would have been just run of the mill. She gave him a little smile and winked. He winked back and her feeling of jealousy subsided. A bit.

Lunch was taken outside on the terrace, shaded from the sun by a wide awning. There was a gentle breeze blowing and the temperature was delightful. As they were outside, Mark had brought Carmen, who stationed herself under the table between Emma and Mark, her nostrils flaring as each successive course was produced. The chef had prepared a magnificent cold spread ranging from a vast assortment of ham and salami to halves of lobster, filets of salmon and spicy prawns. There were no fewer than five different salads, made up of a dazzling variety of plants and herbs, vegetables and fruits and tiny little edible flowers.

Emma kept a close eye on Laney, having deliberately seated her between Erasmus and Ethan, as far away from Mark as possible. The actress just picked at her food and refused anything but water to drink. Ethan, on the other hand, dug in and filled his plate, but there was no contest as to who managed to eat the most: Marylou won hands down, by a knockout and two submissions, packing away enough food to satisfy a rugby team.

Emma was pleased to see Ethan and Laney chatting and as the day progressed, she distinctly got the impression that they were getting on just fine.

Later that afternoon, as the shadows began to lengthen and after Erasmus had retired to his room with Katya for another bout of meditation, the others met down at the tennis court for a game. Laney immediately chose Mark as her partner, which meant that Ethan was left with Emma. Laney turned up dressed in a stretchy top that could have been sprayed on and short shorts that left very little to the imagination.

As it turned out, the two sides were pretty evenly matched. Laney was very polished, but lacked power in her shots. It was clear that Mark was a stylish player, but it was also clear that he was a bit rusty. Ethan made up for a lack of technique by hitting the ball so hard, he almost dented the surface of the court. Unfortunately, this same power made him less consistent and his serves more often than not ended up in the net, threatening to tear holes in it. It was a close-run thing, but Emma and Ethan just managed to win the set by a single game. Ethan's reaction was predictably boisterous. As her winning serve went in, he ran across and grabbed her, lifting her bodily into the air and whirling her round like a rag doll. As he set her down again, he deposited a smacking kiss on her cheek and raised her arm in the air like a victorious boxer.

'That's my girl, English. You were dynamite.'

She rearranged her clothing and gave him a smile in return. 'Could have gone either way. A very close game.'

As she was speaking, she saw Laney, not to be outdone, turn to Mark and kiss him on the cheek as well, suspiciously close to his mouth. Emma had to struggle to keep the smile on her face as she and Ethan walked over to the net for them all to shake hands. As always, a simple touch of Mark's hand was enough to send a little tremor through her body. She swallowed hard.

'I don't know about you guys, but I need a shower and a cold drink.'

Mark nodded in agreement. 'If you're all willing, I've asked the chef to prepare some canapés, and we'd like to offer you all a few glasses of champagne later on to celebrate the fact that our first guests are such world-famous names. Would that be okay with you?'

Ethan had no hesitation. 'Sounds great to me, Mark.'

Laney went a step further, grabbing Mark and pulling him towards her so she could stick another smacker of a

kiss on his cheek. 'What a lovely thought. I'd be delighted.'
She glanced across at Emma. 'But you're quite right, first
things first – I need to change.'

Chapter 16

Emma was ready on the terrace at seven o'clock. Marina and Rich were already there, as was Marylou, strategically positioned alongside the canapés. Emma had struggled to decide which dress to wear, torn between the realisation that it was lunacy to try to compete with the most famous and beautiful actress in the world, and the desire to look so good for Mark that he wouldn't be able to take his eyes off her. Short of going topless, she knew that would be an impossibility, but she did her best to look good all the same, putting her hair up, wearing her new shoes, and choosing her smartest and, purely by chance, or so she told herself, her most revealing dress.

When Laney came down onto the terrace, Emma immediately realised that there was a broad gulf between what she considered revealing and what Laney considered revealing. The broad gulf in question was Laney's cleavage that extended right down to the film star's navel. Doing her best to rise above any petty feelings of jealousy – and the sudden overwhelming urge to scratch the actress's eyes out – Emma went over to meet her.

'Laney, you look gorgeous. What a lovely dress.' Not that there was much of it.

'Why, thank you, Emma. And that's a sweet dress you're wearing.'

Sweet? Emma's smile never weakened, but she knew her face muscles were going to hurt in the morning. 'Thank you, Laney. Now do come and have a glass of champagne.'

The actress accepted a glass of the hotel's very good champagne, but made no attempt to drink it. Emma, on the other hand, took a glass from one of the waiters and downed it so quickly, she got the hiccups. Wisely, she decided this would be a good time to go and check on the evening meal. Murmuring an excuse, she went inside and, as she did so, she met Mark coming out. He was wearing a light pink linen shirt and he looked drop-dead gorgeous. Resisting the temptation to throw herself into his arms, she gave him a big smile and a mock curtsey.

'Good evening, milord, you look very smart.' This would have come across a whole lot sexier if she hadn't hiccupped right in the middle of it.

He smiled in return and gave her a little bow. As he did so, she distinctly saw his eyes drawn to what she considered to be her relatively revealing neckline. '*Buonasera signora.* And you look wonderful. That's a stunning dress.'

She grinned, just happy to be in his company. 'If you think *this* dress is stunning, get ready for what awaits you outside. The parting of the Red Sea was nothing in comparison.' She was relieved to have been able to deliver these lines without hiccupping.

Mark laughed. 'Now, why doesn't that surprise me?'

As he spoke, she let her eyes run across his torso and she found herself measuring just where those three wounds on his chest would be. She had thought a lot about them since seeing him in the pool, wondering what might have caused them: a pitchfork, an explosion or maybe even bullets? Had he maybe been in the army? He had told her he used to work for the British government after all. Another hiccup brought her mind back to more immediate matters.

'I thought I'd just pop inside to check what time dinner's going to be served.' This was punctuated by another hiccup. She caught his eye and grinned apologetically. 'Well, to be completely honest, my champagne went down the wrong way and I thought I'd better go into hiding until the hiccups subside.'

His smile broadened. 'Well, I can save you the trip as far as dinner's concerned. We're aiming for eight o'clock – as long as our resident weirdo has appeared by then. As for the hiccups, they'll go away pretty quickly, I'm sure. Come on, if you can spare a few minutes while your hiccups subside, I'd like to show you that romantic spot I told you about when we were in Bordighera. It's not far and you can easily walk there, even in your heels.'

To her delight, he then took her gently by the arm and led her through the lobby and out of a side door. The ground sloped away sharply, but a paved walkway led to a tiny promontory, overlooking the valley. Here, almost hidden by an ancient and luxuriant wisteria, was an equally ancient wooden structure in the shape of a pagoda. He helped her through the narrow doorway until they were standing side by side. When they came to a halt, she waited for him to release his grip on her arm but, to her delight, he kept hold of her as they stood there in silence for a minute or two, looking out over the valley below. She could even feel the beat of his heart through his skin and she wondered if he would notice the way her heart appeared to be engaged in an Olympic

100-metre sprint as her excitement grew. The sun was low in the sky and its rays had tinted both the hill on which the little town of Gubbio was situated and the peaks of the Apennines behind them a delicate rose colour. It really was a delightful spot and she couldn't imagine sharing it with a better man. When he started speaking, it was in hushed tones.

'When I told you this was a romantic place, I meant it. My grandfather proposed to my grandmother here, and my father did the same thing.' He fell silent again and Emma risked a question.

'And what about you? Ever proposed to anybody here?' She crossed her fingers as she posed the question, hoping she hadn't crossed a line. She had to wait a while for his reply.

'Yes… yes, in fact I did.' He released his grip on her arm and pushed his hands into his pockets. As he did so, she felt an acute sensation of regret.

That answered one question that had been floating round in her head for some time now. 'And did she say yes?' She kept her voice low.

Again, there was a lengthy pause, before he turned his head towards her and looked into her face. His expression was serious, but she was relieved not to see that same dark cloud that she had noted back at Rodolfo's restaurant in Tuscany.

'She said yes. We married twelve years ago.' Emma was just reflecting that it would have been the same year that she had moved to the States when he carried on. 'We got divorced seven years later.'

'I'm sorry to hear that.' She thought about asking more, but decided to let him tell her in his own time.

He took a deep breath. 'When we were together, we got on fine. Fundamentally, the problem was my job. I was away from her a lot of the time and, in the end, she couldn't take it any more.'

'You said you worked for the British government. What was it you did?'

There was a distinct hesitation before he replied. 'I worked out of Whitehall, but I had to do a lot of travelling to overseas embassies and the like.'

'So absence didn't make the heart grow fonder?'

She saw his eyes glint for a second. 'It did for me, Emma. It just didn't work the same way for Francesca. Of course, the fact that she had had to leave her home country and start a new life in London didn't help. She's from Perugia and although she did some English at school, she was never completely confident using it. As a result, she didn't make many friends in England, and in the end she just stopped going out and I could see she was spiralling into depression. Divorce was the only logical solution.' He hesitated again. 'Or rather, it was the solution I chose. The other solution would have been for me to give up my job and move back here to Italy. I chose my job over my marriage.'

'And you regret it?'

'Very much. At least, I did.'

'But now you've given up the London job. Couldn't the two of you get back together again? Are you still in contact?'

He nodded. 'More or less in contact. You know, photos on Facebook and that sort of thing. The thing is, she's married now. She got married four years ago and she's got two lovely little children. Her husband's a good guy. He was… is… one of my friends.'

Emma laid her hand on his arm. 'At least you're both happy now.' She caught his eye. 'You are happy, aren't you?'

Slowly a smile spread across his face. 'I wasn't for a long time, but I really think I am now.' To her delight, he leant down and kissed her softly on the cheek. 'Thanks, Emma. Thank you a lot.'

'What've I done?' She was very close to kissing him back – and not on the cheek.

'More than you know.' His voice was so low, she could hardly hear him. 'More than you know.' Suddenly straightening up, he glanced over his shoulder. 'I'm sorry. I took you away from the guests. We'd better get back.' It was clear he was feeling uncomfortable.

Emma let the desire to kiss him gradually fade away, but it wasn't easy. She followed him out of the gazebo and back onto the path. As she came up alongside him, he caught hold of her arm again.

'So, do you think you're going to include that spot in the movie? Is it romantic enough?'

She had already made up her mind about this. She shook her head. 'It's certainly romantic enough but no, it's far too personal to you. I would feel like we were intruding.' She took a deep breath and did her best to sound cheerful. 'But from what I've seen, Umbria's over-flowing with romantic places. We'll find somewhere else and leave you your own special place.'

–

The resident eccentric did indeed turn up in time for dinner – this time wearing a white tuxedo that would have looked better if he had also changed out of his frayed jeans. By that time, Laney was draped all over Mark, simpering in reply to his remarks, her eyes glued on his. Emma, heartened by her conversation with him in the gazebo, managed to subdue the urge to attack her with a fork and concentrated instead on Ethan, who looked and sounded delighted to find himself the object of her attentions. A couple more glasses of champagne also helped her further calm any homicidal tendencies.

Over a magnificent dinner taken on the terrace by candlelight, they talked about the movie. It soon became clear that Erasmus hadn't just been meditating in his room.

'So the female lead, Emily, gets sick, and her guardian goes down with the same thing. Emily gets it real bad and then there's that wonderful moment when the fever breaks and she sees it's Robert who's been looking after her. That could well be the most crucial scene in the movie.'

'Will you shoot that here? Do you want to use one of the bedrooms?' Mark took advantage of a brief moment of peace and quiet as Laney had left the table to take a phone call.

Erasmus shook his head. 'No, we'll do all that back in Hollywood, but we'll need a lot of exteriors of the villa plus some interiors in the main rooms like the dining room and the conservatory.' He turned to Emma. 'Can you make sure you get some good photos of a few bedrooms so we can make the set back in the studio as authentic as possible?'

'Of course. I'll take lots of shots of the dining room, orangery and some of the bedrooms. I'm sure you're right about the events of this place being crucial to the movie.'

'What did I miss? What's crucial?' Laney returned to the table. 'I must confess I haven't had a chance to read the screenplay yet. What's the big deal about this place?'

Erasmus launched into a long and detailed explanation and Emma watched the expression on Laney's face. She was clearly hooked. When he finally ground to a halt, Laney spoke up.

'I love the sound of that.' She slid a sly glance across at Mark. 'These screenwriters – always trying to get me into the bedroom.' He didn't react so she returned her attention to Erasmus. 'How're you going to shoot it?'

As she and the director got technical about overhead shots, lighting and the sort of make-up she would need to make her look close to death, Emma kept her eyes on Mark's face. He was following the conversation intently, either because he was interested in the nuts and bolts of moviemaking or maybe because he was still thinking about Laney in the bedroom. Emma gave a little internal snort. The big star's play for him was so obvious as to be distasteful – at least to her. What Mark thought about it was another matter.

It soon turned out she hadn't been the only one to notice Laney's interest in Mark. She heard Ethan's voice at her ear.

'Looks like Mark's gonna get lucky tonight, doesn't it?' His voice dropped to a whisper. 'I'd heard a few stories, but I hadn't realised we had a cougar on the prowl.'

Emma managed to whisper back to him through gritted teeth. 'Maybe she's just putting on an act.'

'I always thought she was a great actor, but if this is acting, she's the best. No, she's made it pretty clear what she thinks of him.' He grinned. 'Don't get me wrong. I reckon she could do a lot worse. He's a great guy.'

'Yes, he's a great guy.' Emma's smile must have slipped as Ethan came straight back at her.

'To be honest, I thought the two of you might end up together. If that happened, he'd be a very lucky guy. I like you a lot, Emma, you know that.'

'And I love you to bits, Ethan.' She leant across and gave him a little kiss. She was really aiming for his cheek but, after three glasses of champagne, she ended up kissing him on the lips, but only very gently. 'You'll always be my big little brother.' As she sat back again, she saw Mark's eyes on the two of them. She gave him a little smile and he looked hastily away.

Bugger, she thought to herself, *why did he have to see that?*

She spent the rest of the evening drinking water, but feared that the damage had already been done. At the end of the meal, after the chef's take on the French classic *Îles flottantes*, she watched as Laney grabbed Mark proprietarily by the arm and led him off 'for a tour of the park'. As Emma ground her teeth and watched them disappear into the shadows, she felt a hand on her own arm and turned to see Ethan looking down at her.

'Feel like a walk?'

'Yes, I think I do, Ethan.' She affected a carefree tone. 'Have you seen the pool yet? I know my way there.'

'Sounds good to me.'

They headed off along the gravel track. Too late she realised she was wearing her new shoes with the high heels and she had to cling onto Ethan's arm for fear of toppling over on the gravel. He didn't appear to mind. Little lights had come on in the bushes illuminating the path, and they found their way to the pool quite easily. When they got there, they sat down side by side on a bench and Emma stared into the clear blue water floodlit from below. Something big and white swooped past them at speed and she suspected it to be an owl. Some seconds later her hunch was confirmed as an owl hooted in the trees just beyond them. The evening air was warm and once more dry, and she would have been perfectly happy, but for the thought of Mark and the diva somewhere in the shadows.

'So I'm your little brother. Ouch, English, you know how to kick a guy when he's down. You really don't see you and me getting together?'

Emma turned towards Ethan and groaned inwardly. The last thing she wanted to do was to hurt him. She reached across and caught hold of his hand and squeezed it.

'You're my *big* little brother, Ethan. You and I go way back, you know that. I meant it when I said I loved you to bits. You're my very best friend in Hollywood and I can't risk that by letting myself start thinking of you any other way. The thing is, my contract's crystal clear – no romantic relationships within the company. If you and I had a thing, I could lose my job and that would mean I'd also lose you. I don't ever want that to happen.'

He sat in silence for a few seconds before trying again.

'So what? What if I'm really serious and this thing could go all the way? You wouldn't need your job. I'd take care of you.' She felt his hand give her a squeeze. 'You'd never need to work again.'

'Ethan, I don't know how to say this, but I'd hate that. Not you, I don't mean that. I love my job and I really want to do my very best and get ahead. I know you'd look after me, but I would miss it and I don't want to give it up.' Sensing that she needed to give him more, she took a deep breath and added. 'And there's something else. The thing is, you were right – I can't stop thinking about Mark. It's never happened to me before, but I get goosepimples just looking at him. I can't explain it.'

She felt his fingers squeeze hers again. 'I can, Emma. It's a thing called love.' He looked up from the water and turned towards her. 'I know what that's like.'

Emma didn't know what to say. 'I'm so sorry, Ethan, but you do understand, don't you?'

'Hell, yeah.' She could hear that he was doing his best to put on a brave face. 'Of course I understand. Let's just hope for your sake that Mark realises what's at stake here. You're a great girl. He doesn't want to throw that away for the sake of a roll in the hay with Laney.'

Chapter 17

It took Emma quite a long time to get off to sleep that night and when she woke in the morning she wasn't feeling as bright as normal. She glanced at her phone and saw it was just six thirty, but the sun was already up and the sky once more a clear blue. In an attempt to kick-start her brain she decided to go for a swim. So she slipped into her bikini, wrapped herself in a bath towel and set off for the pool. When she got there, she found the wooden gate open and heard the sound of splashing from within. For a moment she hoped it might be Mark having an early morning swim and she hurried down the path towards the water. She was almost there when the thought dawned on her that this might be Laney and Mark indulging in a bit of post-coital skinny-dipping. She almost turned back, but gritted her teeth and decided to press on.

When she got to the pool, she found that the swimmer had four legs and a tail. Carmen was swimming about in the clear water, snuffling happily as she did so. Emma stopped and looked around, but saw nobody.

'Mark! Are you there?' There was no response so she went over to the side and crouched down. 'Ciao, Carmen. Enjoying yourself?'

The Labrador doggy-paddled towards her and scrabbled at the tiles, a broad smile on her face. Emma remembered that the dog had trouble getting out of the pool, so she slipped off her towel and sandals and lowered herself into the water. It was cool at this time of day, but very refreshing.

'So what're you doing here on your own, eh, dog?'

Carmen came across to nuzzle her and Emma swam with her for a few minutes, enjoying the sensation of having a happy dog alongside her and doing her unsuccessful best to banish the thought of who might currently be alongside her master. Was he still in bed? And if so, was he alone?

Although the dog was clearly still full of energy, after a while Emma decided it was time for the two of them to get out of the water. She enticed Carmen to the shallow end and, aping what Mark had done, got behind her and shoved her up the steps and out of the water. She swilled herself off and followed along behind, narrowly avoiding being sprayed with Eau de Labrador as the dog shook herself vigorously. She was standing under the outdoor shower when she heard his voice.

'Hi, Emma. Thanks for looking after Carmen for me.'

She turned off the shower and shook the water out of her eyes. As she did so, she felt a touch on her hand. It was her towel, being offered to her by Mark. He looked apologetic.

'I'm so sorry you had to do that. We were out for our early-morning walk and she suddenly disappeared. It took me a while to realise where she'd gone. I'm going to murder that carpenter next time I see him. It's a nice gate, but if the damn thing doesn't close, what's the point?'

Emma wiped the worst of the water off her hair and face before wrapping the towel around her once more. 'No apology needed. We had a lovely swim.' She glanced across at him and risked a direct question. 'Good night?'

She saw him smile sheepishly. 'Now I know what the fox feels like with a pack of hounds after it. That Laney's like a little terrier when she's after something.'

'Or somebody.'

'Indeed, or somebody.' He sat down on the same bench she and Ethan had sat on the previous night and absently stroked the damp dog who settled down at his feet. Emma followed suit, a discrete distance away until she heard his story.

'So, did the pack of hounds manage to get their teeth into their quarry?'

He shook his head and she felt a surge of relief. Doing her best to sound casual, she queried what had happened. His reply was reassuring.

'I didn't know what to do. I'm not the most observant of men when it comes to women, but even I worked out pretty early on that for some reason she had me in her sights. It put me in an uncomfortable position.'

'I'm sure being the object of desire of the world's most beautiful woman must be extremely uncomfortable.' There was a distinctly ironic note in her voice and he didn't miss it. He glanced over at her.

'Just about as uncomfortable as finding yourself kissing the sexiest man in the world.' There was a smile on his face, but she thought she could spot a glimmer of insecurity in there as well. She gave him an answering smile.

'Indeed. You tell me yours and then I'll tell you mine. How about that?'

'Okay, well, like I say, I found myself in an awkward position. One thing was clear. There was no way I was going to end up in bed with Laney Travers.' This sounded pretty good to Emma, but she just nodded, reserving judgement until she heard the whole story. 'But I knew I couldn't just turn her down flat or she might blow a gasket and maybe even storm off and leave the movie without its big star. So, after a bit of hard thinking, I told her I was already involved with somebody else.'

Emma's ears pricked up. 'And are you?'

'No, or rather, maybe.' Emma didn't have time to digest this as he carried on. 'She wasn't in the least bit interested at first. I'm sure I could have told her I was married with half a dozen kids and she wouldn't have batted an eyelid, but I persevered and she gradually came round to accepting I was already taken.'

'That's what's called thinking on your feet. So she didn't storm off?'

He shook his head. 'No, she wasn't very happy, but definitely no storming.' He caught her eye. 'I've shown you mine. Now it's your turn to show me yours.'

'Ethan's a sweetie. I've known him ever since he was a bit-part actor and I think of him like my brother. It now appears that he thinks of me in a different way, so we came for a walk down here to the pool after dinner last night and I set him straight.' She looked up for a second or two and shot him a little smile. 'And, no, I didn't take a leaf out of your book and tell him I was engaged to be married to somebody else. I told him the truth. There's a clause in all JMGP contracts making it clear that relationships with other employees are strictly verboten. I told him I want to keep him as a friend and, hopefully, we parted amicably.

He's probably a bit disappointed, but he's a big boy. He'll get over it.'

'I'm glad.'

He didn't specify whether he was glad Ethan would get over it or whether he was glad she had rejected Ethan's advances. She almost asked, but decided against it. Instead, she turned the conversation to more practical matters.

'So, any plans for today?'

He nodded. 'Sort of, if you're agreeable. Talking to Erasmus last night it's clear he wants to include at least a cameo of Orvieto in the movie. He and Katya stopped off there on their way up from Rome on Friday and he fell in love with the place. If you like, I thought I could drive you down there today so you can see it for yourself and take lots of photos for your boss.'

'That sounds great, but what about the others?'

'I think Marina and Rich could do with a lie-in and a lazy day.' He cleared his throat and put on a mock-serious concerned expression, belied by the twinkle of humour in his eyes. 'They've been looking a bit tired lately. Erasmus, once he's meditated, said he wants to sit down with the two big stars and go over with them in detail what his plans for the movie are. He's asked them to take a look at the screenplay this morning and then the three of them will get together after lunch for a few hours. He made it pretty clear that he wants this to be restricted to just the three of them, so that leaves you and me in the clear until this evening. So, Orvieto?'

Emma suppressed the urge to leap in the air and cheer. 'Definitely.'

Orvieto was gorgeous, if crowded.

The journey down there in Mark's grandfather's cherished old sports car was more exciting than she had expected. Remembering what Emma had said, he insisted upon letting her drive and she loved it. The roof was down, the sun was warm on her shoulders, and the snarl of the exhaust was as stimulating as Mark's presence beside her. If she were honest, her little Mini probably went faster, but it didn't matter. Just being here in Italy on a beautiful day like this and being given the opportunity to drive such a classic car was amazing. And the man beside her was amazing too.

It took almost an hour and a half, but she wouldn't have minded if it had taken twice as long. They chatted amicably as they drove along and the time passed easily. The road ran through tree-covered hills at first and then down the wide valley of the River Tiber as it wended its way towards Rome and the sea.

About halfway, they stopped at a roadside cafe and had coffee sitting outside underneath a parasol. He told her more about his childhood, about growing up here in Italy, with summer holidays spent with his British grandparents just outside Dorchester. She quizzed him about how he had been able to speak so fluently to Katya and he revealed that her native language was Czech. He told her he had spent time over there while working for the British government and had picked up the language in the process. Under cross-examination he then admitted that he was also 'reasonably' fluent in Russian, German and French. She was impressed, but he just shrugged.

'Languages are just about the only thing I'm good at.'
She didn't believe that for a second.

In return, she told him about her early years in rural Norfolk and the lucky chance that had resulted in her sharing a run-down house while at Nottingham University with, among others, an American girl called Janie. They had become close friends and it had been Janie who had suggested she try applying for jobs over in America. The result had been the job at JMGP.

'And you've been there ever since?'

'That's right. Twelve years and I've loved every one of them.'

'So, what's the plan? Stay for another twelve years?'

'For as long as it takes.'

'To do what?'

'To get where I'm going.'

'And that's the top?'

She nodded. 'Or as near the top as I can get. Of course I'm not stupid – I know I'll never take JM's place. It's a family affair and the top job's going to Rich – we all know. But I'd like to prove to myself that I can get as high as any man could.'

'That's important to you?'

'Yes, I think it is.' She did her best to explain. 'I grew up in a little village. The men worked in the fields and the women produced children and ran the home. All right, I know I'm exaggerating. It's no longer the Middle Ages, but even my parents had no great expectations for me apart from hopefully finding myself a suitable husband. For suitable, read well off. I knew I wanted more.'

'So you really would have had a lot in common with Emily, the suffragette. She was a woman struggling for women's rights in a far less enlightened era.'

'Absolutely. Like I told you, we've come a long way, but there's still a lot further to go.'

'By the sound of it, you're well on your way. If it helps, I'd employ you to head up my media empire if I had one.'

When they left the cafe, she said it was only fair that he should drive the rest of the way, and she relaxed alongside him, admiring the views. Towards the end of their journey, after running alongside a broad lake ringed with trees, they emerged onto a major road in another valley. He pointed through the windscreen straight ahead. 'Look, there's Orvieto up there.'

Emma followed the direction of his finger. On the hill above them was a walled town perched on rocky cliffs high above the valley floor. They drove into the lower part of town through the modern suburbs on the valley floor and then he swung the car onto a narrower road that started to climb and climb. The closer they got to the old town, the more impressive the fortifications appeared. The natural defence provided by the cliff had been reinforced by massive stone walls and Emma felt sorry for any attacking army. Even just marching up here would have been difficult enough, let alone beneath a hail of fire from above. The higher the car climbed, the better the view became across the valley to the line of wooded hills on the other side, punctuated by iconic cypress trees and red-roofed farmsteads.

The road twisted and turned up the hillside until they reached a narrow stone gateway in the city wall. Mark drove through the gate and onwards into even narrower cobbled streets. Signs warned of prohibitive fines for illegal parking and Emma was just wondering where he intended leaving the car when he indicated left and squeezed into a vacant parking space clearly marked for the sole use of residents with parking permits. Unperturbed, he reached into the glove compartment and pulled out an official-looking card which he set on the dashboard. As he did so, he glanced across at her with a little smile and explained.

'This place belongs to Claudio's parents. They live in Rome and only use it now and then so he let me use his permit.'

Emma grinned. 'It's good to have friends.'

They climbed out of the car into the oppressive heat and he guided her barely a matter of a hundred metres or so until the narrow lane emerged into a wide square. She caught her breath. Erasmus hadn't been joking: Orvieto was magnificent.

There, in front of them was the Duomo. The cathedral was built of alternating horizontal rows of white and black marble, and its numerous narrow, pointed spires reached up like fingers into the unbroken blue of the sky. The light cream-coloured façade with its three arched entrances was almost entirely either sculpted or covered in predominantly blue and gold mosaics of biblical scenes. It was breathtaking. Emma caught hold of Mark's arm and looked up at him.

'Absolutely stunning. Shame about the crowds.' And it certainly was very, very crowded.

'It's not as bad as it looks. It's a really small town and there are limited hotel places. Most of the tourists wandering round here this Sunday are probably staying in Rome and have just come up for a day trip. I reckon it should be possible to film here without all the people if you make it an early morning shoot, preferably on a weekday, and before the trains and coaches arrive.'

Emma shot off a lot of photos, some for JM, but some for her own sake as a memory of this beautiful place. They walked around the narrow streets of the pedestrians-only central area, coming upon one architectural gem after another until he glanced at his watch.

'I thought I'd better book us into a restaurant for lunch.' He pointed across to a restaurant with tables out on the street, sheltered from the sun by an awning. 'Okay with you?'

'Very definitely okay with me.'

They both resolved to have a light lunch: they chose bruschetta, topped with chopped fresh tomato and extra virgin olive oil, followed by freshly-grilled sardines accompanied by a mixed salad. Mark insisted she try the local white wine and she found it excellent but not, she assured him, as good as the wine back at the villa.

As they ate she found herself studying him more closely from behind her sunglasses, and there was no doubt about it: even just looking at him really did give her goose pimples. As she had told Ethan last night, she had never, ever, felt this way before. They chatted and laughed together and she got the impression he was enjoying their day out together as much as she was. Whether there was more to it for him was still impossible to read. One thing was for sure, the more she thought about it, the more she realised Ethan had been right: as far as she was concerned, this had to be love, or at least, infatuation. Either way, it was a brand new experience for her.

And if it really was love, so what? As she had just told him in the car, her career was what mattered most to her. Or at least, it had been that way up until now. She counted off the days. Tomorrow they would drive across the Apennines to Bologna, and Tuesday would see them in the historic city of Padua. Then, finally, Wednesday would take them to Venice, and Thursday their little group would split up and they would head off in their different directions. Yes, she hoped she might be able to see him again. Yes, maybe she could take her next vacation in Italy. Maybe he could come over to California to see her as well but, with the best will in the world, there would still be six thousand miles between them for the rest of the year. She sipped her wine and told herself to try to forget him. It was the only way.

Wasn't it?

Chapter 18

On the way back to the villa Emma got an email from Dexter. It didn't surprise her that he was working on a Sunday. Somehow she felt pretty sure he never stopped. The contents of the email were interesting.

> I've just remembered, today is Richard's twenty-eighth birthday. Thought you might like to know. Hope he's doing all right and you've found some great locations. How's it going with the big stars and the director? Dexter.

She passed the message on to Mark and he reacted immediately.

'I'll tell Claudio. At the very least there should be a cake. Shall we make it a surprise? Maybe Marina could jump out of the cake in her underwear.'

Emma grinned. 'Somehow I think he's probably already familiar with her underwear.'

He grinned back. 'Lucky old Rich.'

'Lucky both of them.' And she meant it.

Back at the villa, she found herself the very willing recipient of a cup of tea and a piece of cake on the terrace while Mark went off to fetch his dog. She settled down under the awning and stretched her legs. As she did so, Ethan appeared and, seeing her, came across to her table.

'Hi, English, mind if I join you?'

'Do you need to ask? How did the big meeting with Erasmus go?'

'It went great. He's bat-crap crazy but he knows what he's at when it comes to the cinema.' A waitress appeared and he asked for a coffee and 'a big piece of that wonderful sponge cake'. As she left, cheeks glowing at having been addressed directly by the one-and-only Ethan Dukes, he resumed his report. 'I read through the screenplay this morning – all right, in a bit of a hurry – but I saw enough to know that it's good, very good. I'm getting really excited about it. I've got some great lines and the sexual tension just builds and builds.'

'You and Laney going to be okay with that? Do you think she likes you enough to strip to her underwear and roll around in a hundred-year-old bed with you, with a full camera crew looking on?'

The expression that spread across his face was difficult to define: part satisfaction, part embarrassment, but with a good shot of macho pride. Even before he opened his mouth, Emma realised she knew what had happened. She set down her cup and subjected him to a searching look.

'You two have slept together, haven't you?' His cheeks had the decency to flush a little. 'So when did that happen? This morning?'

'Last night.' He was grinning now. 'After you and I had our walk and our little talk, I went back to my room. You might be interested to know that I took a cold shower.' This time it was her turn to blush. 'Anyway, I'm just coming out of the shower, dripping wet, and there's a

207

knock at the door. I go across and open up and hey presto, it's Laney.'

Emma didn't know whether to laugh or cry. One minute he had been declaring undying love to her and the next he had been prepared to jump into bed with another woman – admittedly the most beautiful woman in the world. The more she thought of it, however, the better it made her feel. She really did like him a lot and she had been worried her refusal might have hurt him irreparably. Such would now appear not to be the case and she was glad for him.

'And she said…'

'And she said she reckoned it would be a good idea if we got to know each other a bit better. While I'm still trying to come up with a suitable answer, she reaches over and pulls the towel off me.' He grinned. 'After that we didn't do a lot of talking for a good long time.'

'And the end result is that you two are now friends?'

'With benefits.' He waited until the waitress set down his coffee and about a quarter of a cake and scuttled off to recover her composure, before carrying on. 'We're good. We really did talk a good bit… afterwards. She told me about all the trouble she's had with the tennis player guy and she even apologised to me for being so sniffy when we first met. I'll be honest, Emma, I find I like her a lot now.'

'That's normally a given when you sleep with some-body.' She grinned back at him to rob her words of offence.

'Yeh, I know, but I really do.' He glanced over his shoulder and then lowered his voice. 'And it was the best sex I've had in a real long time.'

'Ethan, I don't need to know that.'

'Well, anyway, we're all good. Thanks for getting us together.'

For a moment Emma thought about pointing out that she hadn't expected to get them quite so close together, but then dropped the idea. As he said, it was all good now, and she knew her bosses would be relieved and delighted. She had yet to reply to Dexter so she resolved to pass on the good news to him at the same time.

'I'm really happy for you, Ethan. So does this mean you've forgiven me and you still want to be my friend?'

'Of course it does, and the other great news for you is that she didn't get it together with Mark. He's all yours.' He picked up his cake and buried his face in it. 'I'm gonna pay for this tomorrow, but this is one hell of a cake.'

At that moment there was a flash of jet black and Carmen sped up the steps and across the terrace towards them. As she skidded to a halt beside Emma, she reared up on her hind legs and put her front paws on her lap.

'Ciao, Carmen. Now, get off. Be a good girl.'

Emma persuaded the dog to return to the ground and then stroked her until she slid down onto her back, legs in the air, her tail wiping the floor tiles as she did so.

'Sorry about that. She's evidently just very pleased to see you.' Mark jogged up the steps behind her and, once again, Emma's heart leapt. 'Claudio says she's been sleeping all day, so she's feeling very bouncy.'

Emma hadn't been sleeping, but seeing him again, she found herself feeling unexpectedly bouncy as well. Maybe, she wondered to herself, even though she knew it was all going to end in four days' time, she should give in to her physical desires, just as Laney and Ethan and Marina and Rich had done. Better to have loved and lost…

'I've spoken to the chef and he's going to make a birthday cake for Rich. He's even got a box of candles.' Mark sat down beside them and mouthed the word 'espresso' to the waitress. She smiled and ducked back into the villa. 'And he's doing a barbecue out here tonight as it's such a fine evening.'

'This is a great place you have here, Mark.' Ethan swilled the last of the coffee around in his cup and got to his feet. 'I'd better go off and check in with Sinc. He's been making all the arrangements for tomorrow. But it's been a really good weekend and I promise I'll come back once the hotel's open to the public.'

Mark smiled up at him. 'Be sure to tell all your friends.'

'You bet.'

As Ethan headed back into the villa, Mark transferred his attention to Emma. 'He seems unexpectedly happy for somebody who's just been turned down by the woman he described as the most desirable in Hollywood.'

Emma felt the colour rush to her cheeks and rushed to downplay it. 'Hollywood hype. Doesn't mean a thing. But there is a reason why he's smiling.'

'Not Laney by any chance?'

'Full marks, Sherlock. Got it in one.'

'So he got over you pretty damn fast?'

'Precisely.'

'There must be something in the air.'

Emma liked where this might be leading, but she was to be thwarted as Marina appeared alongside Rich and they sat down to discuss arrangements for the following day.

The barbecue was predictably excellent. Not only were there some massive Florentine steaks, the size of Emma's grandmother's old bible on there, the chef had also prepared delicate little pieces of chicken breast, rolled up in the local version of Parma ham, as well as kebabs made up of prawns and cherry tomatoes. Ethan chomped his way through half a cow, while Marylou made short work of the rest. Fortunately there were no horns or hooves or she would probably have eaten those as well. Emma opted for a more restrained meal and helped herself to some pieces of chicken and a prawn kebab.

Laney appeared wearing a stunning, if minimal, silk dress with no bra and Emma grinned to herself as she noticed Mark sitting opposite her, doing his best to avert his eyes. Marina, she noticed, was looking particularly good tonight and Rich, alongside her, was doing a lot of smiling. The dark rings under his eyes were now a distant memory and his whole demeanour had changed for the better. Emma had absolutely no doubt that this Italian interlude had been the best thing for him.

When they reached the end of the meal, the chef appeared with a massive iced birthday cake, loaded with twenty-eight candles and Rich looked genuinely surprised and very pleased. Champagne was distributed and everybody toasted him. Shyly, he rose to his feet.

'This is great, guys. I'll be completely honest, I'd forgotten it was my birthday. This means a lot and I know who to thank.' He held out his glass towards Emma and gave her a brilliant smile. 'Thanks, boss. You're a star.'

To Emma's embarrassment, the real stars around the table all joined in, even Laney, thanking her for organising such a wonderful weekend. Emma tried to tell them it was all down to Mark and his wonderful hotel, but she still had to drink a toast to herself.

Afterwards, as the party split up, she walked across the terrace to the balustrade and rested on her elbows, gazing across at the twinkling lights of Gubbio on the hillside opposite. Above her the sky was a velvety deep purple with a huge full moon so clear she could see the craters. As she leant there, she heard soft footsteps and felt a light touch on her bare shoulder. She turned to find it was Marina.

'Hi, Marina. That was some meal, wasn't it?'

Marina smiled. 'It certainly was.' She settled down alongside Emma for a few moments and Emma wondered if she had something to say. It very soon emerged that she had.

'Emma, can I ask you for your advice, please?' She sounded unusually hesitant.

'Of course. Anything.'

'It's about Rich.' Emma saw her hesitate again. 'Or at least, it's about Rich and me. You see, you may have noticed that we've grown pretty close over the past week and I'm conscious that it won't be long before we get to Venice and the trip will be over.' There was a longer pause and Emma was just wondering if she should say something when Marina continued. 'In fact, I'm counting off the days and I'm dreading Thursday.'

'Because he'll be going back to the States.'

'Because he'll be going back to the States.' She looked up and Emma could see the tears in the corners of her eyes sparkling in the moonlight. 'And my job means I'm supposed to be staying here. I don't know what to do, Emma, I really don't. What would *you* do?'

Emma paused in her turn. If Marina only knew; this whole subject was very fresh and very raw inside her own head. 'Has Rich said anything?'

Marina nodded. 'Yes, he's asked me to go over there with him.'

'What, permanently?'

'We don't know. Maybe just temporarily to see how it works out.'

'And if it doesn't work out, what happens then?'

'I know. That's what I've been asking myself. I love my job and I think I'm pretty good at it.' Emma had to bite her tongue as she heard Marina using the exact same words she had used herself. 'I'd hate to lose the job, but at the same time I'd hate to lose Rich.' She dropped her head. 'He's had such a rough time over the past few years, but he's doing so well now. I've seen a massive change in him just in a few days.'

'He's told you about his problems?'

'He's told me everything – from first experimenting with drugs to becoming totally hooked. He told me he came over to Europe to escape from his life in California and even spent some time in Italy, but it must have been very tough and very squalid. I can't bear the thought of him falling back into that spiral of despair all over again.'

Although Marina's face was turned towards the distant valley floor, Emma could hear the tears in her voice and she stretched her arm around her and gave her a hug.

'You're asking the wrong person, Marina. I don't know the answer any more than you do... I really don't.'

Marina looked up. 'Mark?'

'Mark.' Emma sighed. 'Is it that obvious?'

A gentle smile appeared on Marina's face. 'It was to me. Rich said he thought it was Ethan, but I knew it was Mark.' She reached up with her free hand and wiped her eyes. 'He's a lovely man, Emma. So, what are you going to do?'

'I wish I knew.'

'Hello, ladies. Katya and I are off early tomorrow and I just wanted to say thank you for everything.'

They both spun around to find Erasmus standing close behind them. He had a smile on his face and he didn't look in the least bit weird – unless you counted the white tuxedo, tonight worn with merely a string vest underneath. Emma released her grip on Marina's shoulder and they both turned to face him fully.

'You're very welcome, Erasmus. I'm delighted you've had a good time here.'

'Um, I couldn't help overhearing a little bit of what you were saying.' He held his hands up in front of him apologetically. 'I didn't mean to snoop, I assure you, but nobody ever hears me coming in my bare feet.'

Emma glanced down. Sure enough, tonight his feet were bare. As a look, coupled with the tux and the string vest, it was unlikely to make the pages of *Vogue Hommes*, but he clearly didn't care.

'Would you mind terribly if I were to offer you ladies a word of advice? You see, this is a subject very dear to my own heart.'

Both women looked at him in amazement. Emma was the first to reply.

'Of course, Erasmus. Please.' She was turning his words over in her head, barely able to believe they had come from him.

He gave them a gentle smile. 'Try not to think of it as yes or no, either or, black or white, have him or lose him. Choices are never clear cut. Our lives are complicated enough without erecting extra hurdles. Every problem has a solution, although you may not see it at first. It's just a matter of finding the one that's right for you, for both of you. Marina, if you think you've found the right man, do something about it. In your case, Emma, anybody can see you're in love with our charming host here at the villa, but you refuse to tell him.'

Emma was genuinely gobsmacked. How could this larger than life character possibly have noticed something as obscure as her feelings? Or had she really been walking around with her tongue hanging out, drooling over Mark? And how did he know she hadn't spoken to Mark about her feelings? She didn't have time to pursue this train of thought as Erasmus hadn't finished.

'I have three words for you, Emma, and, indeed for you, too, Marina. *Amor vincit omnia.*'

'Love conquers all.' Emma and Marina exchanged looks. 'But how can love overcome six thousand miles of distance between us?'

His smile broadened. 'It did for me.' As comprehension began to dawn on their faces, he nodded. 'That's right. That's why Katya and I are always together, even if our homes are six thousand miles apart.' He reached out and tapped each of them on the shoulder, almost like a benediction. 'Let love sort it out. It will, you know. And now, I must go and meditate. We're leaving early tomorrow, so goodbye if I don't see you. I look forward to meeting up with you both once more.'

As he started to turn away, he suddenly stopped himself and turned back, looking straight at Emma.

'Perhaps you should start by telling him how you feel? He's a man, after all, and we aren't generally renowned for our perceptive skills in matters of the heart. Now, goodnight and thank you again.'

Chapter 19

After their conversation with Erasmus, Marina went off to bed with Rich, and Emma went for a twilight walk with Mark, now determined to follow Erasmus's advice and tell him she had been developing feelings for him, even though she feared she might discover that he didn't share those feelings.

However, all did not go to plan.

As she and Mark strolled along the gravel track through the woods, her hand resting on his arm ostensibly for support, his phone suddenly started ringing. He stopped to answer it and she saw at once that all was not well. He carried on a conversation in rapid Italian and she only understood occasional bits of it. One word that cropped up time and time again, however, was *ospedale*. Evidently, somebody was in hospital. Finally, he returned the phone to his pocket and turned towards her.

'I'm afraid something's happened to my uncle, my father's brother. He lives on the other side of the valley and he's just been rushed into hospital in Perugia with a suspected stroke. My aunt's freaking out. They have no kids and they've always considered me a sort of son. In fact, I probably spent as much time at their house growing up as I did here with my grandparents. Would it be all right with you if I dash off now to see what's what and to give my aunt a bit of TLC?'

'Of course it would. Just go. If you think Carmen'll be okay without you, I can carry on with her walk and hand her over to Claudio at the end.'

'Brilliant, thank you.' He hesitated. 'Look, Emma, I'm really sorry. I was looking forward to our walk. I'd really like to talk to you, but I suppose it'll have to wait until tomorrow.' He hesitated again and then ducked swiftly towards her, deposited the lightest of kisses on her lips and straightened back up again with an apologetic smile. 'Like I say, I'm sorry. Talk tomorrow. Ciao.'

And he left.

Emma carried on through the woods, her head still spinning as a result of that kiss, the dog apparently unconcerned that her master had left her in the hands of the new girl. They gradually circled the villa until they ended up on the promontory with the pergola. The sweet scent of the wisteria was overwhelming and enticing and she let herself be drawn inside, where she sat down on the bench, overlooking the valley. As she did so, there was a movement beside her as Carmen arrived and sat down at her feet, leaning against her legs. Emma stroked the dog's head as she reflected on their brief conversation.

He had told her he wanted to talk. Might this have been some sort of declaration of affection, or more? Was this to have been the night he told her he felt the same way about her as she felt about him, or was it just wishful thinking on her part? And if this really was his message, what did this mean to her? She thought back to what Erasmus had said and tried to think it through. 'Every problem has a solution' had been his words, but was this really the case for her or, indeed, Marina? For Erasmus, the solution had been to hook up with Katya as his permanent companion, travelling the world together, but surely that couldn't work in their situations.

The hotel here was brand new and it was evident that Mark had to stay for at least a year or two to see it safely launched. As for her, she had high hopes of returning to LA to find herself elevated in rank and responsibility in the company that meant so much to her. As JM had indicated, and as his son had repeated, the sky was the limit as far as her ambitions were concerned. She had no doubt, in spite of knowing him for barely a week, that she loved, or at least felt very, very strongly about Mark, but she also loved her job. Which was she prepared to give up and how on earth could Erasmus's assertion that a solution existed to everything actually be true in this case?

As she sat there on that warm summer night, the hairy body of the dog resting against her feet, she did her best to take a long, hard look at the facts, but, whichever way she looked at it, she kept coming back to how little she knew about Mark. And how little he knew about her.

Apart from anything else, he was a very handsome man; even the most beautiful woman in the world had made a play for him this weekend. For all she knew, there could be several girlfriends stashed away all over Europe. Maybe even in the Czech Republic if he had spent so much time over there. In fact, she only had his word for it that his sudden departure tonight had been to see his uncle. It might be another woman – although the repetition of the word *ospedale* in their telephone conversation had tended to lend support to the story he had given her. The more she thought about it, however, the more she worried that she really didn't know much about him at all.

And then there was the physical side of things. His tiny kiss a few minutes earlier, electrifying as it had been, was the closest they had come to any form of real intimacy. She was reminded of one particular man, an executive from a rival production company, from her past. She had met him at a Hollywood party and had immediately found him attractive. He had asked her out and they had spent several pleasant evenings together as a result. And then he had taken her back to his apartment and his bed and the whole thing had blown up in her face. Within seconds of feeling his hands on her body she had realised that there was something wrong. Although she was hard put to identify exactly why, it had been patently clear that she and he were physically incompatible. Everything had felt wrong and she had mumbled a vague apology and left.

What if the same were to happen between her and Mark? Six thousand miles would be a hell of a long way for him to travel to find himself kicked out of her bed. She stared out over the lights of Gubbio and racked her brains. What to do? She was still mulling it over, quite some time later, when she returned to the villa and handed the, by now, sleepy Labrador over to Claudio.

Up in her room, she set her alarm. Erasmus and Katya had indicated their intention of leaving as soon after sunrise as possible and she wanted to see them off. A quick check on Google had indicated dawn, on what was almost the longest day of the year, at five thirty. Even so, it took her a long time before she finally dozed off that night and when she woke up in pitch darkness at five o'clock, she felt jaded and weary. By the time she had pulled on shorts and a T-shirt she was feeling a bit brighter and the grey light of day was creeping through the curtains.

Downstairs, she found Erasmus and Katya already in the lobby. Erasmus was dressed quite normally and soberly – although shoes might have helped complete his ensemble. Emma accompanied them out to the car park and waved them off. As they disappeared down the drive, she glanced towards the old stable yard and noticed that Mark's car was absent. Presumably he had spent the night at the hospital.

She went back inside and asked if anybody minded if she took the dog for a walk. The porter at the front desk was only too pleased – presumably this might have otherwise been his task – and he went off to fetch her. Carmen arrived looking bright and breezy and delighted to go for a walk. Emma thought about taking her down to the pool for a swim but decided it was better not to get her wet. Wet dog isn't the most appealing of aromas to find in a luxury hotel. Instead, they headed uphill through the trees along the track that the joggers used. Since arriving here, Emma had ducked out of the regular morning runs and she really didn't feel like doing more than walking this early on a Monday morning.

She and the dog had been climbing steadily for almost twenty minutes when she heard pounding foot-steps approaching from behind and turned to see Ethan and Sinclair racing up the hill towards her. Ethan was sweating profusely and had clearly been putting in a lot of effort, while Sinclair looked relatively unruffled. Emma remembered that he had been a world-class athlete in his twenties and was reminded of the rigorous exercise regime Ethan and other Hollywood stars had to endure in order to stay in trim. An early morning run was just a warm-up, and she knew he often spent as much as three or four hours a day in the gym. As they approached, Ethan slowed to walking pace alongside her.

'Hi, there, English. You're out early.'

'Hi, guys. Going far?'

Ethan nodded. 'We're doing three circuits this morning. I ate too much yesterday. Gotta stay in shape.' He grinned at her. 'Otherwise you'll start looking at other men.'

She grinned back. 'You know I only have eyes for you, Ethan.'

'Me and a certain someone? Right?'

Emma felt the colour rush to her cheeks, but she had very few secrets from Ethan. 'That certain someone's been at the hospital all night. His uncle's had a stroke.'

'Sorry to hear that. So that only leaves you, what, three or four nights to seal the deal before you jet off back to the US of A?' He laughed as her blushes deepened. 'Good luck for tonight.'

Doing her best to sound nonchalant, Emma tried to put him on the spot, but all it did was to broaden his grin even further. 'How about you? Have a good night?'

'Good? It was amazing.' He glanced at Sinclair. 'Come to think of it, Sinc, I must have burnt off a good few calories in bed. Maybe I can have another piece of cake for breakfast.'

Emma rolled her eyes at his response. 'What time's your flight?'

This time Sinclair answered. 'Scheduled for 0900. We're flying to London to drop Laney off and then on to Helsinki. Tomorrow we fly back to LA.'

'So, leave here at eight?' She checked her watch. It was still only just after six.

'Great. That gives us time for the three circuits. See you later, Emma.' Ethan blew her a kiss and set off up the hill again at a sprint. Sinclair fell easily into step beside him as if he was just walking down to the shops for a newspaper.

By the time eight o'clock came round, there was still no sign of Mark, so she sent him a text.

> Hope all is well. Going to airport for 0900.
> Should be back at villa by ten latest.

She got a reply almost immediately.

> Uncle doing well. Aunt less well. Could I
> join you guys in Bologna tonight? So sorry.

Emma texted straight back to tell him to take his time, although she knew she was going to miss seeing him all day. What, she asked herself, was it going to be like when she flew back to the States? Parking that thought for now, she supervised getting Laney into the car and dragging Marylou away from the breakfast buffet.

When they got to the airport, Laney air-kissed Emma and boarded the aircraft while Marylou stowed their luggage and Ethan's bags in the hold of the aircraft without breaking into a sweat. Emma gave Ethan a big hug and kissed him on the cheeks. Just before he broke away, he whispered into her ear.

'He's a good guy, Emma, a really good guy.' As he climbed the steps into the plane he turned back and waved. 'And a lucky one. See you, English.'

Chapter 20

Even without Mark, it turned out to be a most enjoyable day. After thanking Claudio and his staff for a terrific weekend and saying goodbye to Carmen with considerable regret, Emma climbed into the back seat of the car and left Marina and Rich in the front. They drove back down into the valley and across to the charming little town of Gubbio, spending most of the morning climbing up and down the narrow streets; some so steep they deteriorated into flights of steps.

The palace, the *Palazzo dei Consoli*, in the square she had seen from across the valley was even more beautiful close-up, built of cream-coloured stone and with crenellations indicating its defensive origins. The square itself was paved with red bricks in the same herringbone pattern they had seen in Tuscany and she felt sure Erasmus would love getting some aerial shots of this. Needless to say, she added this suggestion to her list.

Emma remembered that Mark had said that Graziella, his ancestor, might have had a hand in designing this spectacular building back in the fourteenth century. The fact that he could trace his ancestry back over almost seven centuries brought home to her yet again just how impossible it would be for her to expect him to leave this wonderful, atmospheric part of Italy, his family's home for hundreds upon hundreds of years, just for her sake. She took a load of photos, but the sheer historical beauty of the place reminded her more and more of the impossibility of their relationship ever having a happy ending. Besides, she asked herself yet again, what relationship?

From Gubbio, they headed north, crossing the Apennines. Marina deliberately chose the cross-country route on narrow, winding roads and they traversed ridge after ridge of tree-clad hills, passing through one medieval gem after another: tiny villages boasting delightful Romanesque churches, remote hillsides dotted with spectacular villas surrounded by a variety of trees, and ancient fortresses and defensive towers on almost every outcrop. Clearly, hundreds of years ago, Umbria had been a dangerous place.

As they came down from the mountains onto the much flatter land that Marina told them now extended almost unbroken as far north as Venice, the scenery became more open and more bland, although the towns through which they passed were still beautiful in their own way. Cesena's historic heart was delightful, as was Forlì with its massive fortress, but they didn't spend much time sightseeing and Emma didn't take many photos. In *Dreaming of Italy*, Emily and Robert, now growing ever closer, would have travelled up from Florence to Bologna by train and wouldn't have come as far east as this. Still, after visiting and admiring the amazingly well-preserved castle at Dozza, with its chilling bottle dungeon into which hapless prisoners were once dropped to rot to death, they finally reached Bologna, their destination for the night, around mid-afternoon.

As they drove into the city, Emma received a message from Mark telling her his uncle was getting better and his aunt was finally calming down. Other family members had now arrived and so he was getting the train to Bologna, hoping to arrive at six o'clock.

The hotel was in the very middle of the *centro storico*, not far from a pair of gravity-defying brick-built towers that rose up impossibly high on such narrow bases. The façade of the hotel belied the stunning antique interior with amazing vaulted ceilings covered in murals, and floors clad in marble. As Marina went off to park the car, Emma and Rich stood at the main entrance, underneath the arched portico that circled the square, and soaked up the atmosphere. Emma was impressed.

'Wow, I wasn't expecting this. The centre of Bologna's very grand – sort of like a larger version of Lucca. We've got to get it into the movie.' She took a series of photos; impressed to see that the numbers of tourists here were substantially lower than they had been in Tuscany. It looked as though it would be easier for a film crew to shoot here than in big-name places like Pisa and she was already adding Bologna to her list when Rich asked her a question that immediately returned her mind to more personal matters.

'Emma, do you mind if I ask you something? Are you and Mark dating?'

She felt her cheeks flush as she searched for an honest response. Finally she said the only thing she could say.

'Of course I don't mind, Rich. The simple answer is no.'

'But you'd like it to happen?'

'Rich, there are lots of things I'd like to see happen, starting with a solution to global warming or my winning the lottery.' She was doing her best to sound blasé, but he wasn't buying it.

'I've seen you two together, Emma. He likes you a lot and I can see that you like him too. Surely you want to get together with him.'

Emma sighed deeply and gave in. 'All right, I would, I think, but we all know it wouldn't go anywhere. Or, rather, I'm going back to the US and he's staying here. Where can it go?'

'We're not going back to the States until Thursday. A lot can happen in three days.'

'Of course, but what then? No, Rich, it's better like this. I know I like him a lot. I like Italy a lot too, but I know I can't take it back to LA with me.' She decided to go on the offensive. 'And what about you and Marina? What's going to happen there?'

He nodded slowly. 'That's kinda why I asked about you and Mark. I thought you might have some great plan that she and I could copy.'

'Great plan? You're joking. I haven't got a clue what's happening now, let alone what might happen in three days' time, three weeks' time or even three months' time. It's all in the lap of the gods.'

They spotted Marina crossing the square towards them. Rich turned back towards Emma and gave her a wry smile. 'Looks like we're all in the same boat.'

Emma smiled back at him. 'Without a paddle...'

'If anybody can figure it out, it's you, boss.'

'Some hope.'

The hotel rooms were as gorgeous as the entrance. Emma's room even had a little terrace with two chairs and a table on it and she allowed herself a few moments to fantasise about sitting out here with Mark at her side, gazing over the red-tiled roofs of Bologna's *centro storico*, the skyline punctuated by spires and towers. After a bit, the mirage slowly dissolved and she went back inside to take a shower. Maybe, she told herself sternly, she should follow Ethan's example and make it a cold one.

At just after six, as Emma was sitting at a table outside the front of the hotel under the portico, a taxi drew up and Mark jumped out. As she spotted him, her heart jumped in unison. She gave him a wave.

'Mark, hi. Over here.'

He hurried across to her. 'Hi, Emma. Look, massive apologies once more. I hope I didn't leave you in the lurch.'

'You look hot. Sit down and have a beer. And no, you didn't leave us in the lurch. Don't worry.' She waved to the waiter who came across at once. Mark took a seat and ordered a cold beer. Sitting down alongside her, their backs to the wall, he stretched his legs and wiped his brow.

'It's hotter here than it was in Umbria.' He went on to tell her all about his uncle who was responding well to treatment, while his wife, Mark's aunt, was now finally beginning to get over the initial shock. 'Anyway, I'm here now. What did I miss?'

She filled him in on the day's events, desperately wanting to turn the conversation to more personal matters, but before she could steer him in that direction Rich and Marina appeared and sat down with them. Emma was always pleased to see them but if they had decided on this occasion to go for a stroll on their own she would have been even more pleased. Instead, they ordered drinks and settled down to discuss the itinerary for the next day which, Emma knew only too well, would be their penultimate day on the road. As ever, Marina was on the case.

'We could maybe spend a couple of hours tomorrow morning taking a good look around Bologna and then head north to Ferrara and then Padua. They're both lovely cities, but less well known than Venice and Pisa. I used to live in Padua so I should be able to show you a few places that are off the beaten track.'

This all sounded great to Emma, although her number one priority at the moment was trying to engineer a bit of one-to-one time with Mark so as to do what Erasmus had recommended and tell him how she felt. Annoyingly, the others appeared perfectly happy to sit and chat until sunset and they started thinking about dinner. Mark dashed off to check in and have a shower and Emma very nearly went with him, but bottled out at the last moment. So it was that they were all together at eight o'clock as they walked through the still warm streets in search of a restaurant, with Emma fretting silently.

Dinner was good, but nothing like as good as the food they had enjoyed over the weekend. Marina and Mark told her that Bologna and the flat lands to the north of here were famous for pasta and, of course, she knew the most iconic of all pasta dishes was *spaghetti bolognese*. Mark was quick to point out that this wasn't strictly accurate.

'Rocco, our chef at the villa, told me the locals here would never dream of putting spaghetti with their bolognese sauce. They think thin pasta doesn't collect the full flavour of the meaty sauce and they prefer something chunkier like tagliatelle, or even pappardelle.' He grinned at them. 'Sorry to sound a bit nerdy.'

Rich immediately opted to try the local speciality to see whether it matched up to the American version while Emma limited herself to a chicken salad. She was feeling unusually nervous, still determined to tell Mark how she felt, even though she was ever more convinced that they were on a hiding to nothing.

At the end of the meal, after a powerful espresso, she finally managed to get him alone. Rich and Marina headed off to bed while she and Mark decided to take a stroll around the old town centre. It was still very warm and she felt decidedly sticky, but this might also have been nerves. They walked in silence for some minutes, heading away from the main square and into a maze of narrow streets. It was as they were walking down a deserted lane, little more than a back alley, that she finally heard him start to tell her what she had been hoping to hear for so long.

'Emma, this past week's been the most wonderful week I've spent in years.'

'We've been to some wonderful places.'

'Yes, but I'm not talking about the places. The reason it's been so amazing is because of you.'

Emma caught her breath, conscious that he was maybe reaching some sort of epiphany. She didn't say a word, but just reached over and caught hold of his arm with both her hands, leaning closer to him as he continued.

'I've had a tough few years.' He hesitated and she could tell he was struggling to find the right words. 'Mentally and physically, they haven't been easy.' She heard him take a deep breath. 'My whole life's changed beyond all recognition and it's taken me a long, long time to get my head round it.'

As he spoke, a figure appeared, coming towards them down the narrow lane and she pressed herself tighter against Mark to allow him to pass. But he didn't pass. He stopped, right in front of them, blocking their way, and she felt Mark tense. The man was about the same height as Mark and thickset. His long, straggly hair was unkempt, his eyes wild and his expression menacing. A bolt of fear suddenly ran through Emma and she shrank back.

'*Sono senza soldi. Dovete aiutarmi.*' His voice was low and hoarse, his attitude confrontational, as he told them he had no money and they had to help him. No please, no thank you. This wasn't a request; it was an order. Emma reached for her purse, but as she pulled it out of her bag, the man's hand suddenly snaked out and caught hold of it, tearing it roughly from her grip. Instinctively, she tried to grab it back, but as she did so, there was a movement in the shadows beside them and a second man emerged and, to her horror, he was brandishing a vicious-looking knife.

'Turn around and run away or you'll regret it.'

Emma couldn't quite understand everything he growled at them, but his message was crystal clear. The man holding her purse grinned and turned to Mark. 'But, first, I want your wallet.'

Emma felt Mark push her gently backwards until he was between her and the two men. She saw him reach into the back pocket of his shorts and pull out his wallet. As his hand emerged holding it, he addressed them.

'Here, take it. I don't want any trouble.'

Then, as the first man reached for it, Mark tossed it into the air and, as the man lunged for it, things happened very quickly; so quickly that afterwards, even when she was able to think rationally once more, Emma couldn't recall the exact order of what happened next. Mark somehow sprang sideways and shot his foot upwards at an impossible angle at amazing speed, catching the man with the knife under the jaw and sending him backwards into the wall with a sickening thud. Before this man had even slumped to the ground, Mark's fist caught the other man on the side of the head and, simultaneously, he chopped him to the floor with another kick. Emma saw Mark drop to one knee, there was the sound of another blow, and then silence.

'Emma.' His voice was unexpectedly calm. 'There were two policemen back by the chemist's shop just before we turned off. Can you go back and tell them to come here, please?' As she stood there, rooted to the spot by the speed and violence of what she had just witnessed, he spoke again and she finally reacted. 'It's all right, Emma. I've got things under control. Just fetch the police, would you?'

'Are... are you all right?' Her voice was little more than a whisper.

'I'm fine, Emma, now go. Police. Okay?'

She turned and ran back down the alley as fast as she could and out into the main street again. To her considerable relief the two policemen were still standing a bit further along, under the arches of the portico. As they heard her running footsteps, they turned towards her and she hastened to pass on Mark's message. Her Italian was flaky, but they quickly understood and she led them back into the alley at a run.

Mark and Emma were taken to the police station in a police car while their two assailants were removed in an ambulance under guard. On the way, she was dimly aware of Mark talking quietly to the police officers and when they got to the police station she was given a little plastic cup of strong coffee and asked to wait while Mark disappeared into a side office to give a full account of what had happened.

As she sat on a long wooden bench in the echoing corridor, she did her best to pull herself together. She had no previous experience of anything like this and she could feel her hands trembling. In spite of the warm evening, she suddenly began to feel cold but she did her best to tell herself she was just in shock, and gritted her teeth to stop them from chattering. Mercifully, Mark came back before too long. He must have realised the state she was in as he sat down close beside her and stretched his arm around her shoulders, hugging her tightly against his chest. She felt him lean down towards her and kiss the top of her head. In spite of the circumstances, it felt good and she snuggled even closer against him.

'I've told them what happened. The two men are already known to them and I get the impression they'll throw the book at them. They don't like knife crime here.' She felt his arm give her a reassuring squeeze. 'Anyway, it's all over now and we're fine. We just have to wait until they've typed up the statement and then we can go.' He squeezed her again. 'How're you holding up?'

Considering he had just been involved in a struggle against two men, one of them armed with a knife, he sounded remarkably composed and the thought finally dawned upon Emma's befuddled brain that this obviously wasn't a new experience to him. She looked up at him, suddenly seeing him in a new light as realisation began to dawn.

'Those are bullet holes in your chest, aren't they?' She felt him tense. She had to wait a few seconds before he replied, reluctantly.

'Yes.' He hesitated. 'I didn't know you'd seen them. I don't like to show them off.' He glanced down at her. 'They belong to my previous life.' His voice sounded tired now.

'It's all your dog's fault.' Emma did her best to sound brighter, although her heart was still beating at a furious pace. 'When she knocked you in the pool, remember?'

Mention of Carmen must have helped as she saw the hint of a smile on his lips. Sight of his lips reminded Emma there was something she had to do. Wriggling out of his grip sufficiently so she could reach up toward his face with her hands, she caught hold of him, pulled him down, and kissed him hard on the lips. Her hands still holding his cheeks, she drew back a few inches until she was looking straight into his eyes at close range.

'Thank you, Mark. Thank you for saving my life.'

She saw him smile. 'I probably just saved your purse to be honest. Did you see the way the knife was trembling in that guy's hand? He probably would have dropped it before he managed to stab anybody.'

Emma was very conscious that she herself had only just stopped trembling. 'I didn't see a thing. I was so terrified I couldn't move.' She removed one hand from his cheek long enough to wipe away a tear that had appeared in a corner of her eye. 'Really, Mark, thank you so very, very much.' And she kissed him again. This time she felt him respond and the trembling started again, but now for a very different reason. It was a long kiss and as far as she was concerned, it could have lasted forever, but after a while he pulled away and crushed her against his chest. His mouth was close by her ear and she heard him whisper.

'I didn't... I don't want anything to happen to you. You've become so very precious to me.'

She stretched her arms around him and pressed herself so tightly against him she almost stopped breathing, but it didn't matter. An overwhelming sensation of warmth, security and love flooded throughout her whole body and the tears started for real. As she sat there sobbing, she felt his fingers running softly across her back and his lips at her ear. Gradually, the tears dried up to be replaced by a blissful feeling of well-being and joy.

'*Scusate, signori.*' She became dimly aware of a man's voice and looked up to see a police officer holding a clipboard towards Mark. '*Se volesse firmare, per piacere.*'

As Mark released his grip on her so as to take the statement and sign it, the sensation of abandonment was so strong in Emma that she felt the tears start all over again.

The police gave them a lift back to the hotel and Emma distinctly saw the driver salute Mark before driving off again. Mark came around to take hold of her by the shoulders once more and looked down at her.

'Coffee? Cognac? Grappa? Bed?'

Emma had absolutely no doubt.

'Bed.'

Chapter 21

Emma woke to find herself clinging to his warm body as if her life depended upon it. As her eyes opened, there was enough early morning sunlight coming in through the blinds for her to see Mark's face quite clearly and to see that his eyes were open and trained on hers, a gentle smile on his face.

'*Buongiorno, signora.*'

'*Buongiorno, signore.* Sleep well?' She stretched up and deposited the lightest of kisses on his lips.

His smile broadened. 'Yes, indeed. What about you? No bad dreams?'

'With you beside me? No, I was fine.' She snuggled even more tightly up against his chest and launched into the speech she had been preparing since talking to Erasmus, or maybe even before. 'I've got a confession to make, Mark. Forgetting for one moment the fact that you saved my life last night, I've been trying to get you alone so I could tell you how I feel.' She took a deep breath. 'I've never felt like this before.' Another deep breath. 'You see, although it's crazy, seeing as we've only known each other for a week or so...'

'Eight and a half days, but who's counting?' His voice was low, his tone gentle.

'...for eight and a half days – the thing is, I think I'm falling in love with you.' She looked up into those amazing blue-grey eyes once again. 'I know it sounds stupid and I promise I don't make a habit of going around telling men I love them. You have to believe me, but it's just...'

'It's not stupid. If it helps, I've been trying to find the right moment to tell you the exact same thing. For days now I've been telling myself I'm crazy, but there's no getting away from it. I can't stop thinking about you, Emma. You're amazing.'

He leant forward to kiss her and it was a long time before they started speaking again. Finally, she ran her fingers gently across the little round scars on his chest, one by one, and looked up at him.

'Feel like telling me?'

He nodded. 'I can't tell you much. I'm afraid I had to sign the Official Secrets Act, and, although I gave up the day job a year ago, it still applies.'

'You said you worked for the British government. Were you in the army, like Robert in *Dreaming of Italy*?'

'Not exactly. I worked for SIS, the Secret Intelligence Service. Now I'm no longer part of it, I can tell you that, but please don't broadcast the fact.'

Emma's eyes opened wide. 'So does this mean you were a spy?'

'I suppose you could say that. I was recruited way back when I was still at Oxford. Like I told you, I can speak a few languages and they liked the sound of that. Most of the work – at least at first – was fairly routine and pretty boring, and it isn't as glamorous as the movies would make you think.'

'And these wounds?' She let her fingers run across them again. 'Who did that to you?'

'I can't tell you.' He shook his head. 'It doesn't matter anyway. The trouble was that not only did they almost kill me, they ended my career. My people managed to keep it out of the mainstream media, but the damage had been done in intelligence circles. My name was named and my cover, as we say in the trade, was blown. If everybody knows you're a spy, you aren't much use as a spy.'

'So they sacked you?'

'No, to my surprise they offered me a promotion and a desk job. But then my grandfather died and I knew it was time for me to make the change.'

'And as far as your wounds were concerned, did it take you a long time to recover?'

She saw him nod slowly. 'Physically about six months. Apparently I was very lucky. Mentally, I'm not sure I have ever recovered fully.' He stopped and corrected himself. 'Until now, that is.' He leant down and kissed her softly, first on one eyelid, then the other. 'You say you think I saved your life last night. Well, I think it's the other way round. In a way, you've saved mine. It's been years and years since I've felt as happy as I do now.'

It was almost nine o'clock before Emma made it down to breakfast. Rich and Marina were waiting for her, and appeared relieved to see her. A broad smile spread across Rich's face.

'Morning, boss. We were getting worried. Good night?'

Emma smiled back. 'I had a very good night, apart from somebody trying to rob us at knifepoint.' They both looked horrified and she hastened to explain. As she got to the end of her tale, the other two exchanged looks of astonishment.

'So you're saying Mark fought off two armed men?'

'Let's not exaggerate here. Technically only one was armed.' Emma looked up at the sound of Mark's voice as he approached the table. He looked even more drop-dead gorgeous than before and a wave of emotion swept over her. It must have shown on her face as Marina instantly picked up on it.

'So you got your knight in shining armour, Emma. Lucky you.'

'Lucky me, indeed.'

After breakfast they set off on a walking tour of Bologna. Even though it was the middle of June, there were still crowds of students everywhere. Mark told them that it was very much a university town.

'The University of Bologna's one of the oldest in the world, founded in 1088. Popes, princes and household names like Dante, Boccaccio and Petrarch all studied here. Give or take a Duomo or a Ponte Vecchio, Bologna rivals Florence in terms of antiquity and culture and there's no question it would have been on the route of the Grand Tour.' He glanced across at Emma and smiled. 'So definitely a good choice for the movie.'

'Perfect.' Emma smiled back at him, reflecting that she had been doing a lot of that this morning.

She added these facts to her list and took photos as they walked through the city. They admired and photographed the twin towers, both leaning, although far less spectacularly than the one in Pisa, and walked around the main square, the Piazza Maggiore, stopping to visit the magnificent Basilica of San Petronio. Almost everywhere they went, they were shaded from the sun by miles of covered porticos lined with cafes, restaurants and shops. By mid-morning, Emma finally decided she had gathered enough for her report and they sat down for a coffee under the portico outside their hotel once more.

As they waited to be served, Mark brought up the subject of the movie.

'Venice is the day after tomorrow, isn't it, and that's where the movie ends? What about now? Can I ask at what stage the characters in the movie are by the time they get here to Bologna?'

Emma glanced across at Rich and let him answer. As she listened to him, she realised it might have been less embarrassing if she had told them herself, but it was too late.

'Bologna's the place where Emily and Robert finally get together. This is the town where love very definitely breaks out for them.'

'And why was he so troubled, so hard to fathom?' Marina sounded fascinated.

'The girl he was supposed to marry died of pneumonia a couple of years previously and he was still grieving.'

'I see. So, she actually sleeps with him here in Bologna? I didn't think they did that sort of thing back then.'

Rich grinned back at her. 'They did it all right – or at least they do in my old man's screenplay. In a lovely old hotel, bang in the centre of town. I imagine it being not dissimilar to this one.' Emma was beginning to wonder if it was suddenly getting hotter, as her cheeks were definitely glowing. Rich caught her eye and his grin broadened. 'Are you going to suggest they use our hotel for the movie, Emma? Do you think it's romantic enough for our two lovers? Can you imagine two people who've been in close proximity for days, gradually falling in love, finally ending up in the same bed right here?' Beside him, Marina looked as if she was going to choke.

Emma was still searching for a suitable answer – or for the pavement under her feet to open up and let her drop out of this embarrassment – when Mark stepped in.

'I reckon it would be perfect for any lovers.' He reached over and caught hold of Emma's hand and kissed her fingers. 'Absolutely perfect.'

Emma knew by now that the cat was out of the bag, so she did what she had been dying to do since starting their walk about town. She leant across and kissed him.

'You said it. Absolutely perfect.' She turned back towards Rich and grinned at him. 'In fact, the first thing I did after breakfast was to talk to the manager. He was very amenable and says they'll be only too happy to cooperate.'

–

The drive up the motorway to Ferrara took only just over half an hour and the city turned out to be delightful. It was much smaller than Bologna but there was a similar feel to the place. This, too, was a famous university town and there was a noticeably young population. The centre of town was dominated by a massive castle surrounded by a moat, and Mark told them that this, like so much of the town, had been built in the late Middle Ages. The architecture and the atmosphere of the city was a mixture: parts were medieval, with tortuous, narrow lanes, while other parts were filled with grander-looking Renaissance and more recent buildings. The cathedral, built of white marble, recalled the cathedral in Pisa. Emma and Mark walked around the *centro storico* arm in arm and she was happier than she had been in years. The others, too, joked and laughed and there was a festive air to the four of them. Emma took a lot of photos and by the time they left the city around mid-afternoon, she was feeling well pleased.

As they travelled up the motorway to Padua, she got a text message from Dexter.

> Very Urgent. JM has heard that Rich has found himself an Italian girlfriend. Please can you confirm and give your confidential assessment of the girl. Hope all is well with you. Dexter.

Emma cradled her phone in her hand and did some serious thinking. JM's bush telegraph was legendary in the company, but, even so, she wondered how he had found out. Maybe Ethan or Erasmus or even Rich himself had told his father. She decided to wait until they got to Padua to speak to him about it before replying. Needless to say, she knew she would give Marina a glowing reference, but she needed to be sure she got Rich's go-ahead first.

They got to the hotel at just after five. It was some ten kilometres outside Padua, set among the only hills for miles. These hills, the Colli Euganei, rose from the flat-lands around Venice like massive pyramids from the desert and the views were spectacular in all directions. The hotel was situated on the northern flank of the hills, overlooking Padua itself, with the backdrop of high, snow-covered mountains in the distance beyond that. Over to the right, if they screwed up their eyes, there was a pink smudge that had to be Venice. The hotel was a magnificent Palladian villa and Mark told them all about it as the car climbed up the winding road to get there.

'All around here you'll find Palladian villas. They're built in the style made popular by an architect called Andrea Palladio way back in the sixteenth century, although many of the buildings you see are much more recent than that. He was very much influenced by the architecture of ancient Rome and you'll find lots of magnificent villas around this area built in the classical style.'

Marina turned off the road into a narrow drive that led up to the hotel which emerged into view in all its glory. Unlike Mark's Umbrian villa with its ochre-coloured walls and blue-green shutters, this was a white building with an imposing façade made up of tall Grecian columns. It looked very grand and very alluring.

Emma had been contentedly sitting alongside Mark all day on the back seat of the car and she knew that she wanted nothing more now than to accompany him upstairs to his room and wrap herself round him, preferably forever. However, first, she knew she needed to speak to Rich. She showed Dexter's message to Mark and whispered in his ear.

'I'd better have a word with him. Would you go with Marina and check us in? I'll come up just as soon as I can.' She kissed him long and lovingly. 'I promise.'

She took Rich to one side and showed him the message. He nodded and revealed that he had called his father with the news himself. Emma was pleased to hear this. The last thing she wanted was to be asked to keep secrets from her boss.

'Right, well, I'll call Dexter now and tell him what a wonderful girl Marina is.'

Rich grinned. 'She is, isn't she?'

'You two any closer to coming up with a solution as to what happens when the time comes for you to go back to LA?'

'She's busy with work for the rest of this month and all of July, but she thinks she can get some time off in August. I'll check with my father and try to do the same. Hopefully she'll come over to California and I'll show her around. If she likes it enough, maybe she'll agree to stay. I sure hope so.'

Emma nodded approvingly. Rich was looking good and sounding much more confident. Whether it was Marina or this trip to Italy, something was working for him and she felt sure his parents would note an amazing improvement in him when he got back to LA. She was delighted for him. Her fears that she might end up having to cart a resentful drug addict around with her had been well and truly laid to rest and she couldn't have been happier.

She walked across the car park to a conveniently situated bench, from where she could look down onto the city of Padua in the distance. Her eyes were drawn to a strange bulbous structure that looked more like a mosque than a church and she resolved to ask Mark or Marina what it might be. For now, however, she had other things on her mind, like Mark's bed for example. But first, she called Dexter.

'Hi, Emma, how's it going?'

'Great, thanks. The weekend in Umbria went really well and yesterday we were in Bologna which is lovely.'

She decided to leave out the confrontation with the two would-be robbers. She went on to report that Laney and Ethan had left the previous morning with smiles on their faces, as had Erasmus. Dexter was delighted. She then brought the conversation round to Rich and Marina.

'You aren't going to believe the change I've seen in Richard since coming over here. He looks brighter, sounds happier and he's developed a real interest in the movie. He's contributed a lot of ideas and he's been very useful to me. Please tell his father I'm really delighted with the progress he's made. And part of the reason for this sea change, I'm sure, is Marina.'

She launched into a very flattering, but completely honest, description of Marina as a woman and a colleague, ending with the words: 'If I could think of a job for her in my department I'd employ her like a shot.'

'That all sounds great, Emma. I'll pass it up the line to JM. I know he'll be really glad to hear all that. Now listen, I've got some big news for you. You might be interested to know that the sign writers are coming in this week.'

Emma was puzzled. 'The sign writers?'

'To write your name and *vice president* on the door of a very nice office on the sixth floor. Congratulations, Emma, you're going places.'

'Wow, that's amazing.' She hesitated, hardly daring to believe it. 'But I haven't even presented JM with my report yet.'

'He thinks very highly of you, Emma. The promotion is effective as of today and the report isn't going to change his mind, believe me. You've nailed it.'

Emma thanked him and asked him to pass on her thanks to JM. As she rang off, she realised she hadn't even thought to ask him how the filming of *Sweet Memories* was going. The pre-Mark Emma wouldn't have forgotten. Did this signal a deterioration in her work ethic, or was it a positive thing? Had she suddenly discovered the ability to delegate or was she simply so obsessed with Mark that her mind had no place for such considerations? She sat there holding the phone in the palm of her hand, staring blindly down onto the city below, trying to get her head round what she had just heard.

Vice president was big. She knew there were a few women at a similar level in her industry, but they were still a rarity. Now, suddenly, she had been elevated to a senior position and it felt great. It was all she had ever dreamt of. Her career, which had been climbing fast, had suddenly taken a massive leap forward. Surely this was good, wasn't it?

She stood up and turned towards the hotel, determined to make sure Mark was the first to hear about her promotion. As the thought crossed her mind, so did the logical corollary of this piece of news. Along with this new position would come new responsibilities and, above all, it would tie her ever more firmly to JMGP and Hollywood. Any thought of turning her back on her career and settling down in a beautiful villa in Umbria with this wonderful man was rendered ever more inadvisable. Suddenly, she had even more to lose. Like it or not, this latest piece of good news was another nail in the coffin of her doomed relationship with Mark.

As she headed into the hotel, she determined not to mention her promotion to him yet. At least they would have tonight and tomorrow before harsh reality would have to rear its ugly head.

Chapter 22

That evening Emma and Mark were late coming down to dinner, but she was unapologetic. For their part, Rich and Marina appeared perfectly content sitting in the bar waiting for them. Mark, at Emma's side, looked happier than she had ever seen him and she had a permanent smile on her own face as well. The atmosphere was joyous, but an undercurrent of apprehension lurked just below the surface.

Over the last couple of hours, she and Mark had managed to find time to talk and they had chatted about their lives, their interests, their likes and dislikes. She had finally summoned up the courage to tell him about Dexter's phone call and her promotion. He had sounded very happy for her. The elephant in the luxurious bedroom, however, had been what would happen in two days' time when this trip would end and they would have to head off in their separate directions. Neither of them brought up their imminent separation, although it weighed heavily on Emma's mind, and she knew Mark well enough by now to be sure it was also uppermost in his thoughts.

Over dinner, as much to move the conversation away from this painful prospect for all four of them as anything else, they talked about the movie, and Rich was the first to bring up the subject.

'I had a quick word with the manager earlier on and he told me this place was already functioning as a hotel before the start of the First World War, so it would be okay for Emily and Robert to have stayed here.' He glanced across at Marina and clapped his hands in appreciation. 'Another great find, Marina. Apparently, a year or two later the hotel was taken over by the Italian army as a convalescence home for officers injured on the front.'

'Where was that? Was there fighting here during World War One?' Emma glanced apologetically at Mark. 'I'm sorry, my lack of knowledge of history is shameful.'

He smiled at her. 'There was a *lot* of fighting in the high mountains starting barely forty or fifty kilometres north of here, but that's not a very well-known fact back in the UK. We tend only to think of the First World War as the battlefields of the Somme or Flanders fields, but there was so much more to it than that.'

'So who were the Italians fighting?'

'The old enemy – the Austrians. Believe it or not, almost as many Italians died here in the mountains to the north of us as Brits did in France and Belgium. It was slaughter on an industrial scale. And not just Italians, by the end there were British and French troops fighting here as well.'

'So maybe Robert might have ended up on the front line here in Italy?'

Mark shook his head. 'I doubt it. As a serving officer in the British army at the start of the war, he would almost certainly have been sent straight to Belgium when the

German assault began in August 1914. Italy only joined the war in 1915.'

'And presumably if he was in the war from the very start, it would have been unlikely that he would have survived all the way through.' Emma was thinking of the end of the movie: the heart-wrenching farewell on the waterfront of Venice. 'That makes the last scene of *Dreaming of Italy* even sadder. Almost certainly Emily and Robert really were saying farewell forever.'

The word 'forever' stuck in her head. Could it be that when she and Mark also parted in less than two days' time that this goodbye would be forever, too?

'Statistically, I'm afraid so. Of course, he might have been lucky and just got injured.' Mark was trying to sound positive, but it didn't last. 'That war was so truly awful that men actually considered themselves lucky if they lost a leg or an eye and were invalided out. It beggars belief.'

Rich tapped Emma's arm. 'How's this for an idea? Right at the very end of the final scene, as it dissolves, the shot could cut to a bleak black-and-white image of a devastated battlefield, maybe even with a British officer lying face down in the mud, and the audience would get the point. Or is that too terribly sad?'

A shiver went down Emma's back and she shook her head. '*Dreaming of Italy*'s supposed to be a romance, not a tragedy, Rich. We want the audience to leave with a few wistful tears in the corners of their eyes, but I don't think we want to send them out completely gutted. I'll include that suggestion in my report to your father but, personally, I think it might be better to avoid mentioning the war. He might have survived, who knows?'

'Mind you, though, the war does get a mention.' Rich had clearly done his homework and Emma was pleased to hear it. 'Isn't it here in Padua that Robert gets the telegram ordering him back to his regiment?'

Emma nodded. 'Yes, indeed, and that same day Emily gets a telegram from her father, telling her she has to come home, as war is looking likely.'

'Why was that?' Marina had been following the conversation with interest. 'Does that mean the war had started?'

Mark glanced across at Emma. 'You said the story was all happening just before the war. As far as Britain was concerned, the declaration of war was at the end of July 1914. Are we saying Robert and Emily were over here then?'

Emma shook her head. 'No, according to the screen-play they were definitely here in June, so just *before* the actual outbreak of war. Something must have happened in June to tell everybody that war was on the way.'

'Well, the event that sparked the whole thing off was the assassination of Archduke Franz Ferdinand on the twenty-eighth of June 1914. Emily and Robert must have been here at that time. I imagine as soon as the news came out, everybody with any sense started heading for home and troops started getting the call to arms.'

'Just think, we're in June now. All this was happening just over a hundred years ago, almost to the day. Poor Emily and Robert. Little did they know the horror to come...'

'Nobody did. In fact, most people assumed it would be a fast-moving war that would be over by Christmas. How wrong could they be? Anyway, you're saying it was in Padua that they got the telegrams. That's going to be a pretty dark moment in the movie.' Mark took a big mouthful of wine. 'That's a real pity, seeing as it's such a beautiful city.'

Silence descended upon the table and Emma was still racking her brains for some way of cheering everybody up when Mark got there first.

'Anyway, changing the subject, you'll all be delighted to hear that the carpenter has fixed that damn gate and Carmen is no longer able to go swimming in the pool – much to her displeasure.' He smiled across the table at the others. 'Claudio sent me the good news and he sends his greetings to you all.'

'He's a very good guy, isn't he?' Emma did her best to pick up the ball and run with it. 'Is there a Mrs Claudio?'

Mark told them that Claudio was happily married with three little kids, and his family would be coming to join him at the hotel any day now as soon as the decorators applied the finishing touches to the manager's apartment a bit further along the old stable block from Mark's house. Thought of Mark's lovely house brought another little wave of nostalgia to Emma, but she did her best to stifle it as the main course arrived.

She had chosen a roulade of pork, filled with omelette, walnuts and spinach and accompanied by roast potatoes and, unusually, half a red lettuce that had been roasted in the oven. The result was excellent. As she ate, she turned the conversation to the city of Padua and they decided on a plan for the following day. Seeing as this would be the last full day the characters in the movie – and, indeed, all of them here – would have together, Marina promised to find them some places with a more melancholy feel to them. Emma just hoped this wouldn't result in her bursting into tears herself. Her flight would be early the following morning and she was already counting off the hours. She knew that tomorrow was going to be very tough on the emotions.

The plan was to spend the morning in Padua and then head to Venice in the afternoon. Marina came up with an excellent suggestion as to how to get there.

'A hundred years ago, almost all heavy goods were still being transported from Padua to Venice by canal. The canal's still in existence. How about leaving the car in Padua and taking a boat to Venice? I'll make a few calls and see if we can rent a launch. Our hotel's right in the middle of Venice and of course there are no cars there anyway. I imagine that's quite possibly what Emily and Robert would have done.'

Emma definitely liked the sound of that and it was decided. In her mind's eye she could already imagine the scene as the two heartbroken lovers sailed into the majestic beauty of Venice, their minds filled with foreboding. As for her, this time tomorrow, she and Mark would be in Venice for their last night together, maybe ever.

At the end of the meal, she and Mark wandered out into the evening air and sat outside the hotel watching the sun set over the jagged peaks of the distant Alps. Emma reflected that in less than two days' time she would be at her parents' home in Norfolk, where she was going to spend a night before getting a flight back to LA on Friday. Pleased as she was at the prospect of seeing her mum and dad again, she knew that leaving Mark would be so very tough.

As they sat there, his arm around her shoulders, watching as the swallows in the sky above them were gradually replaced by bats, her thoughts turned, yet again, to just exactly what she wanted out of life. Up until just ten days ago, there had been no doubt in her mind: her job, and her ambition to rise as far up the ladder as she could in JMGP, had been her overriding ambition. Now, with the arrival of Mark, the waters had been irrevocably muddied and Dexter's big news this afternoon had only added to the burden she now carried on her shoulders. The man or the job? She knew full well she wasn't the first woman in history to be faced with this dilemma and she wouldn't be the last, but knowing that she wasn't unique didn't help.

As the shadows lengthened and old-fashioned lamps came on to illuminate the scene, she turned her head towards him, resting her cheek on his chest directly on top of his three bullet wounds. 'Mark, will you come and visit me in LA?'

He glanced down and she immediately knew that his mind had been running along similar lines.

'Of course I will.' He bent down and kissed her softly on the forehead. 'And will you come and visit Carmen and me in Umbria?'

'Just as soon as I can. The thing is… you maybe know that American companies aren't great as far as long vacations are concerned. It might not be a long visit, but I promise I'll come.'

'And you'll try not to forget me?' His eyes were smiling, but his tone was melancholy.

'I'll never, ever, forget you, Mark.' She stretched up and kissed him hard on the lips. 'Never.'

She didn't say anything else as she was struggling as hard as she had ever struggled before in her life to stop the tears from running.

It wasn't easy.

Chapter 23

Emma woke early next morning and peeked out of the side of the curtains from the bed. Today was overcast and the sky matched her mood. She turned her head on the pillow and looked across at Mark beside her. He was still asleep and supporting herself on one elbow she watched him as he lay there, his strong chest gently rising and falling in time with his breath. Without stretching for her watch or her phone she had no idea what time it was, but that didn't matter. What mattered was that he was here beside her.

For now.

She felt herself smiling down at him as her eyes ran across his body and up to his face. As her eyes reached his eyes, they opened.

'*Buongiorno, signora.*' His face broke into a warm smile.

'*Buongiorno, signore.* You looked very peaceful.'

'And I was. How long have you been awake?'

'Not long. I was just lying here thinking.' She didn't tell him what she had been thinking about. The clouds behind his blue-grey eyes made it clear that he knew.

He leant across and kissed her, reaching out with one arm to pull her tightly against his body.

'You're amazing. Did you know that?'

She nuzzled against his chest, gently kissing his battle scars one by one. 'Not as amazing as you.'

He reached over with his free hand and checked the time. 'Six thirty. Our last day together. Let's make sure it's unforgettable.'

–

When they got down to breakfast a couple of hours later, Rich and Marina were already there and it was immediately obvious that Marina had been crying. Rich was sitting close beside her and he was holding her hand. He hadn't been crying but he was looking pretty miserable. Emma immediately did her best to cheer them up, even though their sombre mood so accurately matched her own.

'Hi, guys. Mark and I have just been saying that seeing as this is our last full day together, we need to do our very best to make it unforgettable. I know you two will be seeing each other again in a month or so, but we owe it to Emily and Robert to make sure we give them the very best final day we can.'

She deliberately omitted any mention of when she and Mark might be seeing each other again, if ever, and concentrated on sounding positive and in control of the situation and of her emotions.

At least for now.

'Marina, I want you to book us into the most fabulous, romantic and exquisite restaurant in Venice for dinner tonight. Ideally, make it somewhere that was operating back then before the First World War so I can take a final few photos. Can you do that?'

She was delighted to see a little smile form on Marina's face. 'I've already done that, if you're agreeable. It's called the *l'Antica Trattoria* and it's supposed to have been there since the Napoleonic wars. It's a twenty-minute walk from our hotel and everybody says the seafood there's exquisite.'

Emma smiled back at her. 'I knew we could count on you, Marina. That sounds fantastic. And what about our trip along the canal to Venice this afternoon?'

Once again, Marina was on the case. 'It's a bit pricey, but I've arranged for a water taxi to pick us up partway and take us right to our hotel. They said they'll give us a little tour of Venice en route.'

'Terrific.' The smile still firmly plastered onto her face, Emma did her best to keep the mood positive. 'Right, seeing as we're celebrating today, I think I can allow myself a plate of bacon and eggs.' She glanced across at Mark. 'You going to join me? I think we've earned it.'

He grinned back. 'A double helping for me.'

They drove down to the outskirts of Padua and left the car in a big car park. From there, they took a taxi into the city centre. Marina queried with the driver where he thought they should start their tour and he had no hesitation.

'You have to start with the Basilica di Sant'Antonio. It's one of the wonders of the world.'

Marina turned to the others with a smile. 'Exactly what I thought. Great. First stop the basilica.'

He deposited them in the wide square, directly opposite the massive church. This turned out to be the oriental-looking building Emma had glimpsed from afar the previous evening. Marina took over from Mark as their guide as this was a city she knew well.

'The basilica was started in 1232 and it took almost a century to finish. It's a unique mixture of styles, predominantly Romanesque and Byzantine. See the domes on the roof, for example. And if you wonder how I know that, it's because I used to work as a tourist guide in my holidays when we were living here.'

The bulbous domes were unlike the roof of any church Emma had seen before and there was no missing the eastern origins of the design. Among them were tall, slim bell towers that reminded her of Turkish minarets. Altogether it was an astonishing building and Emma wasted no time in taking a load of photos and adding it to her list. Professionally, what particularly appealed to her was the relative absence of tourists, in comparison to Pisa and Siena and even Bologna. Here, she felt sure, it would be fairly straightforward to find the space for the film crew to operate.

From there, Marina led them into the maze of cobbled streets of the *centro storico*. Emma was very happy to follow her lead, walking hand in hand with Mark. Here among the ancient buildings, there was a real romantic feel and, for once, she abandoned herself to it for a couple of hours and just enjoyed being with him, doing her best to keep her thoughts in the present, rather than the looming future.

Marina took them into the very centre and to two charming squares: the Piazza delle Erbe and the Piazza della Frutta, with the imposing medieval Palazzo della Ragione dividing one from another. This stunning building was composed of row upon row of arches and capped by a long, curved roof like an airship hangar. Dotted around the flag-stoned squares were stalls selling local produce and beneath the porticoes were shops of all kinds. Sight of the shops reminded Emma she needed to buy a present for her parents. As she did so, she remembered Dexter.

'Rich, have you ever seen Dexter's poodle?'

He grinned. 'Seen it? It even peed on my foot one time – damn thing. It's on the small side. I suppose its head doesn't even come up to my knee. Why do you ask?'

'I want to buy him a present and I thought something for the dog might be a good idea.'

Marina turned back with interest. 'If it's a pet shop you're looking for, there's one just down one of these side streets if I remember right.'

A few minutes later, Emma found exactly what she wanted: a very smart doggie waterproof coat with an Italian flag on it. Although it didn't rain too often in LA, she felt sure Dexter's canine companion would cut a stylish dash when the rain did come. By this time Rich and Marina had also decided they needed to go off to buy presents and they all agreed to meet up in the historic Caffè Pedrocchi in a nearby square later on. Marina assured them this was the best-known cafe in Padua and a must for visitors, so Mark volunteered to go and bag a table while they did their shopping.

There was a market in the centre of the Piazza dell Frutta where Emma bought an old-fashioned moka coffee pot and some real Italian coffee for her mum and dad, and a handmade leather wallet for Elliot before making her way along to the cafe to meet the others.

She found Mark sitting at an outside table under the portico of the impressive neo-Gothic building and she took a number of photos of the cafe as she drew nearer. As the place where Emily and Robert were to get wind of the approaching war, it was suitably sombre with its imposing columns and elegant, formal interior with red velvet chairs and pristine white tablecloths. She could well imagine the scene in the movie where a uniformed postman would arrive bearing the two telegrams that would tear the lovers irrevocably apart. This reminder of their own forthcoming separation made Emma walk straight across to where Mark was sitting and throw her arms around him, kissing him with intensity, in spite of the looks of some of the other customers.

As he emerged from her embrace, Mark winked at her. 'What was that about – absence making the heart grow fonder? It's only been ten minutes. If we'd been separated for an hour I suppose you would have ravished me here on the table?'

She took a seat close beside him and grinned. 'You bet your life. And imagine the treat in store for you if I'd been away for two hours or more.'

They sat in silence for a long time before she heard his voice, now no longer jocular.

'I'm really going to miss you.'

'And I'm going to miss you, too, Mark. Terribly.'

At that moment Rich and Marina reappeared and Emma once more bolted on her happy face.

–

After lunch they returned to the car and took it back to the rental company. From there, a taxi took them and their luggage out of the city and onto a minor road alongside a canal. The clouds had cleared and the sun was once more shining down on them. The land all around was as flat as a pancake and disappointingly built-up, with numerous small to medium-sized factories lining its banks. Marina informed them that this waterway was the Naviglio del Brenta that led all the way to Venice but, to Emma, it didn't immediately look promising for the movie. That was, until they picked up their launch.

The boat was waiting for them just before the impressive and historic Villa Foscari. This imposing villa was set in its own extensive grounds and Emma immediately noted this as a very strong contender for inclusion in the film. This mansion, Marina told them, was a genuine Palladian villa, dating back to the sixteenth century, and it was a magnificent piece of architecture with massive columns supporting the neo-classical façade. Once again, Emma could well imagine the pair of lovers passing by this way, maybe strolling through the grounds hand in hand, ever more conscious that this would be their last day together.

The launch was a Venetian water taxi made of highly-polished wood, its comfortable cabin fitted with leather-upholstered seats and with an open deck at the stern. The boatman cast off and they began to follow the ever-widening canal eastwards. The houses and factories alongside them gradually dwindled away until they found themselves running between wide marshy fields that the boatman informed them would flood at high tide. Here it was a lot wilder and they soon spotted ducks and geese on the water and cormorants perched on stumps, wings outstretched Dracula-style as they dried their feathers.

Emma took more photos as this landscape was timeless and virtually deserted. Ideal for the movie.

As Rich and Mark were standing outside at the stern, Marina came over to sit beside Emma in the cabin.

'Not long now.'

'Until we get to the hotel?'

'Until it's all over. Then what're you going to do, Emma? I've seen you and Mark together. I think you're made for each other. Are you really going back to the US while he stays here?'

Emma took a couple of deep breaths before replying. 'I have to, Marina. It's my job.'

She saw Marina nod her head slowly. 'It's tough, isn't it? I've got a job I love, too. But at least I know I'm going to be with Rich again in only six or seven weeks. What about you and Mark? Do you plan on coming back to Italy to see him?'

Emma did her best to sound as positive as she could, although internally she was feeling anything but upbeat. 'I'm not sure when, but I know I'll see him again before long. Maybe in the autumn? I don't know.'

'And is that how it's going to be? A long-distance affair that brings you together for a few weeks of the year and the rest of the time you'll be apart?'

'Seems like I don't have a choice.' Unless, she thought to herself for the hundredth time, she turned her back on her career and followed her heart as so many women had done in the past. But was that what she wanted? Her train of thought was interrupted as Rich's voice called them to come outside and take a look at a beautifully restored canal boat chugging up towards them. As they both got to their feet, Marina caught hold of Emma's hand and gave it a squeeze.

'Remember what Erasmus said. It'll work itself out.'

Chapter 24

They approached Venice from the west. Over to their left as they emerged from the canal was a sprawling industrial complex and docks with a massive cruise ship moored there but, ahead of them, the unmistakable sight of *La Serenissima*, the serene Republic of Venice, greeted them just as it would have done Emily and Robert. The launch headed straight towards a mass of red-brick buildings on the land directly ahead of them, cutting across one of the main shipping channels as they did so. A luxury yacht almost the size of a warship passed very close to them and they slipped into the mouth of a surprisingly narrow canal. This, the boatman told them, would lead to the Grand Canal.

On either side of them were ancient buildings, many that were probably warehouses, with massive tree trunks driven vertically into the seabed in front of them to act as mooring posts. Bright green barges carrying everything from piles of rubbish to crates of beer chugged past, performing the same tasks that vans and trucks would do in a normal city. Carving through them, the long, low *vaporetto* – waterbuses – carried passengers to and fro just like ordinary buses did on dry land. A police launch and a fire brigade boat came past and Emma realised that even cities built in the middle of a lagoon could catch fire or have bank robberies. Gradually, she started to come to terms with this city on the water. It truly was unique.

They passed under a number of modern-looking bridges before they found themselves approaching the railway station.

'Is this where Emily and Robert say goodbye?' Mark was at her side. Emma shook her head.

'No, the big heart-breaking goodbye scene is on the quayside. He goes off in a launch like this.' She hesitated. 'Mind you, I suppose it only took him to the station and from here he would have caught a train to wherever he was going. That is, of course, if there already was a station here in 1914.'

'A station, yes – just not this one. The line linking Venice with the mainland was completed, believe it or not, as early as the middle of the nineteenth century, but this station was built to replace the original one between the First and the Second World War, so it wouldn't have been there at the time of your movie. So Rich's dad's idea of having the big farewell at the waterside makes sense.'

The launch passed underneath the beautiful wide-arched Ponte degli Scalzi and entered the Grand Canal. Gradually the more modern buildings around the station area gave way to ancient *palazzi* with arched windows and ornate render on the walls. Some were white, many a sun-bleached pink and others different shades of ochre from bright orange to palest cream. The mooring posts were no longer bare wood. Many were painted in colourful stripes and whirls and for the first time they began to see the iconic gondolas. Narrow alleys and equally narrow canals led off on both sides and many of the grander houses had their own moorings and entrances directly off the Grand

Canal itself. Emma breathed it in and just knew that the finale of the movie had to be set here.

'Do you intend putting Emily and Robert on a gondola?' Mark had been watching the seemingly effortless skill of a gondolier in his stripy jumper as he sculled a gondola out of one narrow canal and across the main channel before disappearing into an even narrower canal on the opposite side of the Grand Canal.

Emma nodded. 'I hope so, but on quiet backwaters, I would think. It'll depend on Erasmus, but it would be a shame to bring them to Venice and not let them go in a gondola. Have you ever been in one?'

'I'm afraid so.'

'Why "afraid"?'

'You'd think it would be a lovely romantic way to travel, but all it did for me was to make me feel like a goldfish in a bowl. Everywhere you go, you get your photograph taken and I certainly didn't find it conducive to romance.'

'So you're not going to take me on a romantic moonlit tour of the city in a gondola?' She was kidding, but she enjoyed teasing him.

'My darling girl, if you want a ride in a gondola, I'll grit my teeth and come with you, but I'd feel happier wearing Ethan's wig and shades if I did.'

Emma rather liked the sound of being his 'darling girl' so she relented. 'It's all right, I won't force you. We haven't got much time anyway.' That, she knew, was all too true.

From time to time they passed old churches, glamorous hotels or ostentatious *palazzi*. Everywhere they looked there were window boxes brimming with colourful flowers and even a few canal-side gardens boasting palm trees. Many of the buildings had roof gardens overlooking the canal and Emma definitely liked the look of those. She could imagine Emily and Robert, or maybe Mark and herself, standing up there looking out over the fading grandeur of this marvellous city. Remembering what Rich had suggested in Siena, maybe a scene shot at rooftop level might be the best way of avoiding the crowds of twenty-first century tourists.

The further along the Grand Canal they travelled, the more splendid the buildings became. The boatman pointed out magnificent *palazzi* like the Venice Casino, the Cà d'Oro gallery and the Foscari family's Venetian palace as the canal took a right-hand curve and they were confronted with the famous Rialto Bridge. This stunning marble-faced bridge with its covered porticoes was packed with tourists and Emma began to realise that almost everywhere else that wasn't water was similarly crowded. Venice was very definitely full to bursting. Managing to get space for a film crew was going to be near impossible – unless they went up onto the roofs.

The canal continued to wind its tortuous way through the city until the broad expanse of the lagoon was once more visible in the distance. As they finally emerged into open water, the buildings on their left suddenly gave way and they had a clear view of St Mark's Square, the Palazzo Ducale, St Mark's Basilica and the famous red-brick bell tower, rising high into the sky. It was an impressive and beautiful sight and Emma was delighted when Marina told them their hotel was barely a hundred yards or so from here. Emma resolved to come back on foot and take a closer look – in spite of the mass of humanity already doing just that.

Their hotel was exquisite. Marina told them it had been built in the fourteenth century and the interior was like something out of the Arabian Nights – a symphony of marble, fine art and unashamed luxury. She immediately recognised it from a Hollywood movie starring Johnny Depp and Angelina Jolie and wondered if JMGP would use it for *Dreaming of Italy*. Whether they did or didn't, as the place where she and Mark would spent their last night together, it was unparalleled, and Emma could feel a wonderful sense of anticipation growing inside her, even though she knew it would only be short-lived.

As far as the whole 'better to have loved and lost' thing was concerned, she would now at least be able to say she had loved. And in a place like this with a man like Mark, she knew it would be unforgettable.

In spite of the wonders of Venice just outside the door, Emma had no hesitation in spending the remainder of the afternoon in bed with Mark. Marina had somehow managed to find them two rooms with a communicating door linking them together and when she saw him come through the door, with just a towel around his waist, she thought she would explode with joy.

The rooms were at the front of the hotel and looked straight out onto the lagoon. She made them cups of tea which they drank sitting up in bed looking out over the grey-green water, criss-crossed by the wakes of boats of all sizes. The hotel had also supplied some gorgeous chocolate biscuits and she happily nibbled one as she leant against his shoulder. If it hadn't been for their imminent separation, it would have been heaven. His mind must have been working along similar lines.

'I can't think of a better way to spend the evening – the hotel, the view and, of course the amazing room service.' He leant down and kissed her forehead.

She sipped her tea. This really did feel perfect.

'Emma.' His voice sounded hesitant. 'You do know I can't come over to the States with you, don't you? It's not because I don't want to. It's just that the hotel's too new.'

She glanced up at him. 'Of course I understand. Maybe once the busy summer season's over you might be able to get away.'

'Absolutely. And maybe you might be able to get a week or two off at some point?'

'I'll make sure I do.'

They lapsed into silence for some minutes after that, each alone with their thoughts. For her part, Emma was already feeling the gnawing regret that she knew would be with her for a long time to come. She had been faced with the choice and, just like he said he had done years earlier, she had chosen her career over her heart. Yes, she would make sure she saw him for a few weeks each year, but she had no illusions as to the precarious nature of long-distance relationships. Sooner or later he would find someone else and that would be that. She set down her empty cup and wrapped her arms around his body, clinging to him tightly, trying hard to memorise everything about this magical moment that might never be repeated.

Finally, around seven o'clock, as the sun was beginning to drop towards the horizon, they roused themselves and went down to meet up with the other two. Emma wanted to visit St Mark's Square, but first she had to find the location for the final scene of the movie. They walked out of the hotel onto the quayside and Rich demonstrated that he had also been thinking about this.

'All the way down the Grand Canal I was looking for suitable places, but it's all so damn crowded here.'

'When do you reckon you'll be shooting the film?' Mark was staring at the throng of humanity all around them. 'Presumably there must be a time when it's not as crowded as this.'

'I believe shooting's scheduled to start in early October. That's an unusually quick turnaround. As I told you, there's a lot riding on this movie.' Emma knew it would also depend upon other commitments at JMGP and how soon they could get all the filming permits in place.

'I've been here in the autumn and it was a bit quieter than this.' Marina shrugged her shoulders. 'With kids back at school, there were fewer people, but this part of Venice is always busy.'

Emma made a quick decision. 'Then we've got to look in a different area. Any ideas?'

Mark reached into the back pocket of his jeans, pulled out a map of Venice and consulted it. 'It looks to me as though all the big sights are off to the right of us. Why don't we go the other way?' He pointed along the quayside to the left and Emma's eyes followed his fingers. 'If you look way down there, there are progressively fewer and fewer people. Maybe we can find somewhere suitable in that direction.'

Together they set off along the quayside, the water level barely a couple of feet below where they were walking. Emma remembered the awful stories of floods here in Venice that regularly overwhelmed streets, squares, homes, shops and priceless architectural gems. There was no doubt about it – in this era of global warming and climate change, this wonderful city was living on borrowed time.

As they got further away from the centre so, as Mark had predicted, the crowds began to thin and before long they found themselves on a wide quay called the Riva dei Sette Martiri, the Quay of the Seven Martyrs. There were remarkably few tourists to be seen here, and they soon located mooring posts and a set of old stone steps leading down into the water, right opposite a charming old rose-pink *palazzo*. As an added bonus, the building looked all shut up and there were no modern clothes lines or TV aerials to be seen. Best of all, looking back the way they had come, there was a spectacular view up the Grand Canal with a host of unmistakable cupolas, towers and palaces that just screamed 'Venice'.

Emma was well pleased. 'Brilliant choice, guys. This should do perfectly.' She and Rich took a number of shots and she could well imagine Emily and Robert's tearful farewell taking place here. Marina tugged her sleeve.

'Can I ask? How does it end? Couldn't it have a happy ending?'

Emma shook her head sadly. 'I'm afraid not. It's a real tear-jerker at the end as these two lovers are torn apart by war – just like so many millions of couples were in real life. They stand on this quay and kiss goodbye, knowing in their hearts that it's probably the very last time they'll see each other.' She kept her tone studiously level, although she knew that tomorrow morning she and Mark would find themselves in almost the same situation, give or take a brief holiday now and then.

Once they had taken all the photos they needed, they circled back through a maze of lanes and alleys, crossing little humpback bridges over narrow side canals, until they came upon the bulk of St Mark's Basilica ahead of them. As they did so, the crowds began to thicken once more, and by the time they emerged onto the long expanse of St Mark's Square, they found themselves surrounded by a mass of people. It didn't completely spoil the overall experience of this unique historic city, but it definitely made it less romantic – constantly having to change direction to avoid porters with trolleys, families with children, and large groups of many different nationalities on guided tours. Some of the guides even had their own amplifiers and loudspeakers strung around their necks and the noise just added to the chaotic feel of the place.

In spite of the crowds, they managed to find a table outside one of the cafes and sat down for a drink. A number of people around them were drinking a bright orange concoction that Emma knew as an Aperol Spritz. This was a mixture of white wine, soda water and Italian Aperol liqueur and she decided to follow suit, although she knew from experience that it could be very sweet. Fortunately, the Venetian version was unexpectedly refreshing, which was just as well as, after the hazy morning, the sky was once more clear and the residual heat of the sun was still radiating up from the flagstones at their feet, even though they were now sitting in shade.

Emma and Rich spent twenty minutes going over all the places they had visited and she got him to send her a number of his best photos to add to her report. She had been composing this each day as they went along and her original intention had been to complete it here in Venice today, but she knew that wasn't how she wanted to spend her last night with Mark. At least, it would hopefully give her something to do on the flight back to LA, rather than think longingly of the man she had left behind.

From there they walked through narrow lanes crowded with tourists, sometimes even having to take refuge in doorways as large groups pushed past, until they were almost back at the Rialto Bridge. Here, right alongside the Grand Canal, they found the restaurant, *l'Antica Trattoria*. Marina had got her boss to pull weight and he had managed to get them a table outside, underneath the awning, right on the side of the canal from where they had an uninterrupted view of the gondolas, *vaporetti* and other boats going up and down. It was a spectacular place for their last dinner together. Rather than dwell on the fact that tomorrow both she and Marina would be separated from their men, Emma did her best to keep their minds on the events of the movie.

'This restaurant will be amazing for Emily and Robert's last meal together. Yet another triumph, Marina.'

Marina blushed as the others joined in with applause. 'I just hope *Dreaming of Italy* becomes the success you're all hoping for.' She reached for Rich's hand. 'Will you invite me to the premiere?'

'I'll walk you down the red carpet, I promise.'

Emma chose crayfish, followed by an amazing *fritto misto*: prawns, octopus and little fish delicately fried and accompanied with a side salad. At Mark's suggestion they drank ice-cold Soave Classico, and it was a memorable meal. Emma had been photographing some of the more spectacular dishes over the past twelve days and she was determined to include a suggestion to Erasmus that at least one of the scenes should be over a lavish Italian meal, of which there had been many. She added tonight's fish dishes to the list.

At the end of the meal, Rich announced that he was going to stay on in Venice for another night and Emma felt quite jealous. Her flight to England to see her parents the next day would mean leaving the hotel right after breakfast and, much as she wanted to see her mum and dad, she knew that another twenty-four hours with Mark would have been very precious. Still, she told herself, it was all booked and her mum was expecting her so she had to go. Marina had booked her a ticket on a shared transfer to the airport in a water taxi and she didn't need to check her watch to know that this was less than twelve hours away now.

On the walk back to the hotel through the dark streets, she hung back from Mark for a few minutes to talk to Rich.

'I just wanted to say thank you, Rich.'

'You're thanking me?'

'Very definitely. You've been a massive help and I'll make sure I point out to your father which of the photos and suggestions come from you. On a more personal note, I'm really delighted to see you looking and sounding so much happier. I think this trip's done you good.'

'This trip's done me a world of good, Emma. You've done me a world of good.'

'I haven't done anything.'

'It's been great working with you, being treated as an equal. You listen to my ideas and you trust me to do things. You have no idea how badly I needed that. I can honestly say I feel a new man – and that's not just because of Marina, although I'd be lying if I didn't say she's been amazing.'

'Marina's a great girl, Rich. Don't let her go.'

'I don't intend to. Anyway, like I say, thanks, boss. I won't forget this.'

She gave him a kiss on the cheek and returned to take Mark's arm. It had been a very positive experience for all of them, one way or another. The pity was that it had to end.

Rich and Marina decided to stop off in St Mark's Square for a coffee and Emma gave them both a hug, repeating her thanks to Rich and telling Marina how terrifically impressed she had been with her as a guide, chauffeur and companion. As she hugged her, she spoke into her ear.

'When you come to LA, Marina, do come and see me. And if you decide you want to stay I promise I'll do my very best to find you a job. JMGP needs good people.'

Marina beamed at her and kissed her on the cheeks.

'Thanks a lot, Emma. I've really enjoyed these two weeks and I'm sure *Dreaming of Italy* will be the block-buster you want it to be.' As she drew back Emma saw her eyes twinkle in the light of the streetlamps. 'And don't forget what Erasmus said.'

Emma and Mark continued alone. Night had fallen and the pigeons, along with a lot of the tourists, had gone home for the night. She and Mark didn't speak as they walked across the square, but they didn't need to. The moonlight illuminated the magnificent façade of St Mark's Basilica with its host of columns, statues and frescoes, and the magnificence of the Palazzo Ducale alongside it. As they reached the edge of the square they paused to look out over the lagoon towards the island of St Giorgio, savouring the view, conscious that time was running out for the two of them.

Mark stretched his arm around Emma's shoulders and pulled her close. She stretched her arms around his waist and turned towards him.

'I'm afraid I'm going to cry tomorrow morning.'

The full moon reflected in his eyes as he looked down at her.

'I'm afraid we're both going to cry tomorrow.'

Chapter 25

Next morning the sky was once more overcast as Emma and Mark stood together on the landing stage at San Marco, watching the waterbus for the airport approaching, little waves breaking against its bow as it crossed the busy channel. Mark's arm was around her once more and she had been crying ever since they had stepped out into the relatively cool morning air.

As the launch drew nearer, she looked up at him, forlornly, all too conscious that she was turning her back on something very special. The final scene of *Dreaming of Italy* came to mind as she heard him repeating the self-same words used by Robert, the young army officer.

'I wish we didn't have to part like this.' His voice was flat. He looked as devastated as she felt.

As his eyes met hers, she could see them glistening in the morning light.

'So do I.' She took a deep breath. 'But we both know the situation and we'll have to try really hard to meet up again, as soon as possible, and as often as we can.' He laid his free hand against her cheek and stroked it tenderly. She rubbed her face against his fingers and sighed deeply. 'I love you so very dearly, Mark.'

'Meeting you's the very best thing that's ever happened to me, Emma.' A tear fell from his cheek onto hers as he bent his lips towards her. 'I love you, too, Emma, from the bottom of my heart.'

He hugged her tightly to his body and kissed her with passion, his emotion all too visible and all too raw. Finally, unable to ignore the waiting boat any longer, she took a deep breath, stepped back and looked up at him and swallowed hard. All she could manage was: 'Goodbye, Mark.'

She picked up her bag, handed it to the boatman and stepped onto the launch. As the engine revved and the boat pulled away, she stood on the deck, her face bathed with tears, her eyes on the solitary figure on the quayside, until other vessels hid him from her view.

–

Her flight was on time and she got to Stansted airport just before noon. Her tears had stopped by the time the launch reached the airport, but she had spent the whole flight in a daze, barely aware of her surroundings, only conscious of the awful void inside her. Her parents were waiting for her as she emerged from the baggage hall and she did her best to look and sound bright and cheerful.

'Hi, Mum. Hi, Dad. It's really good to see you.'

As she hugged her mother, her fragile emotions took another hit and she found herself crying her eyes out. Her mother's reassuring arms around her, just like when she had been a little girl, only reminded her of what she had lost. Or rather, what she had rejected.

By the time they got out to the car, she had managed to compose herself and was able to spend the next two hours in the car telling them all about her life in Hollywood, her fantastic promotion and the events of the last two weeks in

Italy – almost all of them. It was only after a very late lunch back home, as her dad was snoozing in an armchair in front of the cricket, that she opened up to her mother and told her the whole story, her voice cracking with emotion. Her mum didn't comment until the very end and, at first, that was only to ask if Emma felt like a cup of tea.

However, once she had pressed a mug of hot tea into Emma's right hand and a fresh tissue into her left, she finally spoke up.

'You're a very lucky girl, Emma.'

'Me, lucky?'

'From what you've told me about this man, Mark, you really do love him, don't you?'

Emma just hung her head and nodded sadly. There could be absolutely no doubt in her mind now.

'Not everybody gets to experience that, you know. You're thirty-five now and you tell me this is the first time you've felt anything like this. You should be glad it's happened. Some people go their whole lives without ever having that depth of emotion for another person.' She reached over and caught Emma gently by the chin, lifting her face until they were eye to eye. 'I've been lucky like that twice in my life. First I fell in love with your father, and then there was you. Cheer up and be happy. You've had something very special.'

Emma managed a little smile. 'Thanks, Mum, but now I know what it's like, why can't I keep it?'

'Why can't you?'

'I told you, Mum, my job. I love Mark but I love my job. And I'm good at my job. I don't want to give it up.'

'Not even for love?'

Emma shook her head, but her mother must have sensed her indecision.

'Not even for a wonderful man who loves you back?'

'Oh, Mum…' Emma's head was swimming as a multitude of conflicting thoughts and emotions swirled around inside her.

'Not even for the chance to live in a gorgeous part of the world with his lovely dog and maybe your own family.' There was a catch in her mother's voice that reached into Emma's heart. 'You can't imagine just how amazing the bond of love can be with your own child.' She rubbed her eyes with the back of her hand. 'You deserve to experience that as well, my darling.'

Emma could feel the tears running down her cheeks once more and she let her mother envelope her in her warm, caring arms and hold her until the crying stopped. As the tears stopped, so Erasmus's words came back to her and she knew she was ready to fight as hard as she could to make this long-distance thing work. Maybe, once the hotel was up and running, Mark would be able to take more time off, maybe even do that doctorate in LA? In her new position she would now find herself heading a team at JMGP and, as she had learnt with Elliot and *Sweet Memories*, if she could delegate more, that might give her more free time… She grabbed a clean tissue, blew her nose and wiped her eyes, before looking up at her mother with renewed resolve.

'You're right, Mum. I can't turn my back on him. I love him, Mum. I love him and I'm going to make it work.' As she spoke, her phone started ringing and she saw with delight that it was him.

'Mark, hi.'

'Emma?' He sounded delighted to hear her voice. 'Are you at your parents' house?'

'Yes, I am, Mark. Listen, there's something I need to say. We've really got to—'

'Hang on. Just tell me one thing. Whereabouts in Church Lane are you?'

Emma was stopped in full flight. 'Church Lane? What, you mean my parents' address?'

'Yes. I've been driving up and down for five minutes now and I can't find the damn house.' He sounded frustrated.

'You're driving up and down this road?' Emma was desperately trying to make sense of what she was hearing.

'Yes, and it would be a great help if you people displayed house numbers on your gates.' In spite of his frustration, she could hear joy in his voice. 'Where are you, Emma? I need to see you, to talk to you.'

The penny was beginning to drop. 'Just keep driving. I'll come out onto the road and meet you. We're opposite the playing fields.' Dropping the phone onto the table, she beamed across at her mother. 'It's him. It's Mark. He's here.'

If she had been expecting a whoop of delight, she was to be disappointed. All she got was another little smile from her mum and a pragmatic decision.

'I'd better wake your father and put the kettle back on again, hadn't I?' Her smile broadened as she pointed towards the door. 'So what are you waiting for? Didn't you say something about going out to meet him?'

Emma grabbed her and kissed her before rushing out of the lounge, through the hall and out onto the drive. As she reached the gate, she looked left and then right.

As she did so, a silver car appeared and she realised it was Mark. She actually felt her heart leap as he screeched to a halt and jumped out. She was totally unsurprised to feel tears running down her cheeks.

'Emma...' He caught her in his arms and hugged her to him, lifting her bodily off the ground. 'Emma, my darling, Emma.' His voice sounded choked with emotion.

As he released her and stepped back, she saw that there were tears on his face too. She found herself starting to babble about her determination to make things work between them, but he just reached across and laid a finger on her lips.

'I'd have been here sooner if I hadn't had to get a flight into Gatwick and got caught up in traffic on the M25.' In spite of the tears on his cheeks, he was smiling broadly now. 'I should have done this back at the villa, in the pergola, overlooking the valley, but I missed my chance. But I'm not going to miss another one. Emma, I love you and I want to be with you. I don't want to make the same mistake I made before. Love is more important than work. I know how much your job means to you so I want to come to California to be with you if you'll have me.'

Emma was speechless. 'You want to come to California? But what about the villa, the hotel?'

'It'll be fine. Claudio knows what he's doing and I can pop back every now and then. And if it isn't fine, so what? I'll still have more than enough to live on, for us both to live on, if you'll have me.'

Emma was still struggling. 'And Carmen? What about her?'

'You said it yourself, she needs a passport. We'll find somewhere nice where she'll be as happy as we are.' He opened his hand and she saw he was holding a little black box. 'I know you're going to think I'm out of my mind after knowing each other for such a short time, but I've never been so sure about anything in all my life. When something's right, you just know it. I missed the first flight because I had to wait at the jewellers, but never mind. I'm here now.'

She thought her heart would break as he she saw him open the box and hold it out towards her. 'I'm not expecting you to commit yourself, or to say you're going to marry me or anything. I'm sure you'd think that would be crazy. But please, Emma, take this as a sign of the overwhelming, undying love I feel for you.'

As if in a dream, she reached out and took the ring from him, slipping it onto her ring finger. There were tears in her eyes and a smile on her face as she answered.

'I don't think it would be crazy.' She stretched her arms up and around his shoulders. 'Not crazy at all.'

And she kissed him.

Epilogue

Searchlights criss-crossed the night sky above the Chinese Theatre on Hollywood Boulevard as stretch limousines delivered celebrity after celebrity to the premiere of *Dreaming of Italy*. It was a warm night and the crowds were out en masse, cheering, applauding and clamouring for autographs.

As Emma climbed out of the car onto the red carpet, Mark was at her side to give her a helping hand. He gave her an encouraging grin as he did so.

'You look gorgeous. You know that, don't you?'

She grimaced. 'I look like a Zeppelin, or at least I feel like one.'

'The most beautiful Zeppelin in history.' He glanced around apprehensively. 'So, what do we do? Just walk up the red carpet or do we wait to be called?'

Emma had done this a few times before so she knew the score. 'Unless there's a big star blocking the way, we just get our heads down and make a run for it. Nobody will know who we are so we should get through unscathed.'

'The doctor said no running.' His tone was concerned. 'She also said no stress. I don't know about you, but this is a whole new experience to me and I have to confess I'm feeling pretty stressed.' To reinforce his point, a cluster of flashbulbs popped at the same time, half blinding them. She gripped his arm more tightly and smiled up at him.

'Don't fuss. I'm just having a baby. Women do it all the time.'

'Not always on the red carpet, though.'

'Now that would make for some interesting footage for the newsreels.'

She heard her name being called and looked over her shoulder towards the latest limousine to arrive. Extracting his lanky frame from the car was Rich closely followed by Marina. In his tuxedo, he looked every inch the future Hollywood mogul he was well on the way to becoming, and Marina in her designer gown drew a host of cameras in her direction. Emma had a feeling the gossip pages would be full of the couple tomorrow.

'Emma, hi, how're you feeling?'

She went over to greet him with a grin. 'Hi, boss.' After all, that's what he would be pretty soon.

He grinned back and she was delighted to see him looking so happy and settled these days. 'There's only one boss as far as I'm concerned and that's you, Emma. Well, almost...' He bent down to kiss Marina softly on the cheek. 'Apart from Marina. She keeps me in place.'

Emma kissed them both and assured Marina that her pregnancy was going fine. Rich asked Mark how his PhD at UCLA was going and received a thumbs up from him in reply. As they were chatting, the crowd exploded into a raucous cheer, accompanied by whistles and screams. The big star had arrived.

Emma and Mark stood to one side as Ethan emerged from his limousine looking like the global megastar he undoubtedly was. His tuxedo had some sort of reflecting thread interwoven into the material and he glistened and sparkled in the lights. His shoulders were broad, his hair perfect and his tan just the right shade for the floodlights. Ignoring the waiting TV reporters with their cameras and microphones, he headed straight across the red carpet to Emma, beaming broadly, his arms outstretched in welcome.

'Hey, English, how you doin'? You're looking really great. How long to go now?' His eyes dropped to her bump and he wisely stopped short of hugging her, just depositing a cautious kiss on her cheek before turning to shake hands with Mark. 'Yo, Mark. Looking good.'

Emma answered for both of them. 'Hi, Ethan. You're looking pretty damn good yourself. I've only got a month to go, that's why I look like a blimp.'

'You look just wonderful.' He lowered his voice. 'As for the movie, I've heard on the grapevine that the critics like it.' Although theoretically tonight's premiere would be the first opportunity for critics to see the movie, they both knew that a select group of 'trusted' critics always got invited to an early screening. She had also been hearing great things about the reception the film had received and she nodded in return.

'What I've heard is that they *love* it, Ethan. And they love you and Laney.' She grinned at him. 'You keep going like this and the city of Los Angeles will name a boulevard after you.'

At that moment Dexter appeared as if from nowhere and caught Ethan gently by the elbow. He flashed Emma a smile as he explained that Ethan had things to do.

'Interviews, Ethan. We'd better start with CBS. Hey, Emma, you're looking great. It's true what they say about pregnant ladies glowing. All well?'

'I'm feeling fine, thanks, Dexter, and if I'm glowing it's because I'm hot. How's Pooch?'

'Pooch is just great and she still loves her Italian raincoat.' He looked up at Ethan. 'Sorry, Ethan, but it's show time, I'm afraid.'

Ethan kissed Emma goodbye, shook hands with Mark and headed towards the media. Emma waited until Rich and Marina had set off up the red carpet before squeezing Mark's arm.

'Ready to go?'

'I am if you are.' The look he gave her still managed to send a shiver up her spine. 'Have I told you recently how much I love you?'

She reached up to kiss him. 'Only about every hour.' She grinned. 'But one more wouldn't hurt.'

'I love you, Emma.'

'And I love you, too, Mark, more than you can possibly imagine.' Supporting her tummy with her free hand, she set off with him at her side. 'Now, if you don't mind helping a pregnant woman along the red carpet, let's go and see what the public think of *Dreaming of Italy*.'